Intentional Acts of Kindness

DREA BRADDOCK

Cover Art by Drea Braddock

To Annie & Kate
for making time to support me in those early days
and never making me feel like I'm too much
I heart you

CHAPTER 1
IVY

Jeepers creepers, it's him again! I dip my head down, watching through my lashes in an attempt not to be outright staring. I doubt I'm fooling anyone in this coffee line. I've never been this close before. Close enough to see that his fitted jeans are cuffed unevenly, not hitting the tops of his lace-up boots in the same place. I could reach out and touch the lived-in leather jacket stretching across his broad shoulders. Maybe run my fingers through those short dark curls. Except my first instinct is to wrap my arms around him protectively because it's not his looks that first caught my attention. It was the weight that seems to be pressing down on him, curving his spine, bowing his head, rounding his shoulders inward. He seems worn out. Weary. In need of a hug. Not that I should be the one to give it to him. I have to cross my arms, though, keeping them to myself, to stop the ridiculous impulse to hug a complete stranger. *Keep it together, Ivy, don't be such a weirdo.*

As the weeks go by I see him fairly regularly, from afar. Whether it's ordering two to-go cups in the local coffee shop, The Foundry, or walking through the park bordering the hospital, that weight is ever-present and seems to be increasing. He always has the same worn paperback in his pocket with what looks like a comb as a bookmark. Why a comb? Is that good for the book? Probably not but it's intriguing. I find myself spending far too much time wondering where he's headed, what is making him that sad, and what the book is about. I need to get a life. It's not that unusual for me to spend time watching someone I want to help, but without anything to indicate what he needs, this is feeling stalker-ish. Something tells me an awkward stalker is *not* the one thing he needs. That logic doesn't keep me from thinking about him though. I'm calling him Weary Stranger and he's a puzzle I can't solve. I think about him while I walk to The Birth and Wellness Collective where I work as a doula. I ponder the source of his problems while in yoga. I wonder what I could do for him while sipping my nightly tea. I don't know him, I have no responsibility towards him, but I can't shake my desire to help. Maybe I could fall back on my old standby and write him a note.

I love helping people — doing small, special things to make their day. Sending anonymous cards has a special place in my heart. I've lost count of how many I've written over the years. I can struggle with sharing my feelings out loud but writing is different. I'd never been brave enough to be so honest in person. In an anonymous card, I feel free. I've moved beyond blank cards pilfered from the summer camp craft cabin though. 12-year-old me would be proud of how I've grown my hobby that started with a secret-admirer-style note to the most popular boy at camp. I wasn't one of his groupies, but I did admire his kind nature and wrote to him to tell him I thought that was more impressive than his good looks. That note caused him to stop preening for the girls and become the kind role model the younger campers needed and gave me a way to use my quiet observations to care for others. I'm thankful I now have more options than my sub-par artwork on cheap cardstock! I found this sweet Etsy shop, Reflection Paper Crafts, that sells blank cards with gorgeous calligraphy and simple art that makes a statement. I love being able to build up a stranger inside something pretty! I have the perfect art picked out for Weary Stranger but I'm still struggling with what to say. I haven't seen him enough to know what he needs, just that he needs *something*. I mull it over while I get ready for work.

After a quick shower, I turn on music and get dressed, shimmying my jeans awkwardly over my thighs and hips to the beat. I let my hair dry in its usual loose curls while I go to work on my makeup, Brandi Carlile's emotive voice filling my bathroom. I love a good winged eyeliner and groomed brow. I may not wear a lot, but putting on makeup makes me feel put together and ready for the day. "Putting on my face" as Mama calls it. Ready, but still grossly under-caffeinated, I head out, pushing Weary Stranger's card back to the "it will come to me" portion of my mind.

My apartment is within walking distance of The Birth and Wellness Collective which is within walking distance of the hospital. Weather permitting, I walk to work. Cutting through the park I notice a familiar figure sitting on a bench. I can tell immediately that something is very wrong. Weary Stranger is hunched over, elbows on his knees, head in his hands, fingers knotted in his thick hair. He's shaking. His messenger bag is spilled at his feet but he hasn't even noticed. I stop mid-step, watching him. He no longer looks weary. He looks broken. I'm conflicted watching him. This isn't my place but I can't just walk by, leaving him like that. I need to do something tangible. Words couldn't possibly be enough, but I could give him something. I start walking again, speeding up my steps as I pass him and head towards The Foundry.

The heady scents of freshly ground coffee and baked pastries waft over me as I step through the door. There isn't a line. I lean on the counter, returning the owner Louise's smile.

"Good morning, Ivy! Medium macchiato to go?"

"You know it! But I need to ask you something too." Curiosity shines from her wise blue eyes as she continues to ring me up. "Do you know the guy who has been coming in for the last 6 weeks or so, dark curly hair, black leather jacket, really handsome but looks super sad?"

Louise gives me a little smile that doesn't quite reach her eyes. "Yeah, that's Miles. Why?"

"I wanted to give him a coffee but I'm not sure what he usually orders. Would you be able to help me out?"

"Sure, honey: brewed dark roast, black. Is this like one of your notes?" Louise had helped me before.

"Something like that, yeah. Add a medium dark roast too, please."

I pay for my coffees, thank Louise, and head back to the park. I don't usually interact with whoever I'm helping. Anonymity is more comfortable but this cannot wait. He's in need right now. I breathe deeply, trying to ignore the knots in my stomach, keeping my steps even to avoid spilling the coffee. Why did I buy myself one too? I should have waited until after to get my own. Now both of my hands are full and it's adding to my anxiety.

He doesn't hear me approach and his eyes are unfocused, staring straight in front of him. His hair is a mess like he's been pulling it and raking his hands through it. There are dark shadows under his eyes, staining his tan skin like bruises. The stubble covering his cheeks and sharp jawline doesn't look purposefully groomed, more like he was in a hurry. Before I have a chance to talk myself out of it, he looks up, seeing me for the first time. Eyes a light amber, like liquid gold, hit me like a punch in my already knotted stomach. A beat passes. Then two as I take in the gold flecks and straight lashes. Because I am staring! I'm straight-up staring at him and neither of us has said anything. Could I make this any weirder? *Focus, Ivy!*

With effort I pull my eyes from his magnetic stare, sitting my coffee at my feet to free up my hand. He's still staring at me, probably confused. I would be if our roles were reversed. I reach out and put the hot coffee cup between his hands, using mine to press his around it. Up close I can see there are flecks of color spackled over his long fingers. There's a jolt at the contact, electricity that zips straight through me like he's my contact point to a newly-accessed energy source. I keep my hands on his longer than I should, shocked by the touch, looking up again to find him still watching me. The feel of his eyes looking straight into mine with his hands still underneath my own is too much. Heat creeps up my cheeks and I step back before I can embarrass myself further. I grab my coffee from my feet and walk away quickly, unable to stop myself from glancing over my shoulder as I leave. He's still watching me.

CHAPTER 2
MILES

He's gone. He's gone. He's gone.

No matter how many times I say it, it doesn't feel real. We knew it was coming but I'm still completely leveled by the hole ripped in my chest.

Fuck cancer.

For almost 7 weeks I spent every spare moment at the hospital with Dad. At first, it was bringing him over for the final round of his treatments, then it was to be with him while there was still time. I brought us coffee; even though he lost his taste for it with the chemo, he still liked to smell it and hold the warm cup in his hands. I read to him—he loved westerns. I kept his favorite Robert Vaughn in my back pocket so I'd always have it with me. He didn't like looking unkempt so I combed his hair and shaved his face every day. I kept a hand on him while he dozed, soaking up the familiarity of his strong and calloused hands. I'd sketch him while he was resting or paint by the window, afraid to leave him for long. It wasn't enough.

I held those hands—hands that had comforted me and clapped me on the back and steadied me my entire life—until his skin cooled and my chest felt like it was caving in. And then I ran.

I knew I was going to have to go back, they probably needed

6

things from me, but I had to get away from there. Even though I knew he was gone, I couldn't break down in front of him. He worked hard to stay positive, right up until the end, and even without him here anymore I couldn't disappoint him.

I found myself on this bench in the park, not even remembering how I got here. Sucking in ragged breaths I sink my head into my hands, willing myself to let go. Instead, I sit. Frozen. Brain looping. *Shit. I need to tell Chloe. We'll have to get word to Liam. Is it the Red Cross I'm supposed to contact? What about a funeral home? He never told me what he wanted. How am I going to do all of this alone?* Instead of dealing with all the problems at hand, I'm dragged back to that phone call, not quite two months before, that blew up my life and ultimately led me to this park bench.

I picked up my phone, barely paying attention to who was calling, trying to finish my current project with a deadline looming.

"Hello?" I mumbled, eyes still locked on my computer screen.

"Miles? Son? Are you there?" His deep voice sounded hesitant.

"Dad, what's up? We don't usually chat during the week." I heard him take a shaky breath, but it hardly registered because my mind was still on work.

"Miles, I uh, I have some news. Some, uh, bad news, really. You have a minute to talk?" My stomach dropped and I jerked my eyes away from the screen, all of my attention on his voice.

"What's going on, Dad? Is Liam ok? Is it Chloe and the baby?" Before I got going he interrupted me, his comforting bass cutting through.

"No, no, Liam and Chloe and the baby are all fine. No, it's, uh, it's me, Miles." He cleared his throat before starting again, almost stumbling over his words. "It's cancer. Pancreatic. It doesn't look good, son."

I was glad I was already sitting as all the air left my lungs and my muscles felt like jelly.

"What can I do?" I managed to choke out, hands shaking.

"Now, I know you have a life up there, but I'm worried about our Chloe girl. This is too much to put on her on top of the pregnancy."

I jumped in, already making plans in my head. "Don't worry about that, Dad. I'll leave Philly tonight and be down there in the morning. You shouldn't be alone and it isn't Chloe's responsibility. I'm gonna get packing right now and I'll see you soon, ok? I love you, Dad."

I packed a bag, sent off a quick email letting my clients know I'd be working out of state, and left for Virginia, not even realizing that the next time I was back I'd be living in a world without the strongest man I'd ever known.

I don't know how long I've been sitting here, unseeing, before I realize someone is in front of me. I look up into big, chocolate brown eyes. Beautiful eyes. Concerned eyes. I stare, confused, trying to recall ever seeing such emotive eyes before. Round and tilted up faintly in the corner, deep brown with long, full lashes framing them. Interesting shadows and contrasts, begging to be captured on canvas. Very expressive. Do I know her? She's vaguely familiar. Her pale skin is a stark contrast to the almost black curls tumbling over her shoulders. Light and dark, like a charcoal drawing.

She leans down, putting something on the ground, then her hands are on mine, pressing them around a hot cup. Her soft skin on mine makes me feel more alive and alert than I have in ages, but before I can even react to the sensation caused by the brushing of our skin, the scent of dark roast hits me, making me miss my dad so much I can't breathe. I have to blink the tears from my eyes, even as I'm still taking hers in.

Shit. I'm still staring. I can't seem to stop. It's like my brain is short-circuiting. I don't know what's happening. She looks like a doll with delicate features and a small chin under a little bow-shaped mouth. The tops of her cheeks start to pink—it would be a fun challenge to get the balance of white and red right, to reflect her warmth and fragility without the color becoming saccharine...*FOCUS!*—and she pulls away.

The absence of her hands leaves me cold and reminds me of how alone I truly am. I haven't even managed to form a sentence and she's walking off. I watch her leave, all feminine curves and bouncy curls, taking the warmth with her. She looks back at me, over her shoulder, and my heart skips a beat. *What the hell was that?* I can't process my feelings. They're generally a lot to deal with, but this is beyond overwhelming. I don't know if I've met her before or how to even begin to handle what I have already experienced this morning. I can't even try. Instead, I sit back, stretch my long legs out in front of me, and take a sip from the cup. The coffee trails a path of heat down my chest and makes me feel connected to my dad in a way that I hadn't been able to manage moments before. I stay there, drinking and remembering him until the cup is empty and my cheeks are wet with tears.

CHAPTER 3
IVY

I took the whole morning for me to push past my feelings of utter embarrassment over my awkward staring at Weary Stranger, but I'm finally feeling better for having done something for him and can move past it. There is no more need to worry over him, I did what I could, time to move on. I have clients to meet with, births to attend, and hopefully, I'll be finding ways I've yet to dream up to help people. I finish up my workday and walk a few blocks over to Hughes Florals. The bell over the door rings merrily and I stride in, breathing in the familiar fragrance of flowers.

"Mama? Are you changed yet?" I wave at Barb, Mama's oldest employee, and walk past the register towards the back room.

"In here Ivy! All changed and packing our waters."

I peck Mama's soft cheek before heading into the bathroom to put on my workout clothes. I hurriedly change and pull my hair up into a high ponytail and we're off, chatting easily on our way to our bi-weekly yoga class.

"I'm so glad you still have time to do this with me, Ivy." Mama bumps my shoulder as we walk.

"I love our time together! I wouldn't miss it for anything."

Our class is mostly young moms, squeezing in a workout

before heading home to make dinner, and we love it. The energy is great and they keep it lively and hilarious with their stories about their lives.

"What do you think the gossip will be tonight? Sophie's nanny? Or Lauren's ex?" Mama grins, holding the door open for me.

We enter the studio and get set up in the back of the class. We get the best view from here. One by one the moms fill the room, taking up their usual spots and talking over each other.

"Sophie? How's the nanny" Lauren taunts.

"Ooh, girl, don't even get me started!" Sophie retorts, shaking her pixie cut angrily. "She rolled up this morning in the teeniest skirt I've ever seen with a sweater so tight I could read the tag on her bra!"

"Gross!"

"I don't know what she thinks she's going to accomplish but my sweet Brian is Mr. Motherflippin' Oblivious! He walked right past her, her nipples saluting him, with his head buried in some old book. Goober ran into the door frame!" Sophie giggles and rolls her eyes. Her bookish husband is super cute but he has no interests outside of his family and his academic studies. I often wonder what she did to get him to notice her. On second thought, maybe I don't want to know.

"What I don't understand," another mom pipes up, "is why you hired her if she's constantly parading her barely clothed body in front of your husband?"

"She wasn't like that when we hired her! When I interviewed her she was wearing a grandma cardigan and a skirt straight out of a 1990s homeschooling convention! She took one look at Brian and showed up like an extra from one of those CW shows with adults playing high schoolers!" Sophie's facial expressions are so animated it bumps her stories up to another level.

Lauren rolls out her mat and tosses her bag aside. "What are you going to do?"

"If it was only the clothes I'd probably ignore her, maybe pop some popcorn and watch her self-confidence bomb when Brian never once sees her." She gives a theatrical, evil laugh. "Buuuut she spends so much time looking in the mirror or taking selfies she never gets any work done! We put in a request with the agency but they don't have anyone else available! We're stuck with her for now. I don't have enough days saved to take time off to cover for the trollop."

"Trollop!" Lauren snorts. "Brazen hussy!"

In front of me is one of the newest students, Sasha. She's pulling uncomfortably at her top like she's a little self-conscious. Her belly is soft and I heard her mention her two-month-old son in class last week. Our group has all levels of ability and all different body shapes, but it's obvious that Sasha is comparing herself to the thinner moms. Maybe *I* could boost her a bit.

"Mama? Can you chat with Sasha, maybe ask her how the baby is doing? I need to do something real quick." Mama gives me a wink and steps up in front of me, catching Sasha's eye. I quickly rifle through my bag, finding a card with a bright watercolor sunrise and "to new beginnings" written in Reflection Paper Crafts' distinctive calligraphy.

"Dear Sasha,

I am in awe of you! Your badass body already nurtured and delivered a perfect baby boy and now, two months later, you're caring for him while giving your own body what it needs with regular exercise! The human body is a thing of wonder and what you do every day is nothing short of miraculous! You have a new growing family and a new identity as someone's mom. Give yourself grace as you get used to the role. I hope yoga gives you a chance to appreciate how incredible your body is and that you get to go home to two guys who revel in your gorgeous smile. You are so strong and beautiful! Keep going, young mama!

—A friend."

I slip the card into Sasha's bag and get back to my mat right as class is starting. We move fluidly from pose to pose, muscles loosening and skin warming. I miss the latest gossip altogether, thinking instead about Sasha and hoping she would be able to feel all the caring I poured into my words.

Saturday morning I head down to the shop early, ready to help Mama with a delivery. There's a funeral at the big church around the corner at the same time as a wedding that has been on the books for months. I don't mind helping at the shop, it had been my afternoon and summertime employment for years before I finished my schooling. Hughes Florals is as much my home as the 2-bedroom cottage I grew up in. I open the back of the second van as Mama comes out with her arms full.

"Wow, those are striking! Great work as always, Mama. Am I only setting up on the casket?"

She answers with her head in the van, arranging the box. "I didn't get much direction, just that the deceased had loved the outdoors. I went with a lot of greenery, dark dahlias, and seed pods. It felt masculine to me. You should take the casket spray upfront and then these two vases will go on either side of the framed photo and guest book by the door."

Funerals are a large part of her business so I'm familiar with what is expected. With the arrangements secured I hop in and drive over to the church, parking in back. The funeral won't start for at least another hour but I don't want to be in the way of the family. I see the side door is propped open so I grab the casket spray first. The sanctuary is empty and my footsteps echo as I carefully cross to the casket. I arrange the flowers, making sure the greenery is flat and the piece is in the right place. It is stunning and, just as she planned, masculine. I hope it's what the family was looking for. I go back out to the van, taking a vase in each hand, pushing the door shut with my hip. Walking down the side aisle I catch a glimpse of a dark shape walking out the door. *I should put these in place and get out of the way before the family comes in. They have enough on their plates today.*

The table up front has a photo of a handsome older man with salt and pepper hair and kind blue eyes. His smile is comforting and there's an aura of calm about him. He was a man with a strong yet gentle presence, you can feel it looking at the photo. It makes me think of my father. I sigh, placing the vases on either end, adjusting them until everything is symmetrical.

I can see a guy in Navy dress blues sitting in the office and the minister's voice is coming through the open door. *That's my cue.* I go back down the side aisle, slipping out the same door, stepping into the sunshine. I let out a sigh, momentarily blinded by the change in brightness, and slam into something warm and solid. My purse falls off my shoulder and I can hear the contents spilling on the pavement beneath me. I'm already stammering out an apology when strong hands grab my arms, steadying me.

"Shit! Sorry! Are you okay?" The voice is low and almost coarse, sending goosebumps across my skin. I take in the dark suit, white dress shirt doing nothing to disguise the firm muscles I had just run into, and I have to tilt my head back to see the face that goes with that voice. Liquid gold eyes stare into mine. *Heavens to Betsy!* It's clear he has been crying but it doesn't take away from his masculine beauty. I inhale shakily, smelling citrus and something woodsy mingling with the mint of his breath. His eyes widen in recognition.

"It's you," he whispers at the same time that I gasp out, "Weary Stranger!"

He looks different without his jeans and leather jacket but not enough that I wouldn't have known it was him even from across a room. The stubble is gone but his eyes are still shadowed and his shoulders still seem to carry the weight of the world on them.

I'm suddenly aware of how close we're still standing. My feet are between his and his hands are still gripping my upper arms. His jaw is clenched and his amber eyes are damp and suddenly my need to help overwhelms me. I take one step forward, slipping my arms around him in a hug. Too late, I realize my arms are under his suit jacket and this is now a more intimate embrace than I had intended. *Who screws up a hug, Ivy?* I feel him take in a sharp breath as my hands slide up the planes of his back, stopping to rest against his shoulder blades. The top of my head doesn't quite reach his chin and my face fits perfectly against his collarbone. Hug perfection.

I'm about to pull away, embarrassed by how much I've overstepped when his arms come around me, holding me back. I allow myself a moment to enjoy his warmth, imagining all my caring reaching into him like a physical sensation. I feel his face tilt down, the tip of his nose touching my hair as his chest expands with a deep breath. *Is he smelling my hair? Of course not, that's silly. Why would he be smelling my hair? He probably needed a deep breath after I squeezed him in an unexpected hug. Why am I so weird?* I close my eyes, listening to his heartbeat, my hands moving on their own, running softly up and down his back.

I move my chest back slightly, intending to turn my face up to tell him I'm sorry but his mouth is right there. He's looking down at me, his eyes intent but unreadable. His lips are parted and his breath traces a tingling path across my mouth. I push up on my toes slightly, my body pushing to be closer before my mind can form the question: *what the crappity-crap am I doing?* His arms are still holding me against him and my hands have stopped caressing and are now resting on his belt, fingertips brushing his firm backside.

Has he realized I'm about a fingertip away from fondling his butt?

Please, Lord, no.

I can't move them now, that will make it even more obvious!

I breathe him in, apparently committing to my current course of overstepping the bounds of polite society. He leans down the tiniest bit more, eyes never leaving mine. *Is it a tick, unintentional, or is he meaning to get closer?* I look down at his mouth as his tongue slips out, wetting his bottom lip and touching mine in the process. I gasp, the featherlight touch sending shockwaves through me. Realizing what he's done he jumps back, dropping my arms but not my gaze.

Crap, why was my mouth so close to his?

Can I die now?

Great request at a freaking funeral, Ivy! Golly.

His low voice gives me goosebumps again. "I'm sorry. I shouldn't..." he takes a step back, "I didn't..." and another, "this isn't..." and another step, "I've gotta go." He brushes past me as he runs to the front of the church leaving me to pick up my scattered belongings and even more scattered thoughts, alone.

CHAPTER 4
MILES

What the hell was that? What is wrong with me?

I had run out to my car to grab my tie and suddenly she was there, the coffee girl from the park. I only meant to keep her from falling over. Then she was watching me so carefully and her arms were around me. Her hands slid up my back and they were warm. So warm. Comforting. I don't even know if I contained my gasp at the surprise of how good it felt to be touched. She laid her face against my chest and fit perfectly against me, like a missing puzzle piece filling the last empty spot to complete the picture. I should have patted her back or something and got myself out of there. Instead, what did I do? Pulled her closer and hugged her back. Don't think I didn't notice how her breasts pressed against me, stupid traitor body picking the worst possible time to wake up. And then to make it worse, I leaned down and smelled her hair. She smelled like lavender and coconut and her hair was soft against my face. There's no way she missed me sniffing her hair like a psycho. Fuck, I hope she did, though.

She was running her hands up and down my back. When was the last time that happened? I mean, really? Just basic human contact. I'd pretty much become a recluse even before I was spending all of my time at the hospital. She was very comforting, I let it go to my head. That's no excuse, to be sure, but I'm blaming the hug and the recluse thing. She turned her face up and I fully intended to say thank you and go back inside. That was the plan. Her eyes were concerned and I swear there was kindness pouring off of her. I paused, soaking that in. Except then I was licking my lip AND HERS.

Fuuuuck. It was just a touch, the tiniest brush, but it lit me up like a Christmas tree. She gasped and my brain caught up with me. I don't know this woman. She was probably being nice considering she had come out the door of the church.

THE CHURCH.

I'm at my dad's fucking funeral.

I should be punched in the junk. What kind of asshole almost kisses a stranger in the church parking lot when he's supposed to be inside for a private viewing before his dad's funeral begins? I don't even know what I said to her. I tried to apologize, to tell her I shouldn't have presumed or I didn't mean to lick her or this wasn't the time for anything like that but I'm not sure I got anything intelligible out. I ran. *Moron.*

I round the corner to the front of the church, slowing to a jog, and duck into the office we'd been sitting in, lifting my chin at my brother. He's still talking to the minister, arms around Chloe. I don't blame him. This is an awful reason to get emergency leave during a deployment, but he's been gone for 5 months and they haven't stopped holding each other since he got home. I turn towards the mirror on the wall, using the moment to get myself under control. My cheekbones and jaw look too sharp. I've lost some weight since that call from Dad. I've always struggled to gain weight but I'm bordering on sickly. I should take better care of myself and get back to the gym more regularly. I need it. Once my tie is in place and my jacket is buttoned I've managed to get my heart rate down to a more reasonable level. I can still feel her lip on my tongue, the phantom touch taunting me.

We opted for a closed casket. Cancer made dad waste away

and in the end, he looked like a hollow shell of his former self. No one needs to see him like that, especially not Liam. When he left, Dad was strong and healthy, looking forward to Liam's homecoming and the birth of his first grandchild. They were able to video chat during a port visit, but that isn't an option in the middle of the ocean. I feel guilty that I got to be with Dad through his entire battle, as brief and painful as it was, and Liam only got one video chat and an emergency message from the Red Cross bringing him back home just long enough for the funeral. As much as it hurt to hold Dad's hand as he left his body, I wouldn't trade it for anything.

The three of us make our way to the front of the sanctuary, Liam and Chloe a tight unit, as always, and me a few steps behind. Thank God they have each other. We rest our hands on the cool lacquered wood of the casket. The flowers are perfect. I had no idea what to tell the florist. She was kind and understanding. Something about her made me know, without a doubt, that I could trust her to take care of it. I'm glad my intuition wasn't wrong. We stand that way, not talking, hands resting above what is left of our larger-than-life father until the minister clears his throat, getting our attention and letting us know people are starting to arrive.

I don't remember a single thing about the funeral. A couple of dad's oldest friends got up to talk about him, or so the program said. Liam spoke. I sort of recall him leaving our pew. The minister spoke briefly. I assume. The sound of their voices washed over me like gentle, lapping waves. I didn't take in anything that was said. I didn't contribute anything. I just sat, holding Chloe's free hand and remembering my dad.

After the longest day of my life, we put our feet up on Dad's coffee table, glad to be done but also still in disbelief that it's over. Liam grabs us both a beer and hands Chloe a mug of chamomile tea. She snuggles into him and he rests his hand on her growing belly. Liam's flying out tomorrow night, going back to his ship, and I'm about to suggest they head out so they have as much time together as possible when he speaks up. His voice is so much like Dad's that it's jarring. I'd never made the connection before.

"Do you remember when Dad took us fishing? He got us up super early. Dragged us out of bed. We kept bitching and moaning but he took it all in stride. He drove forever, at least it felt that way, to some lake, took us out in a canoe, and when we got out in the middle of the lake I noticed we didn't have any fishing poles with us." He barks out a laugh.

"I had forgotten that! We were in such bad moods! And Dad laughed. He opened the little cooler, handed us sandwiches, and told us it was fine that we forgot the poles. He said we could still enjoy the day if we decided to. And we did. Man. It was a great day." I lean back and take another swig. "Do you remember when Mom had planned for weeks, gotten a babysitter, bought a new dress and everything, all for some big anniversary date night?"

"Yeah," Liam sighs, "she looked so pretty, all dressed up. She had those box braids and Dad kept calling her his queen. They were going to an outdoor concert."

"The babysitter was there and they were heading out the door when Dad heard that it was canceled because of weather. Mom was so upset. Dad sent us up to bed..."

"...but we snuck out and watched them from the top of the stairs," Liam remembers with me.

"He lit candles and turned off the lights and they danced."

Chloe chimes in, "Caleb had this quiet way of making ordinary things special."

We sit, not speaking, for a few minutes, before Liam asks, "remember that time, after Mom, when Dad pushed us into the truck after school and drove us out to Shenandoah National Park?"

"Yeah," I take a sip of my beer. "We got cheeseburgers at that diner and he let us have pie. *With* ice cream. After we got to the park he had us lie in the back and we stared at the night sky. I had never seen stars that bright or clear before."

"The air was crisp. It smelled like trees," Liam adds. "And he never explained why we were there or what we were doing. He drove us out there, told us to look out at the sky, and after a while, he took us back home. He was always that way about the stars though. Climbing on the roof to lie out and stargaze, planetariums, camping...it was an endless repeat of *Look at the stars boys*! I remember that trip felt like a secret adventure, the three of us in the truck."

Chloe takes a sip of her tea, watching us both. "He was gruff and not a confident speaker, but he knew how to find the beauty in everything."

We shake our heads in agreement, choked up by her observation. "That was Dad alright."

CHAPTER 5
IVY

It's been two weeks since the funeral and the...lip lick. Life is marching on as usual but I find myself reviewing those few minutes far more often than I'd like to admit. I haven't dated in a long time, so I can't put much stock in my borderline obsession. Two years without any physical affection. And nothing *before* that is anything I want to remember. Of course, I'm making it more than it was. It was a one-sided, super-charged moment in my otherwise mundane life. That's all, I'm sure.

In the meantime, I'd coached a new mom through an arduous 27-hour birth, had bi-weekly yoga with Mama, and snuck in a couple of cards: one to the cutest old man who regularly feeds the ducks and another to the sweet grandma who spends every morning sitting on her patio chair, waving at the kids walking to school.

I put the finishing touches on my makeup before heading out to work. I give myself the once over, liking today's soft, dusty rose sweater dress, tights, and tall boots. I'm cozy and comfortable but still girly, just the way I like it. It won't be too toasty in the early spring air but will keep me warm enough in the office's always-too-cool interior. It's particularly difficult to find the right balance this time of year.

I walk through the Birthing Center's doors on time, getting stopped by the receptionist before I can reach my office.

"Ivy, listen, Janice had to go out of town last night. Her mom is in the hospital and she's not sure how long she'll be gone."

"Oh no, I hope she's ok! Should we send flowers? Do you need me to get a card for everyone to sign?" Janice is a sweetheart and one of our most popular doulas. She's like everyone's dream grandma, amiable and no-nonsense.

"Don't you worry about that, I've got it covered. But she was supposed to be meeting with a mama this morning. Can you take over? It could be a little awkward, stepping into someone else's spot a couple of months before delivery but Janice was adamant that you were the right person to take this one."

I straighten my back, proud that Janice trusts me to look after one of her mamas.

"No problem. What time will she be here?"

"5 minutes?" Victoria grimaces. "I should have called you sooner. Sorry."

"It's fine. I'll go grab a cup of coffee and look over her file before you send her back."

I drop my purse and coat off in my office and hurry back to the break room. I'm pouring my coffee when I hear Victoria walking down the hallway, explaining why I would be taking over for Janice. Crap. Guess I won't be reading over that file after all.

Their backs are to me, getting settled as I stride in, setting my coffee mug down and dropping into my seat with more energy than necessary. I overcompensate for my bouncing chair with a too-big smile and forced expression of what I hope reads as confidence.

"Hi, I'm Ivy Hughes and I'll be taking over for Janice as your doula," I start. And then I look at the couple and choke on my words. The woman is tall, athletic-looking, and intimidatingly attractive. Her long blonde hair cascades over her shoulders, highlighting her enviable figure, even with the baby bump. Big blue eyes are watching me, full lips pulled into a welcoming smile complete with perfect, white teeth. But she's not what stops my heart. Sitting next to her, with his leather jacket and mesmerizing golden eyes that stare right into my soul is Weary Stranger. The Lip Licker.

I know I'm staring at him again but this time it's not because I'm struck dumb by his hotness or frozen by his proximity. My mind is racing. He has a baby mama? Or wait, she's wearing a ring. A WIFE?! Why did he maybe almost kiss me? Or, well, at least hold me and sort of lick my lip? I've been fantasizing about someone who is a cheating asshat! Or maybe not a cheater, but at the very least unavailable. I'm confused and giving myself mental whiplash. She clears her throat and I blink rapidly, trying to will myself to say something, anything. *Do not look at him.*

"Right. Excuse me. Sorry. Uh, as I said, I'm Ivy. It sounded like Victoria told you Janice is caring for her ailing mother. I'm sorry this has created a hiccough in your birth plan but I have every confidence that together we can give you a birth experience that leaves you feeling empowered and ready to step fully into motherhood."

Beautiful Blonde sits forward and extends her hand to shake mine. "I'm Chloe Bennett. Thank you so much for fitting me in. Having someone consistent who can support me and help me see this through is exactly what I need to make all of this less stressful."

I shake her hand with a smile. I hope it doesn't look as strained as it feels. "That's what I'm here for. I'm embarrassed to tell you I only found out about this a few minutes ago and I haven't had time to look through your file, but I promise to be up to speed the next time we meet."

The rest of the appointment is pretty standard. Chloe is friendly and personable. Lip Licker, or Miles right? I think Louise said his name is Miles. Miles and Chloe Bennett. Cute. They should be on the cover of some magazine with their dumb good looks. It would be a study in contrast with his dark hair and quiet smolder—even his clothes look freaking broody—setting off her bright and golden energy.

Miles doesn't contribute anything and the whole vibe is weird. Other than patting her hand, he never touches her and he doesn't seem to care at all about being part of the process. I don't get why you would come to meet with a doula if you want to be hands-off, but it's Chloe's problem, not mine. After it becomes obvious that he isn't going to be any actual help to his wife, I pointedly ignore him. We decide to meet again next week, giving me time to review everything that way we can talk more about what is most important to her during the delivery. They stand up to go and Chloe shakes my hand again, thanking me for stepping in for Janice. Lip Licker lingers behind her like he wants to talk to me. *No thank you.* I head him off, stepping out in front of him and calling over my shoulder to them both, "I have to meet someone at the hospital, see you next week." *So I'm a liar, sue me.* Better to make up an appointment than risk embarrassing myself further.

CHAPTER 6

MILES

C hloe is still happily chatting away, gushing about how comforting Ivy was and how much better she feels about having someone in her corner while Liam is gone. The receptionist stops us on our way out, making eye contact with me.

"Does your wife need to set up her next appointment?"

I shake my head.

Chloe giggles. "Ew, he's not my husband! This is my brother-in-law, Miles. My husband is deployed, but he should be home before my due date." The receptionist apologizes for her mistake and gets everything worked out, getting Chloe's next appointment in the system.

I clear my throat, rubbing my hand across the back of my neck while I watch Chloe practically bouncing with excitement. "Do you think she thought we were married too?"

"Who, the doula? Maybe? Why? Should I have said something? I forgot she wouldn't know."

"Nah, don't worry about it. It's just...we had..." I sigh. "Never mind."

Chloe stops, eyeing me carefully. "Do you *know* her? Is that why there was such a weird vibe? Holy shit! I thought you were both just being awkward so I worked extra hard to be perkier! Was that sexual tension, Milesy?!" Her voice is dangerously close to that screechy register that is highly embarrassing in public.

"Cut it out, Chlo. And lower your voice! There wasn't a weird vibe. There wasn't any kind of vibe. We've never met, not really. I sort of ran into her before the funeral and, you know, let's forget it. It's no big deal."

"Miles Bennett, do you *like* her?" Chloe teases.

"What am I, 12? I don't like her. I don't even know her. I feel a little weird that she probably thinks we're married when the thought of kissing you makes me want to vomit. That's all." Chloe elbows me in the stomach and cackles. She has the funniest, least feminine laugh I've ever heard, and hearing it makes me miss Liam. He's perpetually trying to make her laugh, the more inappropriate the situation the better.

"Sure thing. Now, please tell me we're almost to the coffee shop you like, you promised me breakfast and baby needs baked goods!"

I hold open the door of The Foundry for my sister-in-law, sucking in a lungful of deep coffee smell. She grabs us a table, calling over, "Get me a tea and something yummy, little bro!"

"Roger." I peruse the baked goods case while I wait in line. Louise is behind the register and she pats my hand gently.

"I was so sorry to hear about your dad, Miles. He was a good egg."

"Thanks, Louise." My voice is a little gruffer than I'd like. Maybe someday I'll be able to talk about my dad without the threat of tears. "Can I get a chamomile, a small dark roast, and two of those blueberry muffins for here?"

"Sure thing, honey. Say, did our Ivy girl ever get you that coffee?"

I blink at her, realizing I might have a way to clear up the whole awkward Chloe-is-not-my-wife situation. "Yeah, she did. And it certainly came at the right time. Do you know where I might find Ivy, outside of her office?" Louise takes my money, lips pursed while she considers me.

"Well now, I might. I'm sure you're a nice guy — I can't see Caleb Bennett raising jerks — but women can't be too careful these days. I'm not sure how I feel about giving you her contact info. Let me think about it. Will I see you around this week?"

"I'm sure I'll be by for coffee at some point."

"Ok then, I'll let you know."

She gestures to the woman behind me and I step out of line to wait for our breakfast. That's something. I suppose it's good that Louise isn't one to give out customers' personal information to anyone that asks. I'd prefer setting things straight right now, but I guess I can wait. It's not like I *need* to see Ivy. I want to clear up my relationship with Chloe, that's all. Loose ends and all that. She had seemed so kind and open when I'd seen her before, but this morning she had been almost frigid towards me. We don't have any reason to be friends, but I'd feel better if she didn't think less of me over a misunderstanding.

Chloe and I linger over our muffins, talking about Dad's house, Liam's homecoming, and the baby's nursery. I'm staying at Dad's for now. Once Liam is home we'll have the lawyer and Dad's will and all of that to deal with. Since I can work from anywhere, there isn't a rush for me to get back to my apartment. I want to stay close to home, maybe sort through some of Dad's things, and be here for Chloe, at least until Liam gets back. After that? I haven't thought that far ahead. I don't have a reason to stay, but I also don't have a reason to go. Nothing is holding me anywhere. Without Dad, I feel a bit untethered. We're gathering up our dishes, getting ready to leave when Louise comes over.

"Miles, I had an idea. Possibly a great idea, and this could help with the Ivy thing."

"The Ivy thing?" Chloe looks far too smug for my liking. "What's the Ivy thing?"

"You hush, Chlo," I mutter. "What do you need, Louise?"

"Do you have a card on ya?" I pull a business card out of my wallet and hand it to her. "I'll be honest, I'm hoping this will end up with you helping out my favorite local charity. And working with them could give you an opportunity to talk to her."

"Charity work might be good. My workload isn't too heavy right now either."

"Thanks, Miles. Be expecting a call."

Chloe continues to tease me about Ivy but my heart isn't in the banter. I stay distracted until we leave. I drop Chloe off, spend an hour at the gym, and work on a painting. All the while my mind is mulling over the possibility of this charity. I wonder what Louise is planning? And will I be able to explain myself to Ivy?

CHAPTER 7
IVY

3 1/2 YEARS AGO

I've been home for about six months, but everything still feels temporary. I'm in my old room, in the house I grew up in like I'm still a child. I'm working as a doula but the thrill of my hard work coming to fruition isn't there. Everything is grey. My therapist says it will get better, that color will return, that I won't always vacillate between being numb or angry. It's hard to believe her. There are no outward signs of my brokenness. Anyone who saw me walking down the street could easily assume I'm like any other almost 21-year-old. I'm not sure if it's a good thing that I can hide the hurt or if that pisses me off. Mostly I feel like I'm drifting. Not even work anchors me. Mama has tried suggesting I write a note or do some anonymous act of kindness but I can't. I don't want to admit it to her, but I can't see them anymore. Those good things, hidden from most people but shining out for me, have been dulled by Richmond. There's no good left in me. I'm empty. A shell. A dried, crackling crust that only exists as evidence of where life used to be.

The only thing I look forward to is Krav Maga. When I first got home, the panic attacks were...intense. After the second time I landed in the ER, convinced I was having a heart attack, my therapist increased the dosage of my daily anxiety medication and suggested I find an activity to help me feel more in control. I started with boxing. I thought I needed to beat my rage out. The anger hasn't gone anywhere, but boxing isn't me. Krav Maga though...I like that it takes bits and pieces from different styles of martial arts with the point being extreme efficiency in real-world situations. It's exactly what I need to feel less helpless.

In class I feel like a giant sea sponge, soaking up all the instruction and self-defense tips. I practice between classes, wanting to perfect my throat strikes, palm strikes, and eye gouges. I drill the steps to get myself out of a chokehold or a grab from behind. I stop outside strikes and work on throwing punches. I drop and kick, stomp insteps, and aim for the groin, drilling and drilling and drilling some more to gain that muscle memory.

I'm sweaty and slightly less angry when class ends. It's close enough to walk to Mama's but I don't. I tried in the beginning but ended up having to call her, barely able to breathe, begging for a ride. Now I can at least drive myself. I grab my bag and there's a piece of paper sticking out of the side pocket. I read it right there, where there are bright lights and people around, that need now second nature.

Ivy (I think),

I've seen you in class. You're very determined and work twice as hard as everyone else here. You've made a lot of progress since you started — way more than I have, that's for sure. I don't know what brought you here but it's not often good things that bring women to self-defense classes. I know the places that are still broken in me recognize yours. You look a little haunted, but I wanted you to know that every time you leave class, I see less of the darkness in you. You're a fighter. You're taking back what's yours every time you walk through those doors. I'm betting it won't be long now before you'll know enough to feel safe, to feel in control.

31

Then you won't need this anymore and you'll be ready to move to the next thing. I hope that happens for you Ivy, and soon. I'm sure your next thing is going to be spectacular.

Stay strong,
  A fellow fighter

I hurry out of the class, not wanting anyone to see the tears that are threatening to fall. Safely inside the car, they do, warm streaks tracing down my cheeks and dripping from my chin. I've been seen. I feel a warmth, the soft glow of gold at the horizon as day breaks, seeping through my grey. It's the tiniest hint but it's there: color returning. I wipe my cheeks and carefully fold the note, sliding it safely into my wallet. I was seen. By someone like me. Her broken parts recognized mine. I bet I can do that too. I bet the places inside me that Vance shattered could see fellow fighters. And maybe, just maybe, I could be strong enough to help.

CHAPTER 8
IVY

PRESENT DAY

In preparation for the Bennetts' next appointment, I pull out her file and a notepad, ready to jot down any questions I might have. The first thing I see is a photo that Janice clipped to the top page of the happy couple: Chloe and LIAM Bennett. Face, meet my palm. Liam is clearly related to Miles. They have the same straight nose, strong jawline, and amber eyes. Where Miles is long and lean with a habit of hunching his shoulders in, Liam is broad and bulky with the bearing of a military man. Liam looks strong and vibrant, with no hint of Miles' broodiness. He fits perfectly next to the athletic Chloe, her light to his dark. Lands sakes, imagine the perfect, gorgeous combination of genes that baby is going to have!

Ignoring my discomfort I skim over Janice's notes. Liam wasn't there because he's deployed. That sucks. Janice scrawled in the margins that Chloe was strong and bubbly but could use a calming presence and someone to keep everything in order. Looks like we may be a good fit. I'm hoping I can get by without even mentioning how weird I was during her appointment. I mean, let's face it, I'm often a bit awkward. I should be figuring out a way to apologize to Miles but my phone alarm is telling me it's time to head over to the church. Thursday evenings I volunteer at Fresh Start and I hate being late.

I walk along the side of the building, too aware of what happened the last time I walked through here *(cue replay of the dark suit, the feel of his back underneath my hands, and his tongue lightly touching my lip)*, and cut across the parking lot to the small building on the back of the lot. The lights are already on and the doors are open even though we don't start for another hour. I step inside, wondering if someone has already made the coffee, and standing right in my path is Miles Bennett.

He turns when he hears my steps, a shy smile lighting up his face. Lawdy, I was not ready for smiling Miles. I smile back, tentatively. Might as well get the humiliation over with while I'm still distracted by how his smile makes me feel.

"Ivy, about the other day in your office. Chloe is..." I interrupt him, hoping to rip the band-aid off, so to speak.

"Your sister-in-law? I know. I sat down with her file today and saw a photo of her and your brother. They make quite the striking couple."

"For sure. Always have." He chuckles, tilting his head to the side and running his hand down the side of his neck. Pretty sure I've seen that exact pose in fashion magazines. Freaking model, turning my insides to goo. He looks like he's struggling to say something so when he does start speaking, the subject surprises me. "Chloe moved across the street from us when they were in high school and Liam never had eyes for anyone else. He was single-minded in his pursuit of her. It took him a while to convince her he was worth the risk, though. Chloe was pretty focused on sports and school. But once she gave him a chance that was it for both of them. They've been together ever since. Went to the same college, got married right after graduation, then Liam commissioned. He's stationed out of Norfolk. They've been happy, living close to family." His voice falters at the end but I skip right past it, struck by something he said, details starting to fall into place.

"Liam commissioned and is at Norfolk...he's in the Navy?"

"Yeah. He's a Surface Warfare Officer—he's on ships. That's where he is right now, on a ship somewhere near the Middle East."

"And naval officers wear those dress blues, right? Like a navy blue suit?" I can see the understanding hit his eyes and he nods slowly. "So on that Saturday, when I ran into you here, outside the funeral..."

"Yeah," he almost whispers. "I was on my way inside. For my dad." I move towards him, placing my hand flat against his chest, biting my lip to stop the tears from falling. Now is not the time for the sympathetic tears I can feel wetting my eyes. Nobody needs that. He puts his hand over mine, covering it in warmth and trapping it against him. "That day in the park, when you gave me the coffee, I had just come from the hospital. I didn't even know where I was. I walked until my legs gave out and collapsed on the bench." His eyelids drop and he swallows hard.

"Miles, I'm so sorry." I know from experience that there's nothing else to say. No words will make that burden lighter. I slide my hand out from under his, wanting to give him some space. "While I'm apologizing, I'm also sorry about my behavior in my office. I shouldn't have been cold towards you. It's no excuse, but I was sort of embarrassed and never recovered. I made up that appointment so I didn't have to look you in the eye." He looks up at me, that soft smile reappearing.

"You lied to me? I'm appalled, Ivy." His laugh is warm and sets butterflies off in my stomach. "You didn't have anything to be embarrassed about." He places his hands on my shoulders, the weight grounding me, tiny sparks radiating across my skin. "That Saturday was one of the worst days of my life. I was very overwhelmed. I'm sorry if I acted inappropriately. It wasn't intentional. You'll never know how much that hug meant to me. I needed it." Heat spreads across my cheeks and I'm sure I'm a humiliating shade of pink. I need to get some space between us quickly. I'm not here to flirt with someone who was merely nice enough to talk to me.

"Do you want some coffee?" I point towards the small kitchenette over in the corner. He nods, watching me carefully before dropping his hands, following me as I walk away. While pouring our cups it occurs to me that I haven't asked the most obvious question. "Miles, why are you here?"

He takes a sip, leaning back against the countertop and sliding his free hand into his pocket. I am *not* looking at the way his jeans hang off his hips. While I'm lying to myself, I am also *not* noticing how long his legs are or how the denim hugs his thighs. Nope. Just drinking my coffee, being totally appropriate.

"Ah. The co-director, Walter, called me, on Louise's recommendation. He wants me to design a website for Fresh Start." He takes a sip of his coffee and I'm captivated by the motion of his Adam's apple as he swallows, the prominent bulge gliding underneath tawny skin. I need to get a grip on these hormones!

"That's awesome," I stumble. "I've been telling Walter for a while now that we need an online presence to streamline donations and get the word out about events, but he's been dragging his feet. He has a lot on his plate here but he's not very good at passing on responsibilities to other people." He's studying me and listening intently. I wrap my hands around my mug, needing something to focus on besides him. "A website will be great but I'm still not sure I understand why you're *here*, right *now*. You don't need to be here to design anything, do you?"

"No, you're right. I don't have to be here for the design work. But I think to make a good site, I need to understand what you do here. It's not just that the page should look good and be intuitive to users. I want it to correctly reflect the work you do and its importance to the community. I probably could have gotten the official schpiel from Walter, but I wanted to see everything first hand."

That makes sense. It sounds like not only is he good at his job but he cares about what he's doing. Swoon. "I guess I should show you around, then!" I paste on a smile, the effort to be welcoming and professional more work than it should be.

"You don't have to do that if you have something you need to be doing. I didn't even know you'd be here. That's a bonus."

I feel the teensiest bit sad at his admission that his being here has nothing to do with me. It's silly, but I feel it all the same. Apparently, I wasn't done embarrassing myself. At least this time it's for an audience of one. No one else needs to know.

"Not at all," bobbing my head like a freaking cockatoo, "I'm happy to help." I keep my mug in my hands and walk out of the kitchenette toward the main room. "Here at Fresh Start, we work with one specific group, survivors of domestic abuse. We've cultivated good relationships with a couple of local shelters specializing in helping women who are fleeing abusive situations. They give them a home, keep them safe, help them heal, and get back on their feet — all with absolute privacy. Then we come in. Our goal is to help them transition from the shelter and start a life on their own. We focus mainly on the first step needed for independence: getting a job. We provide a professional outfit for job interviews and we have volunteers — qualified professionals — who give haircuts, help with resumes, and even prep them for interview questions. The clothes are either donated or purchased with monetary donations." As I'm talking I walk him through the clothes racks and show him the shelves of stored supplies. It's getting close to opening time and the other volunteers are finishing the set-up.

"What's in this corner over here?" He points out a small table with chairs, baskets of books, and buckets of crayons, pushed into the corner between clothing racks. Seeing it through his eyes, I'm bothered. It's not enough. I should have done something about it sooner.

"Quite often our ladies flee terrible situations with their children. They don't have the resources to leave their kids with someone while they try to get back on their feet. Right now we have this small space carved out for kids to sit and color or look at books." I feel like I'm apologizing. "I've been working to get volunteers added to provide childcare, while they're here and during their interviews, and maybe tutors for the older kids, but it's taking longer than I'd like."

Miles is staring at me again but before I can puzzle out what he's thinking, Walter is calling me over to welcome our ladies. It's time to start.

CHAPTER 9
MILES

I'm rooted in place, absorbing everything Ivy told me. What they're doing here is unbelievable. I won't have any problem creating something great for them, something that highlights their mission and hopefully brings in more donations. I feel fortunate I get to play a small part in what they do. And I won't be forgetting the way Ivy's face lit up while she talked about Fresh Start. Her eyes sparkled and her passion for her volunteer work made her almost glow, soft rose blooming beneath ivory. It was already difficult not to stare—she's beautiful, and I'm a sucker for genuine passion and interest. If she spends any more time talking about her ideas for helping people, I'll be a goner.

I try not to gape at the generous curve of her hips or the way her tight jeans hug her ass as she walks away but I fail. Miserably. And, just my luck, my ogling doesn't go unnoticed. There is a clear *ahem* right next to me that has heat rising on my cheeks. Caught in the act. Perfect.

"I'm Myrna. I make the coffee and snacks and try to help keep an eye on the kiddos. I see you already appreciate our Ivy?"

I cough out a laugh at her assessment. "Yes, ma'am. There's...a lot to appreciate." Her wrinkled cheeks lift in a big grin. "I'm

Miles. I'm designing a website for Fresh Start. Ivy was telling me all about what you guys do here."

"Well, Miles, did Miss Ivy tell you that all this was her idea?"

My eyebrows lift with surprise. "No ma'am, she did not mention that."

She puts my hand between both of hers, her skin soft and thin. "She's co-director, you know. Could have had the whole position to herself but she asked Walter to share it. Said we need his wisdom and guidance to be successful. Our Ivy is humble, that's for sure. She doesn't like to be the center of attention. Has a heart of gold, that one. She dreamed this up and started wrangling volunteers and donations as soon as she came back home after that trouble up in Richmond. I've never met anyone more passionate about serving others. She's the rare sort that can see straight to what ya need *and* has the drive to help ya get it." Myrna's watery eyes are locked on mine and she squeezes my hand. "You be careful now. Ivy puts so much of herself into everyone around her. She doesn't need someone taking. Not again. Who sees *her*, I ask ya? Who takes care of *her*?" She pats my arm gently and turns back towards the refreshment table. "It was nice to meet you, Miles. I hope we see more of you."

That was a lot to take in. It did help explain the pre-funeral hug a little better though. She is the type of person who sees a need and doesn't think twice about filling it. That's all that was. Now if only I could stop thinking about it. I'll need to be careful about not pushing my attraction on someone that is only trying to help. I'm not sure what is up with that anyway. It's not as if I've never been around a pretty woman before. There's no reason for this particular woman to have me captivated to this extent. Now is not the time anyway. It wouldn't be fair to think about anything beyond Fresh Start or Ivy supporting Chloe as her doula when I'm planning on leaving anyway.

I spend the rest of the evening talking with the women who are there to grab ahold of their fresh starts. One of tonight's volunteers, Phoebe, was part of the first group of women to complete the program here. She grabs me by the arm and has me holding hanging clothes while she talks.

"When I came here, I didn't have any job experience. None. With Ivy's help, I got the opportunity to work as a sales associate and the cutest little boutique." She places a final outfit across my arms and gestures me towards the make-shift fitting room they have set up. "All along this journey I've been met with nothing but patience and positivity. I worked my way up to assistant manager! Can you believe that? Me!" Phoebe's charge comes out from behind the curtains and she gives her an emphatic no before turning back to me. "Now my boss is looking for more ways to help women like me, and it's all because of Fresh Start!"

She goes back to helping while I think about her experience. Stories like hers would be a good addition to the website. I make myself a note and watch Ivy work. She has this calming nature that pulls everyone in. It reminds me a little bit of Dad. He had that same feeling of being a peaceful shelter in a storm. She wipes the tears from a young woman's cheeks, rubbing her arms and talking to her gently until she feels up to meeting with her job counselor. She scoops up a toddler, bouncing him on her hip and handing him an applesauce pouch while she helps his mother choose a blazer. She never stops moving. From one side of the room to the other she comforts with soft touches and kind words, leaving smiles in her wake.

As the last woman is ushered out, a garment bag in her arms, Ivy walks back over to me. Her posture speaks of weariness but she still gives off an air of joy.

"What do you think?"

"I think this place is incredible. What you're doing here is important. I can't wait to get started on the website."

She tucks a stray curl behind her ear, pushing the praise away with one hand. "It's a group effort. We're lucky to have so many people willing to give their time." I know now that there's more to it than that, but I'm not going to press her. It's obvious Ivy isn't looking for acknowledgment, however much it's deserved. I turn, stacking chairs, and Ivy makes a confused *hmm* noise.

"That's not the same book."

"What's that?" I don't know what we're talking about.

"The book in your back pocket, it's not the same as before— the one with the comb."

Remembering that book causes a dull ache between my ribs. I haven't been able to look at it since that day.

"That was the book I was reading to my dad in the hospital. He liked me to help him *look presentable;* I used his comb to mark our place. This is what I normally carry with me." I pull the soft book from my pocket, flipping through the pages to show her. Flashes of graphite and ink amongst the cream pages.

"You're an artist!"

"I am. For work and fun." I slide my sketchbook back into its place. "You were pretty great with the kids tonight." She blushes. "I can see how it could be hard to get everything accomplished that you need to with them roaming around, though. I was wondering, have you ever considered utilizing women who have gone through your program and moved on?" She joins me, stacking chairs and tidying up while we talk. "Speaking with Phoebe got me thinking. Graduates would probably have a soft spot for Fresh Start's mission and other women who are going through what they went through. Maybe if you reached out, some of them would be willing to come in and do the childcare. I don't know what the budget looks like in terms of funds. Maybe they'd volunteer if you couldn't pay them." Her eyes are wide and she sucks her bottom lip into her mouth, nibbling at it with her teeth. I run my hands through my hair, suddenly worried. "Or you've probably already considered that. I didn't mean to imply that I know better. Merely an outsider's perspective. Fresh eyes."

I'm leaning against the back counter, almost sitting on it with my legs stretched out in front of me. She launches herself at me, throwing her arms around my neck in an exuberant hug. I catch her, startled, breathing in her lavender and coconut scent and holding her. I forgot how nice hugs are. How nice *her* hugs are.

"Miles, that idea is perfect!" She gushes. "I can't believe I never thought of that. I'm sure we'd have some interest. It would have to be volunteers for now, but maybe I can find a new revenue stream that we could allocate for paying for childcare."

I'm looking down at her, taking in her excitement, and can see the exact moment she realizes she's between my legs, lying against my body. She breathes deeply, pulling back and putting a step's distance between us.

"Sorry about that!" There's that nervous curl tuck again. "I'm a hugger. I mean, I know random hugs shouldn't last *that* long, I got excited about your idea and distracted by the possibilities." She's back to nibbling her bottom lip.

"No worries. I'm realizing my life is severely lacking in hugs. I don't mind." I grin at her, hoping to put her at ease.

"You've given me a lot to think about. I should probably get home so I can start working out the details. Thanks. I'm glad you came tonight, Miles."

"Me too."

I have a lot to think about as well. As excited as I am to start designing a logo for Fresh Start and working on their website, it would be a safe bet that dark curls, caring brown eyes and exuberant hugs will be taking the center stage tonight. Why again am I thinking about going back to Philadelphia?

CHAPTER 10
IVY

I've spent the last few days buzzing with ideas for the Fresh Start childcare situation. I reached out to a few of my favorite graduates from our first year, to feel out interest. One of them suggested we should also consider their teenage daughters, allowing them to build up job experience early on. I agreed wholeheartedly. That idea builds well on Miles' initial thoughts. Some of these teenagers have lived through situations as scary as what their mothers did, and they've seen firsthand what it looks like to take control of your own life and work to build a future you can be proud of. I can think of two, right off the top of my head, who would likely be happy to get to work with us after watching their mothers go through the program. I add their names to my list. I talk to Walter and meet with him and the church leadership (since they provide the building and graciously help us with funding) to share the idea, making sure to give credit to Miles, and they're all as excited as I am. I'm unfailingly happy to put in time at Fresh Start, but there's a special kind of energy I get with new ideas. It's giving me a bounce in my step.

My first appointment of the day is with Chloe and her midwife and I'm trying not to be nervous about seeing her again.

Our practice has nurses, OBs, midwives, and doulas on staff. We can coordinate appointments, saving our patients from needing to schedule follow-ups with other providers. The proximity to the hospital is also a big plus. I smooth the pleats down on my skirt, happy with how it floats out from my hips. These curves aren't going anywhere, I might as well play them up.

I'm grabbing my notebook and coffee when Victoria buzzes in on my office phone.

"Mrs. Bennett is here and I've sent her back to meet Sarah in Exam Room 2."

"Thanks, Victoria. I'll wait for them in Sarah's office."

I have enough time to return some emails and send out a quick good morning text to my mom before they come out of the examination room. I smile a hello at Chloe and wave at Sarah, the midwife.

"Everything looking good?"

Sarah answers. "Chloe is progressing perfectly! Baby looks good, she's measuring on track and we've even been able to maintain the surprise."

"Oh!" I exclaim. "You're waiting to find out what you're having?"

Chloe's straight white teeth flash as she smiles. "We are! I didn't want to find out without Liam and share such big news through email or a low-quality phone call. This way we'll both find out at the same time!"

Sarah taps her stylus on the tablet she uses. "I know you've reviewed her file, Ivy, but I thought it would be helpful if the three of us went over Chloe's plans together since we're a new team." I nod in agreement and angle my body towards Chloe. "Would you like to tell her, Chloe, or would you prefer I do it?" Sarah asks.

"No problem, I don't mind talking!" Chloe's blue eyes crinkle at the edges with her smile. "I want to do this drug-free. I'm open to using them if I feel like it's necessary in the moment, but my ultimate goal is to do it on my own. With Liam deployed, we didn't get the chance to take any birth classes together. I don't want to be having contractions while trying to explain to him what I need him to do for me. I know, 100%, that my husband will give me everything I need emotionally so I don't want him to have to worry about anything else. He's a doer. If I don't have someone in place with everything taken care of, he'll spend the entire birth rushing around, trying to find me the best ice chips or something ridiculous. I need Liam to *be* with me."

"That's exactly why I'm here. My job is to make sure you're comfortable and you have everything you need, allowing you and Liam to focus on bringing your baby into the world. Will you both be good with me staying in the background, giving him directions when needed?"

"That sounds great. I want him to be a part of it but I don't want him to waste time trying to figure out what he should be doing."

"That information helps me a lot." I pull out my pen and start taking notes. "While you're in labor I'll make sure you have ice when you need it, the lights are how you'd like them to be, the temperature is where you want it, etc. I can text updates to family and handle the music. When you need it we can try different laboring positions, but I'll direct Liam so it's always his hands supporting you. Because Sarah and I work together, you don't have to worry about your providers butting heads, but I hope you know that we will both do everything in our power to give you the birth that you want. Above that though, we want you and baby safe."

Chloe tears up. "Thank you so much! It's such a relief. I can't wait to email Liam, he's been worrying about how the transition was going to go with Janice needing to leave. He hates having so much out of his control."

"Well," Sarah interjects, "I won't see you for another month but you can meet with Ivy as much as you two need before then.

Let me know if you have any concerns and in the meantime, I'm a phone call away."

I stand up, figuring they would need to finish up, but Chloe stops me.

"Ivy? Do you have time to speak with me on your own?"

"Sure! My office?" She nods her assent and I head that way, giving them a moment to say their goodbyes. We sit in the chairs in front of my desk. "What else would you like to go over?"

"I'm pretty good on the birth front. For now anyway. I'm sure I will think of questions or find something else I want to add once I've left." She shakes her head in a cute, self-deprecating gesture. "I wanted to ask you something else." She forges ahead before I have a chance to get nervous. "I was wondering if you'd like to get dinner with me tonight? Maybe that's weird, I'm not sure. But if you're allowed to hang out with me outside of the birth center, I could use a friend. You seem like you'd be a good one. Liam and I have always been a pretty self-contained unit and I didn't put much effort into getting to know the other officers' wives before deployment. I use to get my social fix with my father-in-law but..." she trails off, eyes shining with unshed tears.

"I'd love to!" I exclaim, hoping my babbling will give her time to get her emotions in check if she is wanting to avoid crying in front of me. "Do you like salad? I know that sounds like a chick dinner cliche, but there's this little place in the neighborhood that makes the most incredible salads with homemade dressings and fire-grilled vegetables. They serve it with freshly baked bread and their soups are to die for! My mom and I try to go at least once a month."

She swipes a finger under her eye and smiles. "That sounds killer!"

I grab the file under my notebook, pull out the first page, and type her number into my phone. Her cell dings from her purse. "There, now you have my number. I'll text you the name and address. Does 6 work for you?"

Plans made I hug Chloe goodbye, walk her out so I can tell Victoria she needs to schedule her upcoming appointment, and get back to work.

Tired from a full workday, I walk into Super Salad and see Chloe already seated. "I hope you weren't waiting too long," I sigh, hanging my purse over the back of my chair. The homey, yeasty smell of fresh bread hangs in the air and makes my stomach growl.

"Nope, not at all. I just got settled. Haven't even had a chance to look at the menu yet." The waiter brings by some water and we both take a minute to decide what we want to eat.

"I should warn you," I tell her, "the salads are HUGE! I only get a full-size salad if I intend to take leftovers home for another meal. If you only want salad it would probably be good but I love everything else too much to be limited. I usually order a half salad, a bowl of soup, and bread"

"Yum! Sounds like that's what I need to do then!" We order our meals, asking the waiter to bring everything out at the same time, and sip our waters.

"So, you and Liam are high school sweethearts?" I ask.

"We are! I've loved him since I was 15. I thought he was the hottest guy I had ever seen then and somehow he keeps getting better. Wait, how did you know that? That wasn't in my file was it?"

"No! Janice isn't that thorough! Um, Miles mentioned it the other night. He said Liam was, and I quote, *single-minded* in his pursuit of you."

"That's my man. Single-minded." She grins, looking a little mischievous. "When did you see my brother-in-law?" She waggles her eyebrows at me.

"It's nothing like that! I volunteer at Fresh Start. Miles was hired to design a website for us. I showed him around, talked to him about what we do, that sort of thing. And I kind of had to apologize for being weird towards him during your first appointment with me. I thought you guys were married and it made a previous encounter feel...awkward." That probably sounded even lamer to her than it did to me.

"Previous encounter? Sounds intriguing. Do tell." Chloe steeples her fingers in front of her face dramatically.

"Honestly, there's nothing to tell. I bought him a coffee once. I didn't know who he was, we didn't talk, there was nothing to it. He looked broken... I thought it might help. It was the day your father-in-law passed." I nibble at my bottom lip, wishing there was a way to explain the situation without hurting her more, the loss still being very fresh. "I also sort of ran into him, physically, before the funeral. On accident." Her eyes widened, urging me to go on. "Again, we didn't talk. He looked super sad and I hugged him. That's it." *Liar.* The lip lick flashes in my mind. "But then when I saw you two together in my office I thought I had exceeded what is appropriate and embarrassed myself, giving unasked for comfort to a married man. And like a grown-up, I didn't ask for clarification or give him a chance to explain." I roll my eyes although the disdain is directed at me. "Thankfully he was nice about it so I don't have to go to my grave obsessing over that particular moment of humiliation."

She laughs loudly. "Don't worry about it." Pursing her lips she looks me over carefully. "He *was* pretty flustered when the receptionist thought he was my husband. He even asked me if I thought you made the same mistake. Flustered Milesy is pretty cute."

"Why would he worry about what *I* thought?" Crap. Did I say that out loud?

Chloe snorts which she still somehow manages to make attractive. "Maybe because you're hot and he's a dude?"

"Um, no, I'm sure that's not it. I'm not... no one has ever...

that's just not me. I'm not being all *poor pity me*. I can be honest about my positives as well as my negatives. But guys like Miles would never go for a girl like me." Now I'm flustered and wondering how I let the conversation go in this direction. Maybe I could fake a call and extract myself before I make it worse?

"Oh, Sweets, I didn't mean to embarrass you! But you *have* to know you possess some bangin' curves. Even without that china doll face, a guy would have to be a moron not to notice you! Plus there's the whole sweet-as-pie, caring-and-giving thing you've got going on. I'd hit that." I choke on my water, caught completely off guard by her blunt delivery.

"I think I'm going to like being your friend, Chloe."

"Me too! You can't get away from me now. We're in this thing. Plus you're going to see the most traumatic thing happen to my vagina so you are stuck with me." She snorts again and I fall a teensy bit in love. It's been a long time since I've had a real friend. Richmond ruined that for me. She continues, thankfully missing the dip in my mood. "And don't think I didn't notice you said *guys like Miles*. What did you mean by that, Miss Ivy?"

Now it's my turn to snort. "Psssh! Oh, nothing. Just, he's a whole vibe. He's all cool artist swagger and I've been an awkward dork since birth. I mean, you know! Guys that are tall, dark, and all broody and super sexy." Crappity crap crap. Why did I say that? I got too comfortable with her and forgot to internally edit. I should have been coy instead of brutally honest.

"I feel like I should tease you. Sing-song about you thinking Milesy is sexy. But I won't. I don't think we're there yet in our friendship. I'll move on but *I heard you*, Ivy, and I'm filing it away in my mind vault." She taps the side of her head with one finger and scoots our water glasses to the side, giving the waiter space to set down our meals. I dig into my salad, the peppery fresh arugula and smokey grilled zucchini making me want to dance in my seat. I'm happy to have something to distract her, but she only takes a couple of bites before she resumes our conversation.

"Am I right in assuming you're single?" I nod a yes, chewing my salad. "What's the deal there? No prospects? Sworn off men? Too busy being a secret high-priced escort?" I toss a "pssh" at the last one and consider her question, debating how forthright I should be. Chloe seems honest to a fault, blunt but caring. I like her but I'm not sure if that's enough. The pause has dragged on longer than necessary and she's watching me think.

"What are you wrestling with, Ivy? I promise you can trust me. I want to get to know you better and can't understand how someone who seems so great also seems so alone."

Ouch. She has me there. "It's not that I don't want to be genuine with you," I start, biting into the still-warm bread, the butter oozing down into all the nooks. "I want to. Really. But past experiences have left me wondering if I can trust my instincts."

"How can that be, though? You obviously have great instincts. You never even spoke to Miles but knew exactly what to give him the day we lost his dad, and again the morning of the funeral. You really see people. That's a gift."

"I hadn't thought of it that way. I guess it doesn't make sense to trust my gut feelings when it comes to helping other people but not trust them when it comes to myself. It's hard though." I need to file that away for further examination. My therapist is always reminding me that I should give myself the same grace and consideration I give others. I hate that she's always right.

"What happened? If you don't mind me asking that is." Chloe samples her soup and I weigh the question. I've never really talked about it before. I even kept a lot of the details from Mama. I was too ashamed. I take in Chloe's earnest interest and step over the line I've always drawn. I'm going to be brave.

"It's a lot to go into but bare bones: I went to college up in Richmond. I didn't graduate. After a couple of years, I found it wasn't what I wanted and I got my doula certification instead. I stayed though because it's a nice city and I had friends. That's where I met Vance. It was quite an ego boost for a lonely awkward girl, to be wooed by that type of guy—wealthy and handsome and older. "

I clench my hands under the table, short nails biting into my palms. "It was a whirlwind. He was charismatic and I felt glamorous being romanced by him. I got swept away. I *let* myself get swept away. I moved in with him right away. It all spiraled out of control so quickly!" Chloe's eyes darken and she leans forward.

"He'd go dark but then afterward he'd be extra loving—buying me gifts, showering me with affection, promising me it would never happen again, begging me to understand how much he needed me." I take a sip of water, trying to settle my twisting stomach. "There was a lot of that. Back and forth between scary Vance and charming Vance, too many times I should have left and didn't. Some wounds, too many tears, a lot of fear." My words are spilling out at a faster pace and I let them, desperate to be done. "In the end, he was arrested for assault and attempted rape and I was taken to the hospital to get staples in my head. Then I came back here. The end."

"Holy shit." Chloe breathes out. "What happened to the dickhead?"

"Nothing. It doesn't matter. Mama came and got me from the hospital, I moved back home, and started working on my idea for Fresh Start, wanting to help women who were brave enough to escape abusive relationships."

"Damn. I hope you're including yourself in that, Ivy. You're brave."

"Not really. I didn't leave him. I got hurt and my mom helped me run away while he was in jail." She scoffs but doesn't interrupt. "You know the worst part, though?" I swirl the water and ice in my glass to avoid meeting her eyes. "It wasn't the wounds or the fact that he tried to rape me. It was that he ground me down until I was a shell of a person and made it so that I couldn't trust my instincts about people. It's that I let him in when I shouldn't have. I trusted him. And I couldn't have been more wrong. How can I ever trust my feelings again?"

"Sweets!" Chloe comes around our little table and hugs me. "That's not on you. That's on him." She returns to her chair, crunching on the ice from her glass. "Have you dated since you left Richmond?"

"No. I haven't been with anyone. It's taken this long not to feel physically ill when a man touches me, even innocently. And then there's who I am."

"What is that supposed to mean?" There's fire in her words.

I huff out a breath, frustrated with myself. "Vance PICKED me. The pattern that he followed, the way things progressed from angry words escalating to physical violence, there's no way that was his first time treating a woman that way. Out of all of the women in his orbit, he saw me and *knew* that I would fall for his lines, that I would eat up the compliments, that I was so desperate for love I'd forgive almost anything. Vance saw that I was weak. If a guy ever shows interest in me I'm immediately wary. I know what kind of man wants me. I know what men see in me. That's why I started taking self-defense classes when I moved back. I may not have confidence in my judgment but at least I know I can protect myself physically."

"Shit, every bit of that hurts my heart. What about friends?"

"None of those either," I sigh. "I didn't mend any of the relationships I abandoned for Vance and I was ashamed when it was over. I stay pretty busy, but I also haven't felt very confident in my ability to know whether someone is safe."

"Well, you're safe with me. And I promise, on my life, that my brother-in-law is the best sort of guy. He's safe too. I'm so sorry you went through that." The waiter interrupts, taking our empty dishes and asking if we want anything else. "I'd like a chamomile if you have it."

"Make that two, please. Ooh, do you like gingerbread cake? Theirs is the best!"

"Yes!" Chloe shimmies in her chair. "Gingerbread cake to split, please."

We keep talking, moving on to less heavy topics until Chloe

stops being able to contain her yawns. "Sorry," she grimaces. "This human growing business is no joke." She heads home with a promise to text me to make plans to get together again. The conversation has left me drained but also less weighed down by my secrets. I walk home feeling lighter than I have in a long time. I have a friend.

CHAPTER 11

MILES

The website is coming along nicely. I have a separate portal set up for online donations and a place for people to apply to volunteer. I've also talked to Walter about reaching out to corporate sponsors, maybe finding businesses the program can feed into with guaranteed jobs, even short-term positions, for the right candidates. It's exciting watching it grow. Something about this organization has gotten all my creative juices flowing. I like dreaming up ideas, but I'm not very good at moving forward, putting things into action. It's nice taking that next step.

The one thing I do wish, though, is that I could put a human face to the work. Seeing these women would easily pull at donors' heartstrings, but it simply isn't safe. There's no way we could share online, for anyone to see, the faces of women who have run from their abusers, no matter how much it might help bring in more money. Unless it's with someone who is far enough away from the process that they're comfortable having their story told... I don't need to get distracted by that possibility. That can be something I look into down the road. I need to think of some other way to humanize the mission to outsiders, something to help them connect to the idea and want to know more. I'm not worried. It'll come to me. I finish up what I'm working on, email a rebranding client from Philly, then push away from my desk. Time for something else.

I stretch my back, stiff from sitting in front of a screen for such a long time. My soul needs feeding. I put on Leon Bridges and go back to the sunroom. It started as a porch, but Dad had it enclosed for Mom so she'd have a place to paint. I inherited my creative side from her. Pulling out my watercolors, I let my mind wander as I start to paint. I don't have a plan, nothing specific, I just want to create. I dip my brush, thinking about a nighttime landscape.

The groove of "Smooth Sailing" hits and I put brush to paper, moving instinctually. When I go to reload the bristles though, I don't see a landscape at all. I see dark curls. I turn the paper vertically, eyeing it carefully before adding darker layers to the bottom while the top dries, then add on some lighter streaks, like sunlight kissing the top of her head. I paint feverishly, working from memory while refusing to acknowledge how crystal clear the image is. The soft pink apples of her cheeks, small rosy mouth, and pointed chin spring from the page. Then bold arched brows, intelligent eyes that perfect shade of milk chocolate, full dark lashes. She's strong but delicate. I pull out my favorite Tombow and pen "Ivy" on the bottom. Done.

I'm still itching to do a landscape, picturing those treetops and the dark sky from the night in Shenandoah, but I'm out of time for now. I need to hustle if I'm going to get over to Chloe's place on time for our regular dinner date. Best not to think too hard about why Ivy is the first bright thing I've painted since I left Philadelphia.

I park in front of the little cottage Chloe and Liam are renting and let myself in the front door.

"Chlo! I'm here!"

"In the kitchen, Milesy!"

I follow the sound of her voice, finding her crouched on the ground, belly between her legs.

"What are you doing down there? Let me help before you tip over." I pull her up and sit her in the nearest chair in their little eat-in kitchen.

"I'm trying to find my big pot for pasta. Can you see it back there?"

Pot found, I fill it with water and set it on the stove for her. "Ok, that's done, what next?"

"That's it for now. Come sit with me, tell me what you've been up to?" She rests her hands on her belly, patting absentmindedly.

I pull up another chair, stretching out. "Nothing much, working on a website, finishing up some jobs from Philly. The usual."

"Right, Ivy told me you were doing the web design for that charity. Fresh Start?" She gives me a sly smile that I can't interpret.

"Yep, that's the one. When did you talk to Ivy?"

"Ah," she waves at me breezily, "we had dinner Monday night. She's my new best friend you know."

I raise my eyebrows. "Is she? How did that happen?"

"You know me," she laughs, "I told her she was and that was that."

"You staked your claim, huh? I'm sure there's not a downside to being Ivy's friend."

She gives me that same sly smile. It's starting to make me nervous. Chloe can be a bit devious and usually gets her way.

"There's nothing not to like! Ivy is great. We talked for hours and had such a nice time. She told me about meeting you, you know."

"Really?" I scrunch my lips, worried about playing into Chloe's hands but too curious not to. "How did that story go?"

"Are you fishing for compliments, Milesy?"

"No," I choke out. "I was curious about her perspective, that's all." And maybe a little interested in hearing what she said about me.

"Uh huh. She told me about before the funeral, saying how

she overstepped and embarrassed herself by giving unwanted comfort to a stranger and then made herself feel even more embarrassed when she thought you were married."

I groaned. "I talked to her about that. I even told her how much that hug meant to me." I rub my hands down my face. "Is that all she said about that morning?"

Chloe honed in on me like a missile. "Is there something else she should have mentioned? What else happened?"

There is no way in hell I am telling her I licked Ivy. I would never hear the end of it.

"Nothing, Chlo! You're as bad as Liam."

"Thank you," she replies demurely. "I'll take that as the highest compliment."

"Not how I meant it," I grumble under my breath.

"Anyway," she grins, ignoring my grumbling, "she may have also said some stupid shit about her misinterpreting your reactions to her kindness because guys like you would never go for girls like her."

"What the hell does that mean? What kind of guy does she think I am?" Shit! Was it the hair sniffing? The staring? There are too many embarrassing instances to consider.

"Oh, you know, a guy who is *tall, dark, and all broody and super sexy.* Her words obviously, not mine."

My heart skips a beat. I should be careful about my expression, knowing who I'm sitting with, but I can't help the slow grin that takes over my face. "Did she actually say that or are you just fucking with me?"

"Nope, those were her exact words." She smiles back at me, taking in my glee, but then her smile slips and she is suddenly serious. "Milesy, you should know...shit. It's not my place to tell you her stories. But...she's been hurt. So fucking badly. She has reason to be wary of the type of guys that might be interested in her, to be worried about what they see in her. Tread carefully. I'm not saying you're the kind of guy who would be careless with someone else's feelings—I know that's not you—but please be careful with her. She's put herself back together, but it took a long time. She deserves...*everything*. If you can't give her everything, don't give her anything."

"That's sobering. I don't even know if I have anything to give."

Chloe is throwing up a lot of red flags that I don't understand. I wasn't thinking about starting something, serious or otherwise. It's nice to be seen and wanted, that's all. It's been a while. But that's not fair to Ivy. I put my head in my hands.

"I'm not sure what I'm doing, Chlo."

Chloe sighs, rubbing her belly. "Miles?" Her voice is much softer than her usual speaking volume, it takes a moment for it to register. Chloe is rarely so restrained. "I think I messed up. I wasn't thinking about what it would all mean and I, uh, I sorta invited Ivy over for dinner with us." She grimaces and grabs my hands. "Please don't be mad at me!"

I puff out a loud breath, sitting up straight. Frustration flares hot and I tamp it down. I would have preferred more time, on my own, to figure out my feelings.

"I'm not mad at you. It's fine. I'm going to be seeing Ivy at Fresh Start quite a bit; being friendly isn't a problem."

"Are you sure? It's these hormones, I swear! I was thinking about her saying you're sexy and hoping maybe you'd be interested in her and then I'd have a front seat to your romance, like those silly cable movies I suddenly can't stop watching! I was already hatching this plan before she finished telling me all about Richmond and why she had to come back home. I shouldn't have meddled. Fuck! I'm the meddlesome side character that's always making a mess!" Her eyes get terrifyingly watery. I don't think I can handle an emotional, crying Chloe.

I pull her into a hug, a little awkwardly with her belly in between us. "I still love you, you meddler. Your heart was in the right place. And you weren't wrong. It's not like I'd have to make an effort to be attracted to her. I've been there since the first time I saw her. She's everything I would want. But I still have a job and an apartment in Philadelphia. I don't even know what I'm doing. I'm good to stick around for Liam's homecoming, the baby, and working out what we're going to do with the house. But after that? I don't know. This is all too complicated."

She pats me on the back, swiping at her eyes, and steps away, pulling noodles out of the pantry to drop in the now boiling water.

"Nothing good is ever easy, Miles, but I hear what you're saying. It's probably best that you steer clear of Ivy if you're going to leave again." She looks a little sad. Does she want me to stay? I want to ask but the doorbell rings and Chloe shoos me away, gesturing towards the door. I open the door and Ivy's eyes widen in surprise.

"Miles," she stammers. "Hi. I, uh, didn't know you'd be here. This is Chloe's house, right?"

I chuckle. "You're in the right place. And don't worry, Chloe didn't tell me she had invited you either."

Chloe yells from the kitchen, "It's pregnancy brain! Sorry guys!"

I step out of the way, giving Ivy room to come inside. I'm not bothered by the view, following her in. She looks casual but pretty in tight jeans and a soft wrapped sweater thing that hugs all of her curves and ties at her narrow waist. Chloe clears her throat and I jump because of course she was watching me check Ivy out. What is it about this woman?

"Hey little bro, can you take that pan from Ivy?" I take it from her and our fingers brush, leaving my skin tingling.

"I brought garlic bread, I hope that's ok."

"Yay, carbs!" Chloe crows. Ivy laughs, relaxing her shoulders.

"Can you point me to the bathroom?" Chloe directs her down the hall and then hurries back over to me, slapping me on the arm.

"You were totally checking her out, you perv! What did we just talk about?" I clear my throat.

"I know. Sorry. It's not like it was planned." I scrub my hands down my face. "Those jeans…"

"Right, blame the jeans."

"I'm a mere mortal, Chlo. I'd defy any man to resist the combination of those jeans and Ivy's curves."

"Well keep it together man!"

Chloe goes back to working on the pasta and I pop the bread in the oven to heat them through then check the fridge for veggies. Ivy makes herself at home, pulling out glasses and getting us all water before setting the table. I sauté green beans with garlic and olive oil and serve them up on our plates while Chloe finishes the main dish. The smells of garlic, rich tomato sauce, and butter are making my mouth water. Chloe and Ivy talk easily about her birth plan and making playlists for her labor. That leads to talking about music.

"Is anyone shocked that Milesy likes moody music?" Chloe teases.

"It doesn't have to be moody," I protest. "It has to be genuine. I don't like super polished, empty songs. I want lyrics with depth, voices raw with emotion, things that make me *feel*."

"I like that too," Ivy interjects. "Mama likes to tease me about my love for singer-songwriters and indie rock. She says Daddy was the same way."

"Okay you two, broaden my horizons. I mostly listen to music I can workout to. Give me your favorite female voice that will give me all the feels."

Ivy answers first. "Brandi Carlile."

I extend my fist, bumping hers. "I love her! The break in her voice and how she uses it gives me chills."

"What about guys, Milesy?"

I think for a moment, rifling through my favorite male voices. "Dustin Kensrue. For sure. He was the lead singer for Thrice but has also done some solo stuff. They sing completely different music but vocally he is similar to Brandi Carlile — he uses the grit and break in his voice to show emotion. It's raw and real."

"I'm not familiar with him," Ivy admits. "If you were introducing me to his music, what's the one song you'd want me to listen to?"

"It would have to be 'It's Not Enough.'" I don't even hesitate.

Ivy picks up her phone. "I'm downloading it now."

"You give me one." I pick up my phone.

She closes her eyes, tapping her fingers against the tabletop. "Zee Avi's cover of 'First of the Gang' by Morrissey." I download it, excited to listen to it later.

We talk about live shows we've been to and find we both also love listening to vinyl.

"Liam would say it's because I'm pretentious or desperate to be different," Chloe cackles in agreement, "but I love the warmth and crackle of vinyl. It sounds more real than digital."

Ivy smiles wistfully, crunching on the last of her green beans. "I think I've always had a soft spot for vinyl because of my dad. He died when I was 8 so I don't have a lot of memories of him, but one is crystal clear. I was born in Colorado and we lived in the mountains, pretty far from the nearest town. Our house had these big floor-to-ceiling windows all along the front, completely open without curtains. They helped heat the house with sunshine during the day and the stars at night were incredible." There's a yearning in her expression, her eyes seeming to focus far away, into the past.

"We usually listened to records during dinner but on this particular night, Daddy kept the music going. It got dark but instead of putting on a tv show or getting ready for bed he put on another album and turned off the lights. We threw all the pillows in the middle of the living room floor and piled on, the three of us snuggled close. We looked out at the stars, in the dark, the only sounds coming from the record player. We stayed there for hours. Linda Rondstadt, Chet Baker, Johnny Cash…I can't hear Holst's 'The Planets' without remembering lying sandwiched between my parents, surrounded by their love, blanketed by the stars, completely safe and happy." She sighs softly, sitting her fork down.

I'm afraid to speak, afraid to break the magic spell she's cast. After a moment, Chloe does it for me.

"How'd you end up in Virginia then? Doesn't your mom own a floral shop here?"

"We didn't have any family in Colorado. After Daddy died, Mama decided we should be closer to my grandparents. They helped her buy the shop and worked with her until they passed."

"Wait, your family owns a floral shop? Hughes Florals?" I ask her.

"Yep. That's my mom's."

"I'm pretty sure I've met her. She took care of the flowers for us."

She nods, biting her bottom lip. "That's why I was there. At the church. I was delivering the flowers." I blush, remembering the brief taste of her lips on the tip of my tongue. She blushes too and even though I shouldn't, I hope she's remembering the same thing.

CHAPTER 12
IVY

I wonder if Chloe is trying to maneuver me toward Miles. Surely not. I told her all about Vance, she has to know I'm still not sure about dating again. She's probably being kind since we're both alone and so is she. I did make the mistake of being too candid at Super Salad and now she knows I'm attracted to him. This would be much easier if he looked like a troll. I thought I was going to pass out when he opened her front door. I've never seen him without a jacket. He's wearing a plain white t-shirt and jeans and *sweet son of a biscuit eater*, those arms! He's all long lean muscles and those veins that shouldn't be a turn-on but totally are. His left arm has a full sleeve of sexy tattoos. Who knew I had a thing for arms? Miles Bennett is my kryptonite, I can't seem to function normally around him.

Dinner is delicious and the conversation flows easily. We have a lot of things in common and the more I talk to Miles, the more I find that I like. That makes me feel better since I've been so hyper-aware of him physically. I know it's been a loooong time for me but it was getting silly. It's nice to find that I like him as a person. Maybe I'm not a giant ball of hormones after all. And maybe I don't need to be as wary since my interest is beginning to be as much about who he is as how he looks. Miles and I offer to clean up while Chloe goes to set up a movie in the living room. It doesn't take us very long to get everything washed. Working beside him is easy, comfortable even. At least as long as our arms aren't brushing or his hip isn't coming into contact with my side and putting my body on high alert.

Chloe sits on one end of the couch and I take the other, not wanting to crowd her. Miles goes to take a chair but she drags him down in between us, stretching her legs out across his lap. I'd be more comfortable with him across the room. It would be easier to concentrate on the things I like about his personality when he's not within touching distance, but I'm not going to argue with a pregnant woman. The movie starts—some rom-com I've never seen before. It's depressing watching romantic movies alone so I tend to avoid them. Chloe wiggles her toes, pink lacquered nails gleaming.

"Milesy, will you rub my feet? They're sore from hauling all this extra weight around." She pouts dramatically and he laughs. Every time he does that I feel it all the way to my toes.

"Give 'em here, Chlo. I can't have Liam getting pissed at me for not taking care of you." He glances at me, smiling broadly, and I press my lips together to keep from grinning. I feel on edge around him like I'm constantly on the verge of doing something stupid to humiliate myself. He is way too attuned to my emotions, concern replaces the smile.

"You ok?" He whispers, tilting his head towards me.

"Yeah. Of course. Peachy! How about I take the other foot?" He shifts towards Chloe, keeping her left foot in his hands and I scoot closer to him to better reach her right foot. Our legs are pressed close and I can smell that intoxicating citrusy and woodsy scent. *Jumping Jehosaphat does he ever not smell good?!* I bring my arms underneath his to hold Chloe's foot more easily. Her skin is soft and cool and she sighs as I start rubbing the arch.

"You guys are my favorite. Thank you so much for this." I concentrate on her foot, trying not to dig too hard. "Ooooh! Do you see where Ivy is rubbing? Can you hit that spot on my left foot? It's killing me!" Miles leans over, trying to see what I was doing. I reach across, putting my hand over his. Such an innocent touch should not be this heated.

"It's right here," I tell him, rubbing into the spot directly beneath the ball of Chloe's foot, using my fingers to put pressure on his.

His Adam's apple bobs roughly. "Ah, got it."

I blush as his eyes dart up to mine and I go back to Chloe's other foot, rubbing gently. I try to follow the plot of the movie but can't concentrate with the length of Miles' muscled thigh against mine. I hear a soft snuffling sound and look over at the source: Chloe. I giggle quietly and Miles looks over at her too.

"Looks like we did our job a little too well."

I go to scoot back, giving us some space, but end up rubbing my boob across his arm. He inhales sharply and I jerk my head down, taking in my nipples which are now alert, pressing against my sweater. Why? Can't I go one night without wanting to crawl in a hole to die? I try to act all nonchalant but it's too late, I can see he's already looking at them as well. Real subtle, ladies. Way to dime me out. *Come on Ivy, do something, you idiot!* I turn my body, pressing my back against the arm of the couch. Unfortunately, this seems to put my boobs on display even more, but at least I'm no longer in danger of rubbing my chest on his arm. Progress. I guess.

I look down at his tattoos, distracted by the bright colors and text. I haven't had a chance to look at them close up. I run my fingertips lightly across his forearm, tracing the lines of a vintage-style anchor. Goosebumps erupt on his skin and I smooth my hand across them before going back to tracing it. I peek up through my lashes and his eyes are following the movement of my fingers.

"Would you tell me about them? You're an artist so there have to be stories here."

Miles clears his throat, seeming a little nervous. "Sure." He points his chin to where my fingers are still tracing. "That's for

Liam." He turns his arm slightly to show the back of his forearm where paintbrushes and pens are running vertically. "These are for my mom. And me, I guess. The daisy is Chloe." It's vibrant orange and yellow and brings her to mind immediately. "They're her favorite."

I slide my fingers up his arm, pushing his shirt sleeve up and out of the way. He closes his eyes for a moment before he continues. I trace my fingers over a galaxy with stars and swirls of colors.

"That's for my dad. Caleb and his stars."

My fingers glide back down his arm, running over the text above his inner elbow below his bicep, *Dum Spiro Spero*.

"While I breathe, I hope," he whispers. The font is familiar but I'm too distracted by the feel of his skin to ask more. "And the waves between everything are the ocean, connecting all of us no matter where we are."

My fingertips skate down his forearm, my mind filled with the sensation of the connection between our skin. I trace over his wrist and across the palm of his hands and then slip my fingers between his. The motion is natural. Automatic. His fingers start to curl forward and *suck a puck!* I'm basically holding his hand! *Get control of yourself, Ivy Hughes!* I slip my fingers the rest of the way through his and stand up, suddenly freaked out by the direction I've taken things. Two minutes in arm heaven and I'm one of Lauren's brazen hussies! I step through to the kitchen and grab my bread pan, pulling my coat from the back of the chair with such force I almost knock it over. Miles is gently extracting himself from under Chloe's legs as I hurry towards the door.

"I should go. Early morning and all that. I'll text Chloe tomorrow, I don't want to wake her up." *You're babbling, Ivy, shut it!*

"Ivy, wait." Miles walks towards me. "I'll walk you out."

"You don't have to do that, I'm parked right in the driveway. Will Chloe be alright there?"

"I'll make sure she gets to bed before I leave."

He steps up behind me and reaches around to open the door. For a moment his arm is around me. I spin, taking a step closer, raise on my tiptoes, and press my cheek to his, keeping myself from tipping forward by resting my hands on his chest. Turning slightly I touch my lips to his sharp cheekbone, giving myself a moment to inhale his warm scent. His hand cups my cheek, fingers lightly brushing against my skin. I drop back down, feet flat on the ground, and his hand stays with me. Is it awesome or sad that it's the single most intimate touch of my life?

"Good night, Ivy," his voice rumbles, settling in the pit of my stomach. "Drive safely."

CHAPTER 13
MILES

I feel like I'm coming out of my skin. Everything about tonight was a bad idea if the goal was keeping my distance from Ivy. The more we talk the more I want to know her. She's kind, she's a good friend to Chloe, and I liked talking about music with her. Once Chloe had passed out? Holy. Shit. Fingers crossed she didn't notice that her nipple dragging across my arm had me needing to adjust myself under Chloe's dead weight feet. Ivy's touch makes me feel like I'm coming to life after a Rip Van Winkle-style sleep.

She asked me about my tattoos and her fingertips brushing my skin made it hard to focus. I wish she hadn't rushed out though. I would have liked to talk some more. Music, books, tv shows, I'm interested in knowing more about what she's interested in.

I pick Chloe up, carry her back to her bed, and scribble a quick note to let her know I locked up. I make sure everything is turned off and locked before pointing my car towards Dad's house, my thoughts filled with Ivy.

A week goes by and I haven't had a chance to see her again. I had planned on going back to volunteer on Thursday but an issue came up with another client — gotta love a complete 180 right before I'm set to hand over their new digital logos and website artwork. The rework ended up being epic, way better than what they initially asked for, but fuck if it wasn't down to the wire on little sleep. I love the rush of creating and the buzz is higher when the pressure is on, so I shouldn't complain. I seem to do my best digital work on a tight deadline.

I can't stop thinking about Ivy. I know I should let it be, but it's feeling less and less like an option. She's like an itch I can't scratch, a craving I can't satisfy. Maybe I could get her number. Texting would be fine, right? Just a little scratch.

ME: *Can I get Ivy's number?*
CHLOE: *Stalker much? Why don't you ask her instead of me?*
ME: *I don't want to have to track her down in person to ask if I can text her. I had a question about Fresh Start and would prefer not to wait.*
CHLOE: *K. I'll send her contact.*
ME: *Thanks*

She sends the contact info and I save it to my phone. Suddenly nervous, I type in her name. Am I doing this? *It's a hello, that's it.* Except it *feels* like a step at the edge of a very high cliff and the effect is dizzying.

ME: *Hey, Ivy. This is Miles. Miles Bennett.*

I watch the little ellipses, indicating that she's typing, my stomach knotting up. What do I have to be nervous about? It's only a silly text.

IVY: *Hi Miles, Miles Bennett. I don't recall giving you my number*
ME: *I got it from Chloe. Is that ok?*

IVY: Of course, just messing with you

I pause, not sure what to say next. I didn't truly need to talk to her.

IVY: Is there something I can do for you?
ME: Nah, I saved your contact to my phone and wanted to say hi
ME: Will you be at Fresh Start tomorrow night?
IVY: Yep—5 pm for set up
ME: See you then

The next day drags as I anticipate seeing Ivy. The hours feel like they're slithering at a snail's pace. When it's finally time to head to the church I've changed my shirt three times and consumed way too much coffee. I settle on a dark green henley with the sleeves pushed up and hope it doesn't look like I'm trying too hard. But, you know, also that I tried a little. Chloe insists these shirts are hot. Something about those cable movies and doorways? I don't know. I didn't really get it.

Ivy is already inside when I get there, pulling down containers of supplies from the shelves along the back wall. I step up behind her, blocking her in with my body as I reach up over her head to grab the next box.

"Miles. Um, hey. Thanks for that. I could have gotten it though."

I sit the container at her feet. "I know you could have but I'm here to help." I bow before her, flourishing my arms. "At your service, milady."

She giggles and points down at the two boxes. "Well then, good sir, please bring these boxes over to the vanity, we have a hairstylist coming tonight!"

I follow her lead and we work together to unpack the boxes.

71

There are care packages with shampoo, conditioner, styling products, and makeup, all new. We line everything up on the counter where they'll be easy to grab.

"This group is close to their interviews, almost ready to leave us. Tonight we get to help them feel beautiful and confident in their skin before we send them out to conquer."

Her joy is contagious and I'm swept up in her enthusiasm. For the next couple of hours, I watch in awe as she talks earnestly with each of the women, chatting while the stylist works on their hair. She's liberal with the compliments but not ingenuine. Every single one of them leaves wearing their confidence like a badge of honor.

My favorite of the night is Lynn. She has some wicked scars. They weave onto her scalp and her hair is uneven from where they had to shave it down at the hospital. She sits down in the chair with an air of defeat, apology in her eyes before she even opens her mouth.

"It's ok, I know there's no hope." She tilts her head down, not meeting her own eyes in the mirror.

"Oh, honey, there's always hope! Let me get a good look at ya."

The stylist inspects her hair from all angles, getting Lynn to open up and relax by asking her questions about her life and interests. No one addresses the scars or asks how they got there. The entire focus is on Lynn's life now and what she wants in the future. The stylist ends up working some kind of sorcery with extensions before cutting everything to below Lynn's ears. The reveal causes happy tears, Lynn's shocked giggles bubbling up even as tears streamed down her face.

"I can't believe that's me!"

"Of course, it is, silly. All that beauty was already there, it just needed a hand, that's all. No big deal." The stylist spins her chair around and hands Lynn a mirror so she can see the back.

"I want to do this," she whispers, staring at her reflection. "I want to help other women have this exact feeling."

That leads to a discussion between the two of them about a salon receptionist job and applying for a scholarship to cosmetology school. Lynn leaves with a new hairdo, confidence, and plans for a future she never dared share before tonight. It was AWESOME. I don't get to experience things like that working alone in my apartment, designing business logos.

I help box things back up while Ivy walks the last woman to her car.

"The important thing isn't the outfit or the makeup, it's how you feel in them." Ivy hugs the woman as her sweet voice carries across the parking lot. "You've got this. I know it and you know it. That's going to shine through, no matter how competently you fix your hair or apply mascara. No good employer is going to worry about that sort of thing. They're going to see your resume and hear you talking about how far you've come and know immediately what an asset you'll be. You'll see. I can't wait to hear all about your new job next week." Ivy hugs her again and the woman leaves. I grab Ivy's coat and purse and meet her outside.

"Have you eaten?"

"No, I never have time for dinner between leaving work and set up."

"You wanna grab something? With me?" We're walking towards our vehicles, which are parked side by side at the end of the parking lot.

"Oh. Um, yes. That would be nice," she answers primly. The circles of light from the street lights don't quite reach where we're parked and the noise from Fresh Start closing up sounds distant and muffled. "I can follow you. Then I'll be able to head straight home after without needing to come back here."

"That works."

We've stopped between our cars. Ivy opens her passenger side door and sits her stuff in the seat, closing it with her hip. I move towards her, running my left hand from her shoulder down to her wrist, lightly grasping her hand. I'm running on an emotional high from tonight and the buzz I get whenever I'm near her.

"Hey. You were inspiring tonight. I like getting to watch you work. I hope you know what a difference you're making."

Her lips curve up into a smile and I feel a magnetic pull between us. I don't think about it, I don't question whether or not it's a good idea, my body moves on its own, pulling me to her like the mood pulls the tides. In the span of a breath my right hand is tipping her chin up and my lips are pressing against hers. Her mouth is petal-soft and I kiss her slowly, afraid if I move she'll come to her senses and decide she doesn't want this with me. I angle my head slightly, rubbing my nose up and across hers to adjust the kiss. She increases the pressure, intertwining our fingers and pressing her body into me. I gently suck her bottom lip between mine, nipping it with my teeth, soaking in her textures and taste. She moans against my mouth and licks right inside my top lip with the tip of her tongue. My body is humming and my head is spinning and I want more.

I want to press her back into the side of her car.

I want to delve deeper into her sweet mouth, exploring with my tongue.

I want to taste her skin, wrap my hands in her hair, breathe her in until my lungs are filled with only Ivy.

But I don't want her to think that this was my plan all along, that dinner was a ploy to get into her pants. I tease my tongue along the seam of her mouth, stroking her face with my free hand before pulling back, pecking her mouth lightly, and kissing the tip of her nose. She sighs against me. I chuckle softly, the sound sticking in my chest and vibrating between us.

"You taste even better than I remember."

She giggles quietly, resting her face against my chest. The fingers of her free hand trace over my collarbone inside the collar of my shirt. I shiver, turning my thoughts to the hospital to keep my arousal from becoming obvious against her. She affects every part of my body, every part of me. I kiss the top of her head and force myself to step back.

"How does pizza sound?"

She nods once, pressing her fingers to her lips, and then goes around to get in her car. I'm glad I'll have the drive over there to get myself under control. I don't think I'll ever be the same.

CHAPTER 14
IVY

I don't even remember starting my car. I'm in a daze.
Miles kissed me.
Miles kissed *me*.

And *holey crocheted afghan* it was hot! I've never been kissed like that before. Every touch had me reeling. He tasted like cinnamon and coffee. My entire body is alight and my lips are sensitive to the touch. I want to do that again, for hours. Forever. Just non-stop, never-ending kissing with Miles. Impractical? Possibly but I'd be willing to give it a go. And we're parking so I should probably push this raging crush down a couple of thousand notches. I can do this. I can sit with him and eat pizza. No big deal. I can eat and not jump him in the middle of a public place. That would be the wrong move. Right? Right. Just the pizza then.

The small restaurant smells like fresh yeasty crust and garlic. It makes me realize how hungry I am. We're seated in a small booth and he slides in next to me, our legs and arms touching. Gah, he feels good and he smells good and this is sweet torture.

"What do you like on your pizza?" I ask as much to distract myself as to prepare to order.

"I'll eat anything but I'm not a huge fan of meat on pizza. It's always greasy."

"I agree," I tell him. "Thank goodness! What do you think we should order?" He looks over the menu and then points to one, raising his eyebrows in a question. "The veggie garden? That sounds great."

The waitress comes by and he orders for us, handing over the menus. He stretches his long legs out underneath the table, his jeans rubbing against mine. I want to rest my hand on his thigh or hold his hand but that feels too presumptuous. He saves me from overthinking, asking about what kinds of jobs the Fresh Start women apply for. We talk until the pizza arrives and both dig in.

This isn't a date, I don't think, but I can't remember ever having a better time with a guy. Miles is easy to talk to and I forget to be nervous. I mention something about walking to work most days and he looks surprised.

"I didn't realize you live that close."

I laugh. "Why would you? I only drive to Fresh Start because I'm usually hauling donations, otherwise, I walk most places. Where do you live?"

He pauses mid-bite like this throwaway question, a question I didn't give a moment's thought to asking, is actually a big deal. Why does he look guilty? Why is my stomach starting to knot?

"Well, um," he stops to finish chewing, sitting down his slice and wiping his hands on a napkin. "I'm staying in my dad's house right now. We haven't decided what we're going to do with it yet. I don't want to put that on Liam while he's gone. But...I live in Philadelphia."

My stomach drops rollercoaster-style. How did I not know he was merely visiting or here temporarily until his dad's estate is squared away? He looks uncomfortable. I'm not going to worry about making him feel better when I have my own mental mess to deal with. Nothing has happened, it was one measly kiss! There's no reason for me to be upset, but I'm mad at myself. That dang kiss opened up a whole flood gate of emotions I wasn't sure I would ever feel again. My body is *awake*. For the first time in years, it's like I remember I'm a woman. My body and mind are connected again, working together. I never would have let myself have any kind of feelings for him if I had known he was leaving. He's watching me carefully, so I try to act like I'm not internally imploding. I finish my piece of pizza and carefully wipe my mouth.

"Would you be ok taking the leftovers home?"

"If you don't want them, I don't mind eating this again. Ivy, are you..."

I interrupt him, suddenly desperate to leave. "I can take care of the bill. I don't have any cash on me so it's easier."

"No, Ivy, I invited you, I'll pay for dinner."

I want to argue, pay my half, make this less undefined-date-like but if I do I'll have to stay here and I can't.

"Ok, thanks for dinner, Miles. I need to go."

He tries to stand up but I scoot out of the booth and run out the door, racing my tears to the car. It's only a couple of minutes to get home but I arrive with streaky mascara cheeks and a runny nose. I change into my comfiest pj's, wash my face and make myself a mug of tea. Wrapping up in a blanket, I curl my body into my favorite armchair and hold my mug between my hands. My phone vibrates.

It's probably Miles.

I can't check it.

I should check it. Even with my feelings hurt I don't want to be rude. It's not his fault I read too much into things.

MILES: Ivy, are you ok?

I know I should respond but I don't know what to say. He didn't do anything wrong. He can't help that I let my feelings get away from me before I had all the facts. And I definitely don't want to admit that to him. Experiencing it is bad enough. Having to explain it to him? That would be even more humiliating than running out of the restaurant.

MILES: *Did you get home ok? I'm trying not to worry but I can't help it. Will you let me know that you're alright? I'm sorry if I did something to upset you.*

What do I do here? Why do I constantly make such a mess of things? Needing a friend, I text Chloe.

ME: *I think I messed things up.*
CHLOE: *That's doubtful Sweets. What's up?*
ME: *Why didn't I know that Miles lives in Philadelphia?*
CHLOE: *I didn't realize you didn't know. Is that a problem?*
ME: *No*
ME: *Maybe*
ME: *It shouldn't be but yes*
CHLOE: *What's going on? Do you need me to come over?*
ME: *I don't want to be a bother*
CHLOE: *You're not a bother. I'm on my way. Text me your address otherwise I'll just drive around all night, pregnant and annoyed.*

I send her my address and curl up in my chair, equally embarrassed that I need her and glad that she's coming. I decide to go ahead and make her a mug of chamomile and sit it on the coffee table. In no time at all, there's a knock on my door. I shuffle over, letting her in and she pulls me into a hug. As if I'm not already embarrassingly sensitive, the comfort of her arms around me makes me lose the fragile hold on my emotions and I start bawling.

"Sweets! What is happening right now? Come sit with me. I'm missing Liam and I think we both need snuggles and a hot drink." I let her pull me along behind her until we're both huddled up on my couch, wrapped in a cozy blanket with mugs of tea in hand. "Ok, we're warm and we're snuggly, now tell me what's going on."

Now that she's here in front of me I'm mortified to have to admit what's bothering me.

"Gah, Chloe, this is so embarrassing. I feel like I'm 13 again and that was not a good year for Ivy Hughes." She smiles patiently at me, brushing a stray curl off of my face. "I've been getting to know Miles better recently. No big deal, just some texts and talking while setting up at Fresh Start, that sort of thing. He's easy to talk to and we seem to have a lot in common."

I take a sip of my tea, letting the hot liquid soothe me, and stare across the room. Chloe nudges me with her elbow and I take the hint and forge ahead.

"Tonight, after we finished up at Fresh Start, he said the nicest, most complimentary thing to me about my work there. It felt like I was being seen, for me, for the first time. And then he kissed me." Chloe squeals, bouncing on the couch and almost spilling our drinks.

"Girl! You're great, my brother-in-law is great, what is there to cry about? Was it a bad kiss? Tell me Miles isn't a tragic kisser."

I can feel myself blushing and she squeals again. *Sakes alive,* I've missed having a girlfriend to talk to.

"Um, no. It was hands down the best kiss of my entire life. Possibly the best kiss in the history of the world, no offense to you and Liam."

"Baby bro gettin' it!" She does a little dance. "And you couldn't handle the things that Liam Bennett's mouth can do, so no offense taken."

I laugh, glad to not be sobbing right now. "It was perfect. Absolutely perfect. He was gentle and swoony and he lit me up inside and I wanted to keep kissing him forever until we died right there in the church parking lot from lack of food and water. He didn't push me or try to take things further, he just blew up my world, held me for a minute, then took me to get pizza."

Chloe sets her cup on the coffee table and wraps her arms around me, laying her head on top of mine.

"So...you had a magical earth-shattering kiss and went for pizza. Then what brought the tears?"

I blow out a shaky breath. "That was it. We grabbed some dinner. If it had been a date it would have been the best date I've ever been on. But it wasn't a date. It was just two acquaintances getting food. We agreed on the best toppings, we talked about Fresh Start, and I couldn't stop thinking about the kiss." Too late, I realize I've pressed my fingers to my lips again, remembering how they felt afterward, and I drop my hand like I've been burned.

" I *felt things*, Chloe! I was scared that wasn't possible for me anymore. And then I found out he doesn't even live here. He didn't exactly say he was counting down until he goes back to Philadelphia but he also didn't say he was staying." I feel the tears pooling, threatening to stream down my face again. "It was humiliating. He didn't do anything wrong, it was all me. I read too much into it. I projected feelings on him that couldn't have been there. And instead of acting like an adult, maybe admitting my mistake so we could laugh about it, I high-tailed it out of there and ran home."

Chloe strokes my hair and hands me a tissue. "I don't know what to say. Of course, my greatest wish is that Miles will move back here. I want my baby to know Uncle Miles and I know he doesn't have anything holding him to Philadelphia. But I don't want to push him. Miles has never liked being told what to do. He needs to figure things out for himself. I'm not sorry you kissed. Maybe your magic lips will make him want to stay! I am sorry, though, that you didn't know he's only here temporarily."

I sigh. "I don't think I would have risked getting to know him if I had known."

"You regret the kiss?"

I think about it carefully. "No, I suppose not. I guess being too risk-averse would have had me missing out on that magic. But

I do wish I had done a better job of guarding my heart. I don't know if I'm ready to feel things if my heart is going to get broken again."

"I know it's easier said than done, but let's not worry about that yet. You know now. And Miles hasn't decided anything. I think you're safe with him as long as you're honest. In the meantime, maybe you will sway him to the dark side." She laughs maniacally, messing with me before the laugh turns to her normal cackle. "Have you considered maybe you're putting too much pressure on yourself?"

"How so?"

"You didn't think you'd even consider kissing Miles if you knew he lived in Philly. You're worried about getting your heart broken. Isn't that too much too soon? What if you get to know him? Let him get to know you? What if you don't freak out about what might happen in the future and simply enjoy the fact that a guy you're attracted to wants you? You're allowed to have a good time, Ivy, without stressing about the future."

"That's...new. Is it dumb that I didn't even consider that?"

"Nah. But maybe you should. Be gentle with yourself!" I hug her and decide it's probably time to respond to Miles. Chloe offers to make more tea to give me some space.

Me: *I'm home. I'm safe. Chloe is with me.*
Miles: *Good. I was afraid something had happened to you.*
Me: *Sorry to make you worry.*
Miles: *Are you mad at me? Was the kiss too much? Do you want me to back off?*
Ivy: *No, the kiss was*

I unintentionally hit send but the mistake gives me a moment to process. Having Chloe here makes me feel braver. I can do this. I can talk to Miles about this honestly without melting into a puddle of abject humiliation. Be honest about how you feel and where you're at. Simple. Totally doable.

MILES: *The kiss was what? Terrifying? Gross? Ivy, are you trying to let me down easy? Is there someone else? Wait, are you secretly pining for Walter?*

ME: *Yeah, I have a thing for giant grey caterpillar eyebrows. Anyway, Walter has been married for 40 years*

MILES: *Ivy! Stop stalling! I don't care about Walter's lengthy marital bliss. WHAT ABOUT THE KISS?*

ME: *IT WAS PERFECT. The kiss was perfect*

MILES: *Shit, you scared me!*

MILES: *I thought it was perfect too. I was starting to get worried that it was all one-sided*

ME: *It wasn't*

MILES: *Ok so we agree that was the kiss to end all kisses. We both felt that*

ME: *Did I say that?*

MILES: *I guess I was projecting. It was the kiss to end all kisses for me*

ME: *I suppose I might label it similarly, if pressed*

MILES: *[fainting gif]*

MILES: *So...why did you run? What did I do? I was having a really good time with you. Best date I've ever been on*

ME: *That wasn't a date*

MILES: *Sure it was. We kissed, I asked you, I paid...DATE*

ME: *If it was a date then I should have been aware*

MILES: *I thought it was implied. I don't just go around kissing random people. There was intention there*

ME: *Intention or not, you can't imply a date. Both parties have to be aware*

MILES: *Noted. I'll be clearer next time*

ME: *Next time?*

MILES: *Of course. Do you think you can be one half of the most perfect kiss ever to be kissed and not have a repeat?*

ME: *Miles, I'm gonna level with you. I would like nothing more than to experience that kiss again. And again and again and again*

if I'm honest. But I'm struggling a bit with the fact that you don't live here
MILES: *That's not the best news*
MILES: *What can I do, Ivy? What do you need me to do?*
ME: *I don't know*
MILES: *I don't want to never see you again. Please say that's not the plan*
ME: *I don't know*
ME: *Chloe is here. I don't want to be rude and ignore her while I'm on my phone. Can we come back to this later? I don't feel able to make a decision right now but I'm NOT brushing you off*
MILES: *Ok*
MILES: *I can respect that*
MILES: *Good night Ivy*

It's getting late and I don't want Chloe driving so I convince her to have a sleepover with me. I pull out the bed in the sofa—a hand-me-down from my mom—grab us every pillow I own and we talk late into the night, watching movies and giggling. All in all, even with my emotional breakdown, today was one for the memory books.

CHAPTER 15
MILES

I spend the next week hoping Ivy will clarify where we stand, constantly reminding myself not to push her. We still text and chat but I'm careful not to ask her for more. I'm battling impatience though. I fill my evenings with work for Fresh Start, seeing it as a way to help her since I can't be with her. I keep going back to that night, wondering what I could have done differently. I don't know why her question surprised me so much. It hadn't occurred to me that she didn't know I'm here temporarily. As soon as I realized it I felt guilty, like I was purposefully keeping it from her. I had been counting down the minutes until I could kiss her again, wondering if I could just go for it right there during dinner, and suddenly she was running out of the restaurant looking like she was about to cry. A week later I still don't know what to do.

Art helps. It has been my escape for as long as I can remember. When I was little I used to set up my paper and crayons next to my mom while she painted. I've boxed up everything I painted while Dad was sick. It's all too dark. Looking at them feels like pressing on a bruise. Since he passed my work is still blue but there are glimpses of light in there as well. It can be easier to feel hope, to identify the brighter spots in life, with a paintbrush in my hand.

85

I've been told, more than once, that I'm often too melancholy, that I focus too much on what is lacking. That's the main reason I got the Latin tattoo: to remind me that as long as I'm alive, I have hope. I don't remember ever not feeling like I have a hole in me. The lack, the space that keeps me apart from everyone else, has always been there. As a teenager, I leaned heavily into that, full of youthful angst and hurt. Between my not-easily-determined ethnicity, the emo-tendencies, and my tall, overly skinny frame, I was prime bully fodder. Mom had been gone a long time by then, but Dad pointed me back to her. He told me that there was nothing wrong with feeling things deeply and appreciating the beauty in the darker parts of life. Then he reminded me that Mom would want me to use it and create something meaningful, not dwell on it and make everyone around me miserable.

It makes me smile now, remembering him trying so hard to find the delicate balance between motivating me and outright telling me I was obnoxious. He mostly found it. Social interactions were easier once I stopped expressing all of my feelings through my clothes and bullies backed off once Liam started taking me to the gym with him. I still feel the lack, I still find myself dwelling in the dark, but now I work on letting art pull me back and use exercise to keep my mind clearer.

This last week I've been using acrylics more. I have this idea for a tryptic for Liam. He likes to take photos of the ocean for me, all over the world. I turn on Durand Jones and the Indications, cranking the volume up. I have a few of Liam's photos taped up along the window for inspiration. I want each panel to represent a different piece of water, the colors blending across. The deep blue of the Mediterranean, the blue-green of the Atlantic, the turquoise of the Indian Ocean. I've been layering the paint, simulating waves. I let the thrumming sounds of soul, the driving groove, set my rhythm. I'm quickly absorbed in the task.

I have the base of each where I want it and am working on the highlights and shadows. Light playing on the water is magical when it's right. But can I get it right? That's the challenge. One album ends and the next plays while I work, in the zone. Eventually, I want to try adding something, maybe mica flakes, to the white for the wave caps. I'm not sure how successful any of this is but it feels good to try. It feels like stepping into the light.

Thursday I head over to Fresh Start early, eager to set up what I've been working on. Being around Ivy makes me want to put in more effort, to see dreams through to the action stage. I find Walter carrying in some bags of clothes and help him before unloading my car.

"You can set up over here, Miles. I brought in a desk for you like you asked."

"Thanks, Walter. This is exactly what I had in mind." I get busy setting up the computer I had talked one of my clients into donating. Next comes the new printer and an ergonomic desk chair. I sit down, roll into place, and turn everything on. I'm logging in, noting all the pertinent information on a notepad for easy reference, when I hear Ivy come in. It takes everything in me not to vault out of the chair and run to her. I feel her walk up behind me, her very presence lighting up the air around me.

"What's all this?" She rests a hand on my shoulder and my heart leaps. Touching has to be good, right?

Walter jumps in. "Miles talked to some of his clients and convinced them to donate a good computer and a printer! And he picked up this nice chair!" I swivel around slowly, taking my time before meeting her eyes. Her hair is pulled up, leaving her delicate neck exposed. I'm surprised just how much I've missed seeing her.

"You did all this, Miles?"

I have it bad—even her voice makes me feel like everything is right in the world. "I hope it helps. It will be easier to type up the resumes and look up job listings. I also formatted a couple of fill-in-the-blank type resume forms that you can use to make the process faster. Wanna see?"

I stand up, motioning her towards the chair. Instead of sitting down, she puts her arms around my waist, pressing her face into my chest. I wrap my arms around her, tipping my head down to rest it against the top of hers.

Everything. Is. Right.

"Thank you," she mumbles into my shirt.

"You're welcome."

As much as I'd like to stand here, holding her, I know she's got a lot to do and I don't want to keep her from it. I let her move away and get busy myself. While she's working with the ladies I set up a router and get Fresh Start connected to the church's network. It's nice having a role here. I'm struggling to think of anything back in Philadelphia that I found fulfilling. I really should have left my apartment more. I'm absorbed in my work and miss the ladies going home, everyone cleaning up, and I almost miss Ivy leaving for the night. I shut everything down quickly and jog after her.

"Ivy! Wait up!"

She stops near her car and turns to face me, watching me as I approach. "Thank you again for not only getting all of that for us but setting everything up. It's going to make such a big difference." She rubs at the back of her ankle with the toe of her shoe, looking down shyly.

"Glad I could help. It wasn't much."

"It is. It's a big deal. I can't thank you enough."

"You have. I like getting to volunteer here. And I like getting to do it with you. This is my favorite part of the week."

"Mine too. But don't get a big head," she grins. "It's been my favorite part of the week for a few years now."

I roll my eyes at her, walking past her to sit on the back of my car. She hops up next to me, tucking her right leg under her left and bringing her left knee up, wrapping her arms around it. She rests her chin on her knee, looking out, not at me.

"Can we talk?" I venture.

"Yeah, we can talk." She glances at me out of the corner of her eye but keeps her face forward.

"I'm sorry you didn't know I don't live here. I'm still not sure what I'm going to do. It's something I'd like to talk over with Chloe and Liam, once they're both in the same place. I need to consider them when I make my decision. And I'm starting to think I might like to consider you as well. If you'd let me. I've liked getting to know you, Ivy. I'd like to continue getting to know you."

"I think I'd like that too." She tilts her head to look at me.

"That's good. I like the direction this is going. Let's keep up that momentum. Would getting to know you better include kissing? Because I'd like to lobby for that inclusion. It's not *just* about the kissing, mind you, but I'm hoping that's not off the table."

She drops her knee so she's sitting cross-legged, what our elementary teachers liked to call "criss-cross applesauce" and swivels her body to face my left side. I turn towards her and pull my legs up, mirroring her.

"I'm gonna show all my cards here, Ivy. I like you." The bottom drops out of my stomach at the admission but I press on. "I like you a lot. You're smart, kind, you take care of people, you're dead sexy, and kissing you is about the only thing that occupies my thoughts lately. Could you maybe consider *not worrying* about where I live for now? Could we see where this goes?" I take a deep breath, gulping down the impending panic over whether or not I've said too much and scared her off. Her pale skin is glowing in the moonlight, seeming to reflect the silvery light.

"I'm scared, Miles." Her breath is shaky and the silence between us feels taut, like a guitar string, vibrating with unvoiced hopes. "But I'd like to try. I'd like to have fun and get to know you." Her shy smile leaves me breathless. I can hardly dare to believe what she's said.

"You said yes? Yes, you'll give us a shot?"

"Yes."

I exhale slowly, running my hands through my hair and shaking out my arms.

"Can we get started on that kissing bit?" She winks.

I laugh and she does too, tipping her head back. I reach for her and grab her thighs, pulling her forward to overlap her legs with mine. She's still laughing, then gasping out my name, when I lean over and kiss a path up her throat. She grasps my biceps, steadying herself, as I move my mouth along her jawline, grazing the bone with my teeth. She brings her chin back down and I claim her mouth. It starts slow and soft, my hands still holding her thighs. There's no hurry. She said yes.

I'm settling in, finding a gentle rhythm when she parts her lips and her tongue darts out. She traces my lower lip, then my upper lip. I tilt for a better angle, deepening the kiss. My heart is racing and she's pushing the pace. Her hands are running up my arms until she grasps the collar of my jacket, pulling me closer. I unfold her legs, pulling them to either side of my body and dragging her closer still. Her knees are bent up under my armpits and I rest my arms on them, running my hands along her sides.

These curves! I keep my hands moving up and down, my palms grazing right to the edge of the swells of her breasts, down the curve of her waist, and back out over her hips before tracing the path back up again. It's more than enough right now. I don't know how long we stay like that, hands caressing and tongues tangling. I sigh against her mouth.

"I can't get enough of you, Ivy Hughes." I trail kisses up the bridge of her nose and she playfully bites my chin.

"You're really, really good at this," she breathes out.

I bring our lips together again, drinking her in before pulling back to look at her. Her lips are kiss-swollen, her eyes a little dazed. I trace my fingers across her features, wanting to commit her to memory just like this. I wish I had watercolors with me.

"I don't think I've ever enjoyed kissing so much."

She looks down, shy once more. I slide my fingers down her neck, feeling goosebumps trailing behind their path. Fingertips slipping over the skin above the neckline of her shirt, close but not close enough to push things further. Flirting with the line, never crossing it. I lean in and kiss her again with the lightest pressure. I trace my fingers back up, trailing across her exposed collarbones then dip back down to the scooped neckline once more. She gasps against my lip, the sound a prize. I skim my hand over her shoulder and down along her spine, back on safer territory. The kiss stays gentle and I caress her softly.

I don't want this to end.

I don't want to take this too far.

I want Ivy to trust me.

I want to be trustworthy.

She ends the kiss and I sit back. I can't stop smiling.

"Let me walk you to your car." I help her down, holding her hand. She gets in her car and rolls down the window and I lean in, kissing her one last time. I love Thursdays.

CHAPTER 16
IVY

All Friday I struggle to focus. It is quite embarrassing. I'm constantly gazing off in the distance, replaying every delicious moment sitting on the trunk of Miles' car. That guy can KISS! He made me feel desired and cherished. I'm trying hard to be cautious, though. Not because of Miles, because of me. I want to get to know him better and allow myself to have fun. I don't want to let myself get swept away and lost again. The kisses and interactions with Vance weren't anywhere near as sizzling and look how that went! I need to be careful.

Since I don't have any afternoon appointments, I head over to the shop early, figuring I can help Mama with anything she needs to do until it's time for yoga. I store my stuff in the back and join her at the counter. A gorgeous bouquet is sitting out and I spin it around to inspect it. There's tall and delicate stoebe acting as a backdrop, a striking blush pink protea, and mossy eucalyptus, with peachy ranunculus filling it out. The color tones are dreamy and incredibly feminine.

"This is absolutely stunning, Mama! Why is sitting out here?"

"Would you believe I had a man call this morning first thing, wanting a bouquet that represents his girlfriend? He said it needed to be special, girly, soft, and joyful."

I nod along with her list. "Check, check, check, and check! I think you pulled it off. When is he picking it up? Or is it here because you need me to deliver it?"

"Nope. It's here until you take it home." She glares at me but I know her expressions. This is all an act. "Anything you'd like to tell me, Ivy Leigh?"

"Wait, this is for me?" I squeal. "Miles called you?"

"Apparently you have a boyfriend. And he's sweet and thoughtful." I turn the vase again, appreciating the arrangement even more knowing it was created for me. It's so beautiful!

"I was planning on telling you today when I got here. It's new. Brand new. We decided last night to give it a shot and see where things go." I hug her. "Thank you for making this! You outdid yourself and I love it!"

I snap a quick photo and text it to Chloe. I'm sure she'll love it as much as I do. Mama pulls up two stools so we can sit, handing me a thorn stripper and placing a container of long-stemmed roses between us. I strip thorns and Mama cleans up the stems. We've done this task, and similar ones, so often we barely have to look as we talk.

"Tell me about him. How'd you meet? What's he like?"

"You've met him. He came in and ordered those funeral flowers that I delivered."

"I remember him. He was so weighed down by his grief his shoulders were bowed. And having to take care of all of the arrangements by himself! That's so hard."

I pause, thinking about how that must have been for him. It makes my heart ache. "His dad died. And his brother is deployed so it was all up to him. He told me how much he appreciated how you helped him. He was pretty overwhelmed."

"That poor man," Mama chides. "It was the least I could do."

I tell her about seeing him at the funeral and again at Chloe's appointment before meeting him at Fresh Start. She laughs with me, poking fun at my tendency to create embarrassing situations I then run from. I tell her about everything Miles has done for

Fresh Start and my growing friendship with Chloe. We close up shop and get changed, continuing to talk as we walk to yoga. I hear my phone chime and stop to dig it out of my bag.

"It's Miles!" Mama shakes her head knowingly.

MILES: Hey beautiful! Did you get the flowers?
ME: I did! They're gorgeous! Thank you so much!
MILES: I wanted you to know I was thinking of you today
ME: I hope I don't need to buy you a bouquet every time I'm thinking of you. I don't think anyone has that kind of space.
MILES: 😊
MILES: I've never gotten flowers before
MILES: What are you doing right now?
ME: Walking to yoga with my mom
MILES: Is this a regular thing?
ME: Yup. We go together twice a week.
MILES: Can I come?
ME: Nope. This is our thing. It's sacred. Mama and Ivy yoga time. Plus our class is all women. Dudes not welcome.
MILES: Bummer. I'd like to watch you being bendy in yoga pants.
ME: I can feel your eyebrows waggling from here.
MILES: That's on you. Be less sexy and I won't be interested in ogling you.
*ME: *snort**
ME: I've never heard anyone use the word "ogling" IRL
MILES: I'm full of surprises
MILES: How about I meet you after yoga?
ME: Usually we go back to Mom's to get cleaned up and eat dinner.

"Mama?" I ask, looking up from my phone. "Can we invite Miles over for dinner?"

"Of course, Sweet Pea. It's nothin' fancy but I'd like to meet him if he's game."

ME: You wanna have dinner with us?

MILES: *Love to. Shoot me the address and I'll meet you over there.*
ME: *Will do. You can park at the shop and walk over.*
MILES: *Cool. See you in about an hour.*

"He's gonna meet us after." I send him the address and then tuck my phone away. We set up in our usual spot in the back. We're some of the last to arrive and the other ladies are in rare form. It is loud today! Sophie is complaining about the nanny's latest outfit. Sasha is showing the woman next to her photos of her son on her phone. Lauren is cackling.

"Hair plugs! Can you believe it? He looks ridiculous!"

Sophie cackles back, the sound making me think of Chloe. "Is it really that bad? How much did they cost him?"

"I have no idea how much he wasted, I'm just glad it's not my money anymore! My ex-husband's mid-life crisis is wildly entertaining now that he's my ex. Picture the worst hair plugs you can imagine, and then multiply that by 50. It probably rivals your bimbo's favorite crop top for most vomit-inducing."

Everyone around her roars with laughter and the instructor claps loudly from the front. I block out the chatter, focusing on the feel of my muscles as we start moving through our poses. I warm up quickly and work on stretching farther. The class flies by. I feel energized and centered. I'm reaching down for my water when Lauren's voice cuts across the room.

"Who is that? And where can I get me one?"

I look up, seeing Miles standing outside. He looks good enough to eat. His sleeves are pushed up, leaving his toned forearms and tattoos on display. He stretches his arms up and his t-shirt rises with them, exposing a strip of tawny skin above his jeans. I glimpse a hint of hip bone and a trail of hair leading below his waistband. *Yum.* He shakes out his shoulders and steps inside the door. His eyes find me and his smile lights up the whole room.

"Wowza!" Lauren stage whispers. My mom laughs.

Miles props his arms on the open countertop of the reception area. "You two about ready to go?"

I grin, blushing under his gaze. It's easy to forget there are other people here when he's looking at me so intently.

"Whoa, is he here for you, Ivy?" Sophie almost screeches at my back as I walk over to him. Miles leans over the counter, placing a firm kiss on my lips, lingering until my toes are curling. I vaguely hear loud catcalling and cheering in the background but I'm lost in the feel of his soft lips and the scratch of the stubble on his face underneath my fingertips.

"You kiss like that with your Mama watching girlie?" Sophie interrupts.

"Her Mama isn't too old to recall kisses like that, Sophie. She's fine!" Mama sasses right back. Miles chuckles. I pull back, laughing too. I turn around, taking in the group of rowdy ladies, all smiling at us and not even trying to hide their interest. I guess it's fair. I usually keep to myself, eavesdropping from the back. This is the first time I've felt like I am part of the group.

"Simmer down ladies! This is Miles."

"Her boyfriend," Miles adds, raising his hand towards them. I swear they let out a collective oooooh like a bunch of middle schoolers. "I'll go back to waiting outside while you pack up."

He squeezes my hand and leaves. Mama has already gathered our things up leaving me to merely grab my share. Everyone has started to file out and I catch snippets of their conversations as it seems like each one stops to say something to Miles. He's probably regretting asking to come here. Or maybe he likes the attention? How would I know? When we step outside the studio he's leaning against the outer wall, hands in his pockets. He straightens up, approaching my mom first.

"Hi, Mrs. Hughes. It's nice to see you again, especially under better circumstances." He reaches out and shakes Mama's hand.

"You too, Miles. And it's Kathleen. Kath. Call me Kath. Shall we walk?"

Miles takes my hand and shortens his stride to match mine. Has holding hands ever felt this nice? I've missed simple, casual affection like this. We walk to the house I grew up in, Mama asking Miles about his dad.

"Dad was a real salt of the earth kind of guy. He worked hard but never cared too much about money or possessions. He was supportive of my dreams, which I know is rare for a blue-collar dad. He never tried to talk me out of pursuing art and even questioned when I focused on digital art and web design in college. He was worried I was giving up my passion in pursuit of a paycheck! Once I assured him I had no intention of abandoning my paints, he was behind me 100%. That's just who he was." He clears his throat, raw emotion visible on his face.

"He took Chloe, my sister-in-law, on weekly dates whenever my brother was underway or deployed. He was so proud of Liam and his choice to serve with the Navy." I squeezed his hand gently, hearing his voice wavering. "He couldn't wait to be a grandpa." He pauses, his Adam's apple bobbing. "We've put off the reading of the will and all of that until Liam is back and we can face everything together. The immediate future feels a little unsure right now but I'm gonna be there to meet that baby. Dad would have wanted that."

Mama takes over the conversation, giving him a break, and ushers us into the house. It's a humble little place, but Mama created a space for us that has always felt bright and open and homey. Miles sits his bag by the front door and asks Mama what he can do to help with dinner.

"Oh, sugar, the chili is already done in the slow cooker! Sweet Pea," she directs at me, "you go on and take the first shower while I make the cornbread." I pause long enough to kiss her cheek, then his, and head back to wash off the yoga sweat. I can hear Miles offering to help with the cornbread as I close the bathroom door.

CHAPTER 17

MILES

Kath refuses to let me help with the cornbread but she does relent and allows me to set the table. I can hear the shower shut off as I pull the chili toppings out of the fridge.

"There's beer in there too if you'd like one. Grab one for me, if you don't mind. Ivy tends to avoid alcohol after Richmond but I bet she'd appreciate some ice tea from the pitcher in there."

That's the second time Richmond has been mentioned in connection to Ivy. It has to have something to do with all those vague comments Chloe made. I file it away to ask about later. Something tells me it's too big to bring up this soon. I hand Kath her beer and she motions for me to sit with her. I sit across the table, leaving Ivy the spot between us. "If you don't mind me asking, what about your mama? I haven't heard you mention her." I take a swig from the bottle to give myself a moment.

"My mom died when I was a kid. Car accident. A young guy fell asleep at the wheel, crossed the lanes, and hit her head-on. She had gone out to meet some girlfriends. Dad felt guilty about it for a long time because he had insisted she go. I know she wouldn't have wanted him to, though. I remember him telling someone once that he didn't want to stifle her. She was a woman with a full life before they married and she deserved the same afterward. He tried to give her regular opportunities to meet her friends or take time away to paint. I don't think my dad even thought about dating again after. He said she was it for him, one in a million, and there wasn't any point in trying to catch lightning in a bottle twice." She reaches across and puts her hand over mine. I can smell lavender and coconut wafting down the hall.

"What was she like?"

"Fun. Vivacious. Mom was a ball of energy. Affectionate. Dad was stoic but she'd climb in his lap, pulling his arms around her, cracking his shell. They were constantly touching and sharing secret smiles and laughing. She was funny and tenderhearted and swore worse than any Navy sailor! She painted and loved to blast reggae and dance while she cooked." I shake my head at the image of her grooving, apron on and spoon in hand.

"She changed up her hair all the time—big wild curls, a short afro, long box braids, once she even buzzed all of her hair down to her scalp. Dad called it her '*African Queen*' look. He did his best. He did a great job, honestly. But there was less color after we lost her."

That sweet Ivy scent hits me full-on as she wraps her arms around my shoulders from behind, burrowing her nose into my neck. Her damp hair sticks to my skin. The timer beeps and Kath busies herself with the cornbread. I reach up for Ivy's arms while she keeps hugging me. She gives good hug. It's an underrated gift, that's for sure. She rubs her nose against me, kissing my neck with barely-there pressure.

"I hope you don't mind that I was listening. I didn't want to interrupt."

"Nah. It's been so long, it's not as painful to talk about my mom." I feel her nod in understanding.

"It's like that with my dad too. I miss him, but for me, I almost miss the idea of him more." Kath gives us both a sad smile.

We eat and Ivy tells us about an intense breech birth that morning.

"It was the mama's fourth baby so Sarah and I were confident in her ability to deliver him safely." She gives me further explanation while Kath nods in agreement. "A first-time mama would have a harder time with that, but her body knew what to do. Plus, muscle memory and the natural stretching make it easier with each subsequent vaginal birth."

"She delivered a backward baby naturally?" I didn't know that was something that happened. Whoever dubbed women the weaker sex was a moron.

"She did! Baby came out feet first and Mama growled through it all, propped up on all fours like a primal warrior woman. It was incredible to be a part of! I spent the rest of my day riding that high."

Kath entertains us with stories about crazy customers and her most outlandish orders — one involved tiny plastic dicks on sticks! — until our bellies are full. My heart feels full too. I've been on my own for too long. I almost forgot what it feels like to be with a family. It makes me feel guilty about the family I do have. I finish off my beer, thinking about Chloe and Liam and wondering if family dinners might be an option in the future. If I don't go back to Philly, that is.

Ivy pushes her mom into showering while we clean up. There's not a lot to do and I'm content as long as I'm with her. We move out to the porch swing, Ivy tucking herself against my side and bringing her legs up. I put my arm around her, scooting her closer.

"I like your mom. She's pretty great." I run my fingers along her arm. It's pretty fucking awesome touching her like this, casually making an intentional connection.

"She is, isn't she? I'm glad you guys get along. Not that I was worried about it. She's easy to get along with. I mean..." she trails off.

"Don't worry, I know what you mean."

She brings her face up and kisses me softly. I don't know what I did to get to be in a world where Ivy Hughes is kissing me, but I hope nothing changes. She slides her outside arm across my stomach, gripping me in a one-armed hug. I trail my fingers down her now exposed side, reveling in the feel of her curves under my hand. She kisses me again, punctuating it with a peck, and snuggles her face into my chest. I could get used to this. Who knew I was starved for affection? I've always thought of myself as a loner. I'm an introvert and have never minded being by myself. I'm starting to see, though, that I closed myself off after I moved to Philadelphia. I haven't had anyone in my life for a long time. I turn to get my arms around her and pull Ivy into my lap. She's still sideways. I end up holding her like a child cradled to my chest.

"Miles!" She giggles against me.

"Is this ok?" I ask into her hair, the still-damp curls tickling my face.

"More than ok." She slips her arms around me and I wrap mine around her, holding her tight. We rock that way, cradled together, not needing to say anything. Her face is nestled in the hollow of my neck and her breath warms my skin. Occasionally I drop a kiss on the top of her head but otherwise, I don't move. I rock us and hold her and time stands still, freezing around this perfect moment. In my mind, I compose a sketch, but it can't convey the emotions here. It's too flat. The front door creaks open a while later, and Kath steps out, looking cozy in a robe with slippers on.

"Don't get up you two. I'm old and about ready to get on with my evening routine. You're fine here as long as you want to stay. I just wanted to say good night. Ivy, you can lock up when you leave. Thank you both for tonight, it was lovely to have you here." She rests her hand briefly on my head and then does the same to Ivy. It's such a motherly gesture I feel myself tearing up. I smile up at her.

"Thank you, Kath. I enjoyed talking with you tonight."

"Good night, Mama. I'll talk to you tomorrow."

The door shuts behind her and we go back to rocking. It's not late and there's nowhere else I'd rather be. I scoot forward on the seat of the swing to recline a little more.

"Still comfortable?" I adjust Ivy against my chest and let the back of my arms rest against the swing.

"I'm great." She sighs against me, hugging me tighter. "Are you ok?"

"Perfect. I honestly couldn't be better." She kisses the hollow of my throat, her soft lips sending shockwaves straight to my heart and I let out a hum of contentment. "Couldn't be better."

CHAPTER 18
IVY

CHLOE: *Sweets, I need you!*
ME: *What's up?*
CHLOE: *Liam's coming home this week!!!!!*
ME: *YES! How can I help?*
CHLOE: *I've been full-on nesting, focusing on the house and the baby stuff, but I forgot about me*
ME: *Well that's no good! What does mama need?*
CHLOE: *Something pretty to wear on the pier! And lingerie. And brunch. Mama NEEDS brunch. Are you free?*
ME: *Anything for you! Why don't we hit up the MacArthur Center?*
CHLOE: *Great idea! I'll drive*
ME:
Chloe: *Pick you up in 30*

T'm already dressed for the day. I only need to freshen up my coffee and put on a little makeup. I'm washing out my cup when my phone dings.

CHLOE: *I'm in the parking lot*

Purse? Check. Keys? Check. Phone? Checkity-check. I lock up and pretty much skip down to Chloe's car.

"My, aren't we chipper this morning! What has you bouncing and grinning?"

I drop my purse between my feet and fasten my seatbelt before answering. "Would it be awkward to admit it's your brother-in-law?"

"Nope," she laughs, pulling out onto the road. "I'm fully apprised of the Bennett boys' more swoony qualities. Did you guys figure things out?" Unsurprisingly, Chloe is aggressive and competent behind the wheel.

"I pulled back, trying to keep my distance, but Miles came in swinging! He got some really necessary donations for Fresh Start, designed resume templates for us, then laid it all out for me in a way that was so open and un-dating-game-like ever. He told me he likes me and asked me to consider giving us a chance to see where things go. It's impossible to resist someone who is so willing to be vulnerable with his feelings *and* works to support my passions!"

"That's our Miles. When he's not too stuck inside his head he's good with the feels."

"And *great googly moogly*, Chloe, THE KISSING!" She lets out a Chloe snort. "We made out on the trunk of his car like a couple of horny teenagers before curfew!"

"Woot woot!" She yells.

"The first time wasn't a fluke. The kissing is epic. EPIC. I mean, that's all we've done and it's almost weird that it's enough. I don't feel like he's racing to hit the next benchmark or going through the motions until he can push me for more, ya know? With Vance...you know what? Pardon my French but screw, no... FUCK that." Chloe hoots and my heart races at the curse. I'm not good at swearing. "No more comparing everything to Richmond. It's over. I'm done." Chloe pumps her fist in the air.

"I swear, Chloe, only kissing has never felt like so much. But it's not just the kissing. He sent me flowers! He jokes with me and compliments me in a way that never leaves me feeling like an object. We talk about work and art and music. Last night he came to my mom's house for dinner and he held me in his lap on the porch swing for a good hour or more. We didn't even talk! It was quiet companionship. Like the longest, most comforting hug."

"Day-um! I didn't know Miles had that much game!"

"I think...I really like him."

"It sounds like he really likes *you*. Miles never dated much. This isn't the norm for him. He mostly keeps to himself. It doesn't surprise me, though, that he's a good boyfriend."

"He really, really is."

Chloe parks and we head in. We find a maternity store first and Chloe quickly selects a dress for homecoming. She knows what she likes and shops like she's on a mission. The deep blue brings out her eyes and the cut highlights her assets without looking slutty. It's a line she's very adamant about not crossing.

"Every homecoming there's a handful of young girlfriends on the pier that look like they're about to go on shift at a strip club, bless! I want to show Liam what he's been missing but not embarrass him in front of his command. It's a delicate balance."

I love her candor. I didn't expect her to choose a maxi dress, assuming she'd want to show off her long legs, but she tells me she found out the hard way on their first homecoming that the pier tends to be super windy. That's quite a visual. I sneak in my own purchase—soft socks with grippy soles for the delivery room—while she's busy picking out a couple of comfortable nursing bras. Next up is lingerie. I'm not sure if it should feel awkward helping my boyfriend's sister-in-law pick out fancy underwear, but it doesn't.

"I can't decide what I should be looking for. Pregnancy has made the girls pretty nice!" She pushes her breasts up, appraising them thoughtfully. "I want to play that up. I'm not usually curvy though. I'm not sure how to do the super feminine thing."

"What do you mean you don't have curves?" I scoff.

"I'm not talking about this belly! That doesn't count. I've always been tall and athletic. On the boyish side. It's sweet to have some boobs for once, but I've never had the stereotypical girly body."

"Ah, gotcha. But one, clearly Liam loves your body. And two, I'm looking at that butt and it's all kinds of curvy!"

"Muscle, Ivy. I don't have yummy curves like you, I have muscle."

"Thank you for referring to my curves as yummy, but it's all semantics. Muscle or fat, your ass is enviable."

"Nice! So pregnancy boobs and an enviable ass! How do we work with that?" We walk through the racks, touching lace and satin, considering the options.

"If I were you I'd go with a sexy, sheer bra and some of those cheeky panties."

"Cheeky panties?"

"You know, the ones that aren't quite a thong but have minimal coverage in the back to show off your cheeks. Cheeky."

She laughs loudly, drawing the attention of the cashier who comes to ask if we need help. Chloe tells her what she's needing. I find a comfortable bench by the fitting rooms and wait while she tries some things on.

ME: Hey boyfriend
MILES: Hi girlfriend, what are you up to?
ME: Shopping for lingerie with Chloe
MILES: Lingerie huh? Should I be excited or prepared to rinse my brain out with bleach?
ME: The latter LOL
MILES: That's cruel! I'd much rather think about you in lingerie than the kind of show Chloe is planning for my brother. Gag
ME: Be nice
MILES: I am nice! I love them both immeasurably, but that doesn't mean I want to think about them having sex
ME: Then you probably *shouldn't* think about them having sex
MILES: I'll think about you instead. Problem solved.

"Ivy? Earth to Ivy, are you with me?" Chloe is waving in front of my face. "I'm all set. Let's get you a dress now!"

"What? Why would I need a dress?"

"For homecoming! You're coming aren't you?" She glares at me. "You are coming. That's final." She pulls me out the door, marching us towards more shops.

"I'll come if you want me there! As long as you're sure I won't be intruding."

"You won't be intruding. I want you to meet Liam. Plus with you there, I won't have to find some excuse to abandon Miles so I can go home and have my way with my husband!"

"Right, like you wouldn't announce to everyone that you were ready to go have sex."

"You're right, that does sound like me. Still, now I won't need to! That's probably better for everyone involved. You make me more considerate!"

I don't particularly enjoy shopping for myself. I struggle to find clothes that flatter my figure. Either things are so clingy I feel too exposed or they're too loose and I look like I've gained 30 pounds. Chloe pulls a deep emerald wrap dress off a rack and hands it to me.

"This is the one. This color will look good with your complexion and wrap dresses were made for hourglass figures!"

I guess it can't hurt to try it on. She also finds me a deep v-neck top in the same color. It has a tie around the back that cinches in the waist and the bottom is light and drapey. Coming out of the fitting room to show Chloe the results I have to admit she was right about the dress. It's flattering.

"Ivy, you look hot!" I blush, watching my reflection in the three-way mirror. I do like it. "Now show me the top! Hop to it!" The top also works better than I would have guessed seeing it on the hanger. Chloe squeals when she sees it.

"Isn't the front a little too low?" I worry. "I don't want skanky cleavage," I turn towards her, nibbling my bottom lip.

"It's not skanky. There's a *hint* of cleavage. Tasteful but sexy.

You're buying it, the end. I think you should wear that to homecoming with the jeans Miles likes. You'll look pretty *and* you won't have to stress about the wrap dress giving anyone a peep show. That can be a date dress!"

"Miles likes my jeans?"

"That's putting it mildly, Sweets" She raises one eyebrow and the corner of her pursed lips. "I recall him saying something about the power of your sexy curves in those jeans being too much for a mere mortal man to resist. He's such a weirdo. Way into you, so kudos, but a weirdo all the same."

I feel like I could drift to brunch like a boat on the Elizabeth River. The last man to address my curves said I should diet because I was getting a fat ass. I mentally flash a big red stop sign in my brain. Stop, no bad Richmond thoughts. *Move. On. Ivy!* Now there's Miles. I can't imagine him talking about *anyone* that way. He's not a malicious guy. Chloe's voice cuts into my thoughts, bringing me back to the present.

"Let's go get crepes, baby is starving!"

CHAPTER 19
MILES

It's homecoming morning and the weather is cooperating. It's balmy, sunny, and not too windy. Bonus: the air carries the tang of saltwater and not fuel. It can often trend the other way at the world's largest naval station. Chloe's been in a frenzy for the last week, cleaning and organizing and basically driving everyone crazy. I took the finished tryptic canvases to their place and helped her hang them up to surprise Liam. I told her Liam wasn't going to care about the house but she retorted that she was doing it so she wouldn't have to think about anything outside of their bed once he was home. I may have pretended to puke. I plan on giving them LOTS of space.

We had to go through the hassle of getting me a pass to drive on base but it was worth the trouble. Now they'll be able to go home without needing to act as our taxi. I may joke about being grossed out by them, but I love how deeply they love each other. It's cool to see that they're still so connected and attracted to each other after all these years. I'll do whatever I can to let them get back home, alone, as quickly as possible. They deserve that.

The crowd around us is cheering, waving homemade banners and tiny American flags. Music is being played through large speakers and the Family Readiness Group has a table set up, selling flags and baked goods. There's a tent with chairs but we opt to stand in the sunshine. It's crazy crowded! I'm glad Liam is on a destroyer and not a carrier. His ship only has around 300 people on board instead of 6,000. Those homecomings must be a circus. The ship is already in sight but it will still be a while before they make it in and dock. Chloe is pacing around us, full of nervous energy.

"Are you sure I can't get you a chair, Chlo? No one would begrudge the pregnant lady a seat." She shoots me a smile but keeps pacing.

"Nah, I couldn't sit, I'm too antsy. I hate this part! They're so close but still too far away." I can barely make out the whites of the uniforms of the men and women manning the rails. I wonder if Liam is out there or if he's busy inside. I pull Ivy in front of me and wrap my arms around her.

"How are you feeling, Chloe?" Ivy asks. "Cheeky?" Chloe grins in a way that tells me it must be an inside joke.

"So cheeky. Enviable even." They both laugh and I'm grateful that Ivy is distracting Chloe. The ship is close enough now that we can make out the sailors on deck. "Liam said he'll be down in combat so it will be a while before he gets out. The first wave will be new parents who are meeting their babies for the first time, then those that won the F.R.G. raffle for First Kiss and First Hug. Thankfully, by the time Liam comes out, we won't have to dodge the news crews to get to him!"

Now that the ship is preparing to dock Chloe seems to settle down. They're here, they're safe, and the wait doesn't feel too bad now. Ivy digs through her bag and hands Chloe a bag of mixed nuts.

"I thought you might need some protein."

"Aww, thanks, Sweets! You're so good to me. I'm going to need my energy this afternoon, if you know what I mean." Chloe wiggles her eyebrows and digs into the snack greedily, grinning over at me. "I mean sex, Milesy. I'm talking about sexing up your brother."

"Chlo, gross! You know how much I don't want to hear that."
I groan but laugh along with her. 15 years together and they've
still got it bad. I hope to be that lucky.

"The things I'm going to do to that man..."

"If you don't cut it out, I will take your snack and make you
go sit with the old ladies under the tent. They'll probably give you
outdated advice about birthing and ask you a million intrusive
questions about your pregnancy."

"Alright, alright. I'll be good! And don't threaten my snack.
Nobody wants me to be hangry *and* horny." She shimmies her
shoulders, dumping the rest of the nuts into her mouth.

Ivy bends over to get Chloe's water bottle, giving me the
drool-worthy view of her denim-clad ass. She looks over her
shoulder, catching me staring, and gives me a sassy wink. She
hands Chloe the drink and Chloe takes it, smirking saucily.

"Feeling like a mere mortal over there, Bennett?"

I shrug, grinning. "I'm powerless, Chlo. Absolutely
powerless."

Chloe turns back to watch the ship's progress, drinking her
water. Ivy walks back to me slowly, watching me watch her.

"Were you staring at my butt?"

"100%. I'm pretty much always staring at it. It deserves poetry
written about it. In fact, let's see, a haiku in its honor." I count the
syllables on my fingers for her.

> *"A thing of beauty*
> *A squeezable work of art*
> *I love Ivy's ass."*

She giggles and steps closer, putting her palms on my chest,
then sliding them up and over my shoulders. The shoes she's
wearing today, some sort of cute, chunky clog-looking things with
wooden heels, give her a little more height but she still needs to lift
on her tiptoes to kiss me. I relax into the kiss, taking in the scents
and sensations that are all Ivy. I slide my hands down her back,

slipping them into her back pockets, squeezing lightly. I did warn her.

"Miles! Chloe is right there!" She doesn't pull away but holds me closer.

"It's fine. She already knows how I feel about your ass. We don't even need to talk about it anymore. Old news, Ivy." She giggles again, our mouths pressed together, and I squeeze her ass. Fuck me, she feels incredible. Her tongue explores mine and I forget where we are. The noise around us gets louder, indicating that they've docked and sailors are starting to disembark but I don't even care. She whimpers a little in the back of her throat and I groan in response. "You have no idea what you do to me."

"I think I have some idea," she jokes subtly moving against the evidence of my arousal. The feel of her against me has me hard as steel like we're not standing in a huge crowd of people, waiting for my brother.

"Shit." I pull my hands out of her pockets and place them on her hips. "I'm going to need you to stand here while I think about Chloe sexing up my brother until I'm out of danger of embarrassing myself." She laughs softly, running her hands up my arms and resting them underneath the sleeves of my t-shirt.

"I like this, personally, but I'm not sure this is helping you. Do you need me to put some space between us?"

"Maybe a step. I don't want you to go anywhere though." She takes a small step back, giving me breathing room.

"I'm not going anywhere." Her teeth snag her lip and I have to look away. Don't think about Ivy's mouth!

I need a distraction. "Did you end up listening to that Dustin Kensrue song you downloaded?"

"I did and I loved it! You were right—his voice and the build of the song give me goosebumps every time I listen to it. Which was...a lot. It was on repeat all last night. It's so powerful. What did you think of the song I recommended?"

"It was so good I ended up buying the rest of the album! I had never heard of Zee Avi but I dig her whole vibe. I've been listening to it while I paint. Let's do another one. Something unexpected, that I'd be surprised you like." There's more room in my jeans and I can resume touching Ivy without concern.

"I'm game! Let me think." Ivy tips her head back, scanning the clouds. "Got it! 'Bangs' by Brick + Mortar. Although I love that whole album. Honorable mention would be DNCE. It doesn't qualify as something you'd like — there's no depth or raw emotion—but sometimes I just want something fun!"

"Nice. I'll listen to them both! Is any particular song your favorite by DNCE?" I search for it on my phone while I'm talking.

"Probably 'Toothbrush' would be my favorite." She admits, blushing.

I download them both while I'm deciding on my recommendation. "Mine would have to be Thievery Corporation's 'Letter to the Editor.' That album is a painting jam."

"Guys, he's coming! He should be on his way any minute now!" Chloe runs her fingers through her hair nervously. Ivy hands Chloe a breath mint and gives her the once over.

"You look gorgeous! Deep breath, then go get your man."

We're all watching the flurry of movement on deck so we see Liam at the same time.

"BABE!" Chloe yells, waving. Liam only has eyes for her. I doubt he even realizes we're standing behind her. His dress whites are especially bright against his skin and it looks like he's put on some new ribbons and medals since the last time I paid attention to that sort of thing. He makes his way down the gangway, watching Chloe the entire time. The moment his feet hit land he's running until he reaches her. He cradles her face in his hands, kissing her like they aren't surrounded by hundreds of people including old ladies and children. Even I can admit it's a romantic movie-level kind of kiss. Out of the corner of my eye, I catch Ivy dabbing at the corner of her eye. Liam crouches down, careful to keep his white pants off the ground, and gently kisses Chloe's belly. Damn, that one got *me*. I swipe at my eyes and grab Ivy's hand. Liam links his fingers with Chloe's and walks back toward us.

"Miles! Good to see you, bro!" He gives me a one-armed hug, unwilling to let go of his wife.

"Glad you're back!" I pat his shoulder before joining Ivy again, this time putting my arm around her and tucking her against my side. She reaches up, intertwining her fingers with mine.

"We haven't met, have we? I feel like I missed something important." Liam's eyebrows scrunch towards each other.

"Babe," Chloe elbows him, "I told you all about her, don't act like you don't know what's going on. This is Ivy. My best friend, my doula..."

"My girlfriend," I interject.

"Well damn. I leave for a hot minute and suddenly we're a foursome! You seem to be filling a lot of roles there, Ivy."

"That I am. I was the doula first. I took over for Janice. Then Chloe demanded I be her best friend and Miles didn't want to be left out." She laughs, giving me the side-eye.

"I'm not sure that's quite how it happened," I cut in. "I did see you first." Liam laughs, kissing Chloe again.

"Do we have plans today or are we heading home?" Liam looks at Chloe and Chloe looks at Ivy. I get the feeling that Chloe is going to blurt out something incredibly blunt and crude, then Ivy speaks up.

"It was really nice meeting you, Liam! I don't know how this works. Are we supposed to ask you how the trip in was? Chit-chat about the docking? I'm looking forward to getting to know you better, but as her doula, Chloe has been on her feet for a while and would probably be more comfortable at home. I appreciate you guys including me in your homecoming, but we have the whole day ahead of us and I was kind of hoping Miles might take me out. If that's ok with you, I mean. I don't want to ditch you five minutes after you get back." Liam grins, catching on.

"No problem. You two go have fun. I'll take my wife home. Get her off her feet."

"I bet you will," I mutter. Chloe grins and wiggles her eyebrows at me.

"Have fun, Cheeky!" Ivy trills.

"Oh, you know I will! Thanks for being here!" They saunter off, Chloe grabbing Liam's ass and Liam leaning over to nibble on her ear.

"Get a room!" I yell. Liam flips me off, not even looking back, but he's laughing and Chloe is cackling gleefully.

CHAPTER 20
IVY

I feel like I'm settling into this whole girlfriend thing pretty well. We've gone to the movies, worked side by side at Fresh Start, and he's even surprised me with lunch at work! And I surprised him with a flower delivery. I've never given a guy flowers before but he did mention it. And Miles is a fairly unique guy. If any guy would appreciate a bouquet, I figured it would be him. Mama put together something really special with tall sword ferns, big bright green spider chrysanthemums, and tiny verdant button spray chrysanthemums accented with delicate white sinuata statice and soft peachy miniature carnations. She put it in a bamboo cube and Miles loved all the different textures and colors so much that he immediately painted it. Mama has the finished painting hanging in the shop now! I'm not sure what I did with my time before I met the Bennetts. Watched a lot of tv? I'm sitting on a bench at the park, enjoying my lunch in the sunshine when I hear my text alert.

CHLOE: *I'm going on a babymoon!*
ME: *Nice! Where?*
CHLOE: *Some fancy-schmancy hotel in Virginia Beach. Liam*

*booked us massages! He said his plan was for me to be pampered
and then for us to never leave our room*
ME: *Sounds perfect! When do you leave?*
CHLOE *This afternoon. We're only staying two nights since we'll be
so close to home*
ME: *Pack your sexy lingerie*
CHLOE: *Or maybe I'll pack nothing at all! Woot woot!*

She is too much! I finish my sandwich and brush the crumbs
off my lap. I have an inkling of an idea but I need to let it marinate
for a bit. I get up and walk, letting my mind wander as I take in
the beauty around me. It's always easier to think surrounded by
large, leafy trees, feeding off the dappled sunlight like I have
chlorophyll. I think this could work, but I'll need Miles.

ME: *Two things: One, what are you doing tonight?*
MILES: *Hopefully seeing you*
ME: *Excellent. Two, can you get into Chloe and Liam's house?*
MILES: *I have a key for emergencies, what's the plan? A little light
B&E? Horse head in their bed? Stopping up the sinks Wet Bandits
style? House party?*
ME: *You are ridiculous*
MILES: *So that's a no to the horse head?*
ME: *[eye roll gif]*
ME: *I want to do something for them. Will you help me?*
MILES: *Anything for you*
ME: *It's for your brother and Chloe*
MILES: *Nah. Screw them. I'm doing it for you.*
MILES: *Joking*
MILES: *Mostly*
ME: *Will you meet me at the Food Lion over here at 5:30?*
MILES: *See you then*

Miles parks at 5:30 on the dot. He kisses me slightly longer than is appropriate for a grocery store parking lot, but I'm not complaining.

"Where's your car?"

"I walked. Do you mind driving me tonight?"

"Happy to. What's the plan?" He asks, weaving our fingers together. I pull out my list and he grabs a cart, awkwardly, with his free hand.

"Before we get started, do Chloe or Liam have any food allergies or things they will not eat?"

"No allergies. They eat pretty healthy but aren't picky."

I read over my list, glad to hear I won't need to make any major adjustments.

"That makes this much easier. I want to make them freezer meals for after the baby is born. Chloe is going to need extra calories if she's breastfeeding and it will make things easier if she doesn't have to adjust to life as a new mom plus do a bunch of cooking. We can make bigger recipes that way they'll get a couple of dinners out of each meal we prepare. And we can write the instructions on the containers, leaving as little work for them as possible." I prop the list on my purse in the child's seat, talking while we walk.

"I read that there can be an adjustment period after deployment, where they both have to get used to being together, living in the same space again. With Chloe close to her due date, that's going to add another level of stress. I thought we could do something to take a little bit of the load off of them. With them gone for the next two nights, we can use their kitchen, savings us the job of transporting the finished meals."

I'm ramping up, talking too fast, nervous to explain my idea, when Miles pulls me into his arms and kisses me. I melt into him, clenching the front of his shirt in my hands. Soft lips and warm breath meeting, his touch lifting my heart. I hear a polite cough and we break apart. There's an elderly man right behind us, grinning.

"Just needing some grapefruit. Don't mind me."

"Excuse us," I apologize, blushing.

"Sorry, didn't mean to maul you in the produce aisle," Miles whispers, kissing me again, gently this time. "You're the best, you know that?" I push up and kiss him back. Once, twice, looking in his eyes as I press my lips to his a third time. Every touch reminds me this is real. He is this sweet. "Thank you for doing this. It's a great idea. We're lucky to have you in our lives, Ivy."

We wind through the store, grabbing all the items on my lengthy list including easy containers to store, freeze, and reheat the meals. Miles insists on paying for half of the bill. I like that this gift will be from both of us.

Once we're at Chloe and Liam's house we divide all the ingredients up on their kitchen table. Miles turns on an album I've never heard with a cool, old soul sound. The first song about a brown-eyed lover starts and he twirls me into his arms, holding me close to sway to the beat. The comfort of his strong arms encircling me, the rhythm of his heart under my cheek, and our hips moving in tandem is a moment so perfect and simple, I tuck it safely in my heart. With a soft kiss, Miles steers us back towards the food as the song ends.

I have a notecard for each recipe and I chose meals that have ingredients in common to cut down on the prep work. We spend the next 4 hours chopping, mixing, sautéing, and boxing up the food. Miles sneaks off to order us pizza while I'm writing out all of the instructions. By the time the delivery guy rings the bell we have 14 dinners lining their freezer and 4 dozen lactation cookie balls bagged up, ready to be baked.

"We can clean everything up after we eat. Let's take a break." Miles takes my hand and leads me to the living room.

"What's this?"

Spread out on the floor is a blanket. There's iced tea and a little bunch of wildflowers in a jar.

"Pizza picnic!" His grin melts me. We sit side by side, scarfing veggie pizza in companionable silence.

"Thank you for dinner, that hit the spot." I lean my head

against his shoulder, sighing happily. "I'm so full. And tired." Miles stands up, taking the pizza box to the trash and clearing up our picnic.

"Here, hop up on the couch. We can put something on and I'll rub your feet before we tackle the kitchen."

"I'd be crazy to say no to a foot massage." Their couch is deep and soft. Miles hands me a pillow to prop up behind me and pulls my feet into his lap. I groan as he digs his fingers into the tender arch. "That's perfect!" I use the remote and put on Doctor Who. It's my favorite and I've seen it so many times it doesn't matter if my brain is too mushy to follow the plot. Miles is still massaging the tension from the soles of my feet as my eyes grow heavy and the tv sounds fade into the background.

It's dark and there's a line of weak sunlight cutting right across my face. I breathe in deeply, smelling something like fresh trees with a hint of citrus. Mmm, Miles. Wait, that's not right. I open my eyes more and recognize Chloe and Liam's living room. Miles is tucked behind me on the couch, spooning me. My head is resting on his left arm while his right is draped over me, holding me close. I let my eyes fall back closed, soaking in the feeling of Miles' body around mine. I'm safe. I feel him stirring behind me and try to stay still, not wanting to break the spell. He shifts, dragging his arm up, brushing over my breasts before sweeping my hair off of my neck.

"Good morning," he rumbles into the back of my neck, kissing a trail from my hairline down. With my hair out of his way, he drags his arm back down, grazing my breasts again before pulling it tight against my ribcage. "Sorry for the boob grazes." He chuckles, giving me goosebumps. "I mean, I'm not actually sorry at all. But I think that's the sort of thing I'm supposed to apologize for."

I tilt my head down, giving him better access to my neck and he obliges, kissing his way to the tender spot where neck meets shoulder and biting down over the tendon. I arch my back involuntarily, pressing my backside into him. He places a kiss over the spot and I can feel his hardened length pressing against me.

"I should go make us coffee before I get myself in trouble." He pushes up and over me and the shifting of the cushions rolls me onto my back. He stops, bracing his hands on either side of my shoulders and propping his knee between my legs. He smiles down at me, staring at me like it's the first time he's ever seen me. He kisses me slowly, teasing my lips with his. "I don't think I've ever enjoyed waking up more." I don't think I have either.

I watch him swagger into the kitchen and the smell of coffee helps me wake up a little more. I'm almost afraid to go to the bathroom and see what I look like, but it's necessary at this point. My hair is a bit wild and my mascara is smudged. I'm honestly surprised it's not worse. I go ahead and wash my face. No makeup is better than day-old smudged makeup. I don't have a toothbrush but I rinse with a little of Chloe's mouthwash. It helps.

Leaving the bathroom I catch movement out of the corner of my eye. The bedroom door is open. There are three long, vertical canvases behind the bed that look like ocean waves. I want a closer look but Miles is shirtless, rummaging through a dresser drawer. *Sweet Mabel's nanny,* I need a bib to catch this drool! I'm pretty sure my jaw has come unhinged but there isn't enough blood in my brain to do anything about that right now. I'm not into beefcake-type guys, giant muscles are kind of a turn-off. Although maybe that's because Vance was...nope, not thinking about him. But Miles? *Daaaaaang.*

He's long and lean with ridges of muscle I want to explore with my hands. And my tongue. He looks like he doesn't have any body fat. He's told me he works out but he doesn't look like a gym rat. His jeans are hanging off his hips and there's the hint of that v muscle. I thought only celebrities had that! I'm straight up gawking at him, forgetting that I am not, in fact, invisible. He pulls out a grey t-shirt and turns, seeing me standing in the hallway. I still haven't worked out how to close my mouth.

He smirks at me.

Freaking. Smirks.

"You ok over there? I'm gonna borrow one of Liam's shirts. Mine smells like hours of cooking." He walks towards me, shirt in hand. My mouth is still open. How do I fix that? Come on brain, help me out!

I think I say something smooth like "*Eep*." He closes in on me, hard muscles within my reach, laughing eyes watching me.

"See anything you like?" I gulp like a guppy. *Focus on his face, Ivy.* Maybe if I don't look right at the muscles their power will weaken. It's working, I think. Some of my brain function is returning. It's already been too long since he spoke to me but I can't help that now. There's no passing off my reaction or pretending I wasn't staring. I channel my inner Chloe and go for saucy instead.

"I'm not sure. You were all the way over there. I probably need a closer inspection before I can say one way or another." I wink and he grins at me, dropping the t-shirt on the floor. I step up, making a show of looking closely. I run my fingertips across the top of his chest, tilting my head like I'm considering something. Oh Lordy, he's even hotter up close. I purse my lips and he laughs. I trail my fingers down, lightly scratching across his nipples. He hisses through his teeth, breath shaking, and I smirk. Not laughing now, is he?

I'm in control and I like it. I trace the lines of his abs, letting my fingers rest right above his waistband, dropping just inside the tiniest bit before sliding around to his back. I glance up at him. His eyes are closed and his breathing sounds almost ragged. I run my hands up the planes of his back, smoothing them over his shoulders and back down his arms. Tawny skin and bright tattoos, all right here for me alone. I lean forward, my breasts brushing against his back as I softly kiss my way up his spine. He tries to reach for me but I duck under his arms and around him, facing him again. I feel bold, confident even. I put my hands on his waist and make my way up to his chest, a trail of licks and kisses. He growls low in his throat and it spurs me on. My tongue darts out to lick his nipple and I graze it with my teeth.

"Ivy," he groans, dragging me upwards, his hands clamped on my arms. He kisses me hungrily and making him feel this way makes me feel powerful. I match his intensity and he rakes his fingers through my hair. He's clutching me tightly, his lips a hot, wet brand on mine, marking me as his. The dizzying sweep of warm tongues has heat pooling within me and my breath catches in my throat. I've never felt like this before—the intense want and need matching perfectly with his. He groans again and slows the kiss back down, cupping my face in his hands. Exhaling loudly, he pulls away and rests his forehead against mine. "Fuck," he whispers, "we should stop. I really don't want to. Tell me that we need to stop, Ivy. You're too special for where things are headed. Not like this. Not here." I nod against him, kissing his left cheek, then his right cheek, the tip of his nose and barely brushing against his lips. Miles is so, so good to me.

"Coffee," I whisper. "I'll pour us some coffee."

CHAPTER 21

MILES

I vy in that hallway, licking her way up my body, has been on constant repeat in my mind. That was the hottest fucking thing I've ever experienced. I get hard thinking about it. Not ideal, particularly now, while waiting in line at the coffee shop. I push my thoughts firmly elsewhere. I'd like to be able to continue coming here without embarrassment.

I take a couple of minutes to chat with Louise while waiting for my coffee then walk down to the birthing center. The receptionist knows me on sight now and waves me past, not even pausing her phone conversation. I poke my head through Ivy's open door, knocking my knuckles against the frame. She's wearing the green shirt from homecoming and she looks like a hot, real-life Snow White with her pale skin and dark hair. How did I get so lucky? She smiles up at me, starting to stand but I wave her back.

"I know you have appointments, I'm just dropping off a macchiato for you. I thought you might need a little caffeine boost this morning." I kiss her, a work-appropriate peck even though the glimpse down the front of her shirt pulls my mind into very-not-appropriate-for-work territory. Why does being around Ivy turn me into Pervy Pete?

"Thank you for this," she lifts the cup. "You didn't have to do that."

"I like taking care of you."

"I'm not used to being taken care of." She takes a sip of the coffee, sighing. "But I like it. Thank you. Oh, before I forget, did Chloe ever say anything about the freezer meals?"

"Not to me. Did she not say anything to you?"

"No, but it's fine. I shouldn't be worried about a thank you. I guess I just thought she would." She looks a little frustrated. It's strange seeing sunny Ivy annoyed.

"Do you want me to ask her?"

"Nope. Forget about it. I'm being petty. It should be about doing something kind, not about being needed or appreciated. Acknowledgment was not the point. I'm sure coffee will help." She gestures with her cup. "Maybe a mental slap in the face."

"I think you're both needed *and* appreciated. There's no shame in wanting reassurance sometimes." I brush a kiss on her cheek and turn to leave, stopping outside her door. "Chloe's plotting something. She wanted me to ask if there is a day this week when you're light on appointments?"

"I'm free after 11 Wednesday. And Thursday morning."

"Awesome, I'll pass that along. Keep Wednesday afternoon open." I text Chloe as I walk out.

ME: Ivy is free after 11 am Wednesday.
CHLOE: Sweet! I'll plan on then.
ME: What exactly are you planning?
CHLOE Beach day! Liam needs to relax. The only way I can get him to stop doing projects at home is to force him out of the house!
ME: Sounds like him. I'm down. What can I do?
CHLOE: Should we go for the afternoon? Or make a day of it? Pack lunch? Go out to eat afterward? I have too many ideas! Help me before it gets away from me!
ME: Deep breath, Chlo
ME: What does Liam say?

CHLOE: *You know he's no help, he's all "Whatever you want, Babe."*

ME: *The 4 of us?*

CHLOE: *yep*

ME: *How about this? I'll pick up sandwiches and chips at Taste on my way to your place. You guys can get stuff to grill for dinner. We'll eat lunch on the beach, hang out and then go back to your house.*

CHLOE: *I knew you wouldn't let me down, Milesy.*

CHLOE: *I'll work out girly details with Ivy, you get her to my house*

ME: *Girly details?*

CHLOE: *Picking out swimsuits and such. Never you mind*

CHLOE: *Although I should probably ask if she has some kind of sun shelter. Sister is WHITE!*

ME: *Rude. Possibly racist*

CHLOE: *I'm white! You're denying she's super pale?*

ME: *She's perfect*

CHLOE: *I agree Milesy! That's why I need to see if she has an umbrella or pop-up canopy we can use. Gotta protect that perfect skin ;)*

Speaking of, I should probably buy some extra sunscreen...

Wednesday morning has me running all over town. Hughes Florals to get Kath's keys, her house for the beach canopy, back to drop off her keys, Taste to grab our lunch, then the Birthing Center for Ivy. She's waiting outside, still in work clothes with a big bag at her feet. I pull over and hop out, grabbing her bag and stowing it in the backseat then sneaking in a kiss on her cheek before opening her door.

"Do we need to make any stops?" She reaches across to clasp

my hand and I rest them on my thigh. Thank fuck she needs to touch as much as I do.

"All done. We're good to head straight to Chloe and Liam's."

"Wow, thank you for doing all of that." She turns the music up a little, humming along under her breath. Her voice is...not good. It's oddly endearing. I can't sing either. We're just a couple of people who love music with terrible voices.

Liam and Chloe are loading up his truck when I park. I start transferring everything from my car while Ivy goes inside to change.

"Let's go!" Chloe yells, climbing in the front seat.

Liam locks up while I straight up stare at my girlfriend walking out. Her gauzy coverup hints at what's underneath, the mystery making her all the more delectable. She comes around to the side of the truck and we slide onto the bench seat behind Chloe.

"I've got surf tunes queued up for the drive!" She cranks up the volume and rolls down the windows. There's not much better than The Ventures on the stereo, salt air blowing through the windows, and Ivy Hughes snuggled up next to me. We pull up to the gate and Liam shows his ID. He tips his chin at the salute and drives back to the parking lot.

"You know, I've lived here most of my life and never been to Dam Neck beach before," Ivy remarks.

"That's not surprising," Liam says, putting his ID back in his wallet. "You have to have base access to get back here."

I grab the canopy and our bags, Liam gets the cooler and Chloe leads the way. We crest the dunes covered in American Beach grass, the tall reeds waving in the ocean breeze, and pick our way down to the beach. We keep walking a ways down, setting up some distance from the entrance for a little more privacy. Dropping everything in the sand, my brother yanks off his shirt, tossing Chloe the sunscreen. Looks like he spent the entire deployment working out. Dude is ripped. Liam is a couple of inches taller than I am, wide, and solid muscle. Chloe makes quick work of his back and pulls her cover-up off so he can return the favor. She looks like she's about to pop. I'd never say that out loud—I value my life. But from behind I could easily assume she's ready to join Liam, trouncing some unsuspecting beachgoers at volleyball. She's a combination of sporty muscles and big belly. The two of them together are enough to make anyone self-conscious.

I toss my shirt in my bag, turning to ask Ivy if she'd get my back, and momentarily forget how to breathe. Ivy's cover-up is at her feet. All I can see is miles of creamy white skin and a little red bikini. She has her foot propped up on the cooler and she's smoothing sunscreen over her shapely leg. Dark curls are cascading down, hiding her face. She switches legs while I gape. She straightens up, turning towards me, holding out the sunscreen. I take it from her and then step back, dragging my eyes slowly from her face down to her toes and back up again. I can't hide my interest, I own it. I shake my head, trying to comprehend this vision in front of me. Everything about her is soft. Lush. *Mine.* The possessiveness surprises me but it's there all right. MINE.

"Ivy." She looks almost worried. "You are so. fucking. sexy." She blushes prettily as she smiles and I can't help but run my fingers across the pink of her cheeks. "You're like...a goddess. Like you should be painted by Pierre Rutz!"

Liam starts chuckling behind me. I shoot my middle finger up over my shoulder, not even turning around.

"I'll stop gushing. Just...damn! Here, let me get your back." It is not a trial to rub sunscreen into Ivy's skin. Every inch is so soft, begging to be explored by my fingertips. I take my time, lingering almost inappropriately.

"I think she's good, Milesy!" Chloe cackles. "Looks like you've got a little drool right there though." I flip her off too. "Testy little bro! You should be nicer to your elders!"

"Here, let me do yours." Ivy takes the bottle from me and

turns me around. I'm sure it's not my imagination that she takes as long as I did. And I enjoy every moment.

Once the canopy is set up we sit in the shade and eat our sandwiches. Liam wants to know what I've been doing since the funeral. I tell him about what I've been painting and about Fresh Start. Ivy jumps in occasionally to answer questions.

"How long have you been volunteering there, Ivy?"

"A few years."

"She's not just volunteering," I tell my brother. "She came up with the idea, started the whole thing, organizes donations...She's the co-director. Fresh Start is her baby."

"Wow! That's quite an accomplishment. What made you decide to start a charity for survivors of domestic abuse?"

Ivy suddenly looks uncomfortable. Nervous even. "Oh, well, I..." she stammers.

Chloe jumps in, talking over her. "That's Ivy, helping people! Hey Babe, wanna hit the volleyball around with me? I've got too much energy to keep sitting."

That was weird. Liam and Chloe start bumping the volleyball back and forth. Chloe passes it aggressively and Liam has to sprint further down the beach to bump it back to her. After a few more passes like that, they're far enough away that we can't hear what they're calling back and forth to each other. We're the only people on the beach. The break here makes the waves pretty loud and the wind is sharp with bits of sand. Ivy still seems a little uncomfortable. Maybe she's nervous around Liam since she doesn't know him as well? She's usually the more personable of the two of us.

"Liam's a good guy. Hopefully, the third degree didn't bother you too much. He's interested, that's all."

"Oh, sure. No big deal. He seems really nice." Her smile doesn't reach her eyes. I know something in that exchange bothered her. But I also know I don't have all the information, there's not a lot I can do. It is pretty hot out here. I can get her out of the sun. I shake the beach blanket out and spread it back out under the canopy. Stretching out on the blanket, I lean back on my elbows to be upright enough to see the waves. Ivy does the same.

"I'm glad you came today," I tell her.

She props her knees up, pulling her legs out of the sunlight. "Tell me about Philadelphia." She drops down onto her back and I copy her so I can reach across and hold her hand.

"There's sadly not a lot to tell." I stroke my thumb along the side of her hand while I talk. "I got a scholarship to the University of Pennsylvania and stuck around after I graduated. I like the city and I like my work. It's not a bad drive so I come down here for holidays. I thought my life was fine. No complaints. But now that I've been back home..." I bring her hand to my lips, trying to figure out how to explain how I've been feeling.

"Now that you've been back home," she prompts.

"I don't know. I'm realizing that my life was pretty empty. I didn't have friends. I didn't do anything particularly fulfilling. I was far away from my family. I'm not sure I was even aware of how lonely I was. And I don't know why I accepted just *fine*."

"So...why did you stay?"

"Laziness?" I crack. "Maybe that is sort of the answer. It was familiar. It was safe. Philadelphia was easy even if it wasn't actually good."

"You know you deserve good, right? You shouldn't settle for anything less, Miles. Familiar and easy isn't always safe." There's a weight in her voice like sadness is pulling her down.

"What were you doing before you started Fresh Start?" She pulls her hand out of mine and crosses her arms over her chest, gripping them tightly enough to leave indents. Everything I say seems to make things worse and I don't know how to steer us out again. I'm driving blind until Ivy trusts me enough to let me in.

"I was in Richmond." Huh. There it is again. Her body language is not telling happy tales. "I went to college there for a couple of years before dropping out to become a doula. I finished my training and... I moved back here." There's no way that's the whole story. Do I ask her or do I wait for her to trust me enough to tell me? I'm not going to push. Ivy deserves more than my impatience.

"Do you go back to visit?"

"No. I don't have any friends there or anything. I haven't been back since I left."

Another dead end. "Thirsty? Do you want me to grab you a drink from the cooler?" Ivy rolls over onto her side, facing me, and props her cheek on her hand. She reaches out, running one finger across my lips.

"I don't really want a drink."

"Ah." I get the sense she's trying to distract me. I kiss her fingertip and prop up on my side, bringing my body closer to hers and smoothing my hand down the dip of her waist and up the swell of her hip. Her skin is like silk. She moves until she's pressed against me, chest to chest, skin to skin in most places. The sensation is overwhelming. So much Ivy, every touchpoint a beacon of desire. She brushes her lips across mine, leading, but slowly. I'll never get tired of kissing her.

She snakes her arm around my waist and I rest mine on top of hers, twining my fingers in her hair. She's tracing slow circles on my back and I mimic them in her mouth, dancing our tongues together. I'm running my fingers down her spine, slipping them underneath the back ties of her bikini when the volleyball hits us. Ivy bolts upright, knocking me over and the ties get caught in my fingers. I can hear Chloe and Liam jogging toward us but my eyes are stuck on Ivy's loosening bikini top. I yank my hand away but that only makes things worse. I'm watching an unintentional striptease and as much as my dick would like to see where this goes, I don't want that for Ivy. She yelps and crosses her arms over her breasts.

"Ivy?" She's muttering under her breath. "Ivy? Honey? Look at me." Her eyes meet mine and she blinks back tears.

"I spend far too much of my life wishing the ground would swallow me up." She deadpans, tears now threatening to spill over.

I breathe out a soft laugh. "Hey, do you see my eyes? They're up here, looking right at yours. I'll take care of this. I've got you. Wait right there." I hop up and jog out of the canopy to intercept Chloe and Liam. "Hey, guys! I'm going to have to stop you right there." I lower my voice, gesturing to Chloe. "Chlo, can you go help Ivy? The surprise from getting hit by the volleyball caused a wardrobe malfunction...she's about 5 seconds away from crying." I stay with Liam, our backs to the canopy.

Liam starts ribbing me. "Dude. Were you trying to get her naked in public?"

"No, asshole!" I bark out in an angry whisper. "Your ball hit us and scared her! She jumped up and the back of her bikini got caught." I'm probably overreacting to his question. I take a breath and soften my tone. "I didn't want her to feel embarrassed in front of me."

"Sorry, bro. We didn't mean to upset Ivy. Chloe will smooth things over." I grab a couple of drinks from the cooler, passing one to Liam. "Hey, while we're alone, I went ahead and set us up with the lawyer on Friday at 4. I can leave the ship a little early." Liam pauses to take a sip. "We need to deal with the will and estate stuff." I nod in agreement.

"It's cool guys! We're all good in here." Chloe calls out. "Can you bring us some drinks?" Chloe is sitting, her belly resting on her outstretched legs and her arm around Ivy's shoulders. I hand over the cans, icy condensation dripping off onto them. "It's ok, Sweets. Don't cry! Why are you so embarrassed?"

"My flippin' top almost came off, Chloe! I'm humiliated!"

"First, I love your granny curses. Second, what's humiliating about that, Ivy? Were you out in public? No! And if you were, screw them! You care too much about what other people think anyway. But you weren't seen, were you? You were hidden inside this little tent with your boyfriend." Ivy sniffs and Chloe rubs her arm in the most motherly gesture I've ever seen her use. "So...why are you embarrassed? Do you think Milesy would make fun of you or laugh at the sight of your naked boobs?"

Liam chokes on his drink and tries to pass it off as a cough. Ivy looks up at me.

I arch an eyebrow, "I can promise you, Ivy, to me, your breasts are no laughing matter."

She giggles and that sets Chloe off. The laughter diffuses the tension.

"Poetic, Bennett." Chloe laughs again.

I reach out to Ivy and pull her up into a hug. "You ok?"

She nods shyly. "Thanks for sending Chloe in."

We spend another hour splashing in the waves, swimming, and talking until we're all hot, sticky, and tired. We're hauling everything back to the truck when Ivy slows down, putting distance between us and my family.

"Miles?"

"What's up?"

"I'm sorry I made that such a big deal."

"It's fine! I'm sorry you were embarrassed. I hope you know that I think seeing you naked would *not* be a bad thing."

"Good to know," she says wryly. "It's...it wasn't you. I know it's stupid but I think I was upset because I wasn't in control. It's not like I was crying at the thought of you seeing my...you know." She waves dramatically at her breasts and sighs. "But I didn't want to be half-naked in front of you, exposed like that, because of something beyond my control. Something that wasn't my choice. Does that make sense?"

I drop the canopy and turn to face her, tipping her face up with a finger under her chin.

"It sounds like you made a big deal out of it because it *was* a big deal. That makes sense to me." I cup her cheek, looking deep into her eyes. I hope she feels my sincerity. "You're in control here, Ivy. We won't take a single step forward until you say so. If I'm the lucky guy who gets to be with you and you only ever want to kiss, then that's what we'll do. I'm happy if you're happy."

"You are the best boyfriend."

I kiss her forehead and pick our stuff back up. "And Ivy?" I wait until she's looking at me. "I didn't look. I only want to see your body if you're willingly showing it to me."

Back at the house we alternate showers and make dinner. Everyone is lounging in sweatpants with sun-kissed cheeks and damp hair. Liam grills steaks and Chloe makes a salad. Ivy still seems a tad timid but she keeps her hand on my thigh while we eat and snuggles up against me when Liam starts a movie. She starts dozing towards the end.

I nudge Chloe with my foot. "You cool with us staying here?"

"We only have the one bed, Milesy." She gets a little wrinkle between her brows.

"Don't act dumb, we'll be fine on the couch. I know we fit, we slept here before."

"What??" She whispers furiously. "When did this happen? Where was I?"

I frown. "Didn't you read the card?"

"What card? You sent me a card after you *slept with my best friend on my couch*?!"

"Yeah, it was one of those official *Thanks for the Sex Couch* cards." I roll my eyes. "Not like that, Chlo! I should have known you didn't see the card, it's not like you to not say thank you. Ivy seemed a little bothered by it. I'll look for it, it probably got knocked off the front of the fridge. Ivy can explain in the morning. It's important to her."

"Fine, now get back to the couch thing."

"We were here late, working on your gift while you guys were on your babymoon. We fell asleep on the couch. That's it. Do you honestly think I'd have sex with Ivy on your couch? Gross. And disrespectful! Even more to the point, do you think Ivy would do that?"

"Who's having sex on our couch?" Liam chimes in.

"No one!" We both whisper.

"Not *no one*," he adds under his breath, earning him a glare from Chloe.

"You're right, Milesy. I know Ivy wouldn't do that."

"Hey! What about me?"

She nudges my foot. "You wouldn't do that either. It's fine if you want to crash here. Just, you know, be careful."

"Ivy is safe with me!"

"I trust you. I do. Ivy has wormed her way into my heart and I don't want her to get hurt. I love my Sweets."

"I love..." I swallow hard. *What the fuck?* Was I about to say that I love her too? Let's take it back a notch, Bennett. "I, uh, love that you love her."

Liam stands up and Chloe puts her hands out, needing his help to get up from the deep cushions. "Take me to bed, Babe. Night, Miles."

I take my shirt off and grab the blanket from the back of the couch. Ivy blinks her eyes blearily and stands up, stretching.

"Where is everybody?"

"Bed. It's pretty late." I get settled on the couch and reach for her. "Stay with me?"

CHAPTER 22
IVY

I smell coffee and something baking. There's garlic and onions, maybe cheese. *Yum.* A shutter sounds and I turn my head, catching Chloe with her phone out.

"Oops! Didn't mean to wake you. You guys are too cute, I had to get a picture. Don't worry, I'll send it to you."

I rolled over at some point in the night because instead of spooning with Miles I'm facing him, recreating our position yesterday, before the bikini top debacle. *Boob-gate.* My face is snuggled against his bare chest, my head resting on his arm. He's holding me close, keeping me from falling off the couch. One of my legs is tucked between his and the other is thrown up over his hip. I breathe in deeply and as I exhale he hugs me closer. I feel his voice rumbling in his chest, scratchy from sleep. "Morning. How'd you sleep?"

"I'm not sure I'm awake," I whisper against his bare skin. "This feels like a dream."

"Is it a good dream?" The gravel in his voice hits me low, the warmth spreading through my body. I snuggle in, kissing his collarbone lightly.

"The best dream." I don't want to move but sleepy snuggling

and kissing while other people are awake and walking around, making breakfast, is weird. "You asked me to stay."

"You stayed."

"Well, in my defense, you're my ride so I was kind of stuck."

"I would have driven you home, but I think having a sleepover here was the better option."

"It's true, Ivy sleepovers are the best!" Chloe calls from the kitchen.

"Wait, you're having sleepovers with my girlfriend?"

"We've already been over this, Milesy, she was mine first."

He laughs and kisses the top of my head. I guess that's my cue to awkwardly extract myself from our tangle of limbs. Somehow I manage to sit up and Miles slides into a sitting position behind me, pulling me back against him. I lean my head back, closing my eyes, and he presses his cheek to mine. His morning scruff is deliciously scratchy and I like how comfortable it is having his arms around me, like I belong here.

"Chloe never saw the card. She still doesn't know about the meals. I thought you might like to tell her about our gift over breakfast." I start to reply but he kisses my cheek and says "Don't be nervous, they're going to love it. How could they not?"

"You already know me so well. That's exactly what I was worried about."

His arms are crossed loosely over my stomach. I absently run my fingers over his, tracing his knuckles, circling fingertips and palms.

"You have artist's hands, I think."

"Is that a thing? Artist's hands?"

"I don't know about officially, but as far as I'm concerned, yes. Your fingers are long and graceful. And you have this callous from drawing. Artist's hands." My mind is getting away from me, touching his hands and imagining them touching me in a more private setting.

"I like it."

137

"I wish I could stay like this but my bladder won't let me." I reluctantly stand up, missing the feel of him behind me.

"Mine either. You can go first." We shuffle down the hallway to the bathroom, taking turns.

"Breakfast is ready, sleepyheads!"Chloe yells. I get there first and pour us both coffee. "Liam made some potato, egg, breakfast casserole thing."

"It smells awesome, Liam." I yawn. "Thanks for letting us crash here last night." Liam simply tips his chin up at me and serves everyone. The food is delicious and we barely talk as we all inhale our meal. We're all almost finished when Chloe addresses Miles.

"What's this about a gift?"

"I still haven't found the card," Miles admits. "It's probably easier, though, if Ivy shows you." I finish the last bite of my breakfast and sit my dishes in the sink.

"Miles and I wanted to do something to make those first couple of weeks at home with baby a little easier." I open the freezer wide and gesture inside, explaining about the dinners and what they'd need to do to cook them. I pull out one of the bags of dough and show Chloe.

"These are lactation cookies. Our consultant at the birth center swears by them. And they're delicious. They're supposed to help keep your milk supply up. I wrote the instructions here on the bag." Chloe jumps up and throws her arms around me.

"Chlo, are you crying?" Miles teases. She flips him off. Liam pats me on the shoulder.

"Stupid hormones! This is the nicest gift, you guys! I can't believe you made us dinner for two fucking weeks!" I have to blink back my tears and Chloe wipes her face on a dishtowel. Maybe seeing the results of doing something nice for someone is way better than doing it anonymously.

Miles drives me home to get ready for work. The coffee and food did their jobs nicely, but it's been a strange start to the day, waking up on someone else's couch in yesterday's clothes. Not the norm for me, that's for sure.

"What did you think of Brick + Mortar?" I ask him, resting my hand on his thigh.

"Another winner! I downloaded the whole album again!"

"Did it surprise you?"

"100%. Especially after Zee Avi. I wasn't expecting it to hit so hard but I dig it."

"I loved 'Letters to the Editor.' She has so much," I pause, trying to come up with the right word, "swag. The rapping, the chorus, the whole vibe is cool. Do you think Thievery Corporation is something your mom would have liked?"

He peers at me from the corner of his eye, one side of his mouth quirking up. "She did. They've been making music for twenty-something years! Mom had them on her regular dinner-dance rotation. My parents even saw them perform a couple of times. I love that you made that connection."

Miles drops me off at home and I take a quick shower before getting ready for work. I'm clean but my hair needs my products or it becomes a frizzy, unmanageable mess. Curly girls gotta plop. I have a new client: a first-time mom who is newly married and the cutest, sweetest thing. I'm looking forward to building her birth plan. She's very prim and organized with definite ideas about what her birth will be like. I'm betting, once we're in the delivery room, all that is going to be ignored and she's going to dig down into her primal female roots. I've witnessed it countless times. I can see her leaving the hospital with a baby and a new, strong sense of her own power. I can't wait. I freaking love my job!

In between meetings, I think about Miles and Philly. He said he didn't have anything fulfilling in his life there. It's like a sand burr in my flip-flops, irritating me. There has to be something that I can do for him. He still hasn't said whether he's going back or moving here, but I shouldn't let that affect my mission. No matter where he ends up, Miles should have something in his life that feeds his soul. I'm packing up for the day, wondering if I might be able to grab a sandwich before Fresh Start, when the perfect thing occurs to me. Hunger forgotten, I hurry to the church to talk to Walter before anyone else shows up.

I thought I might need to do more to persuade him, but Walter agreed immediately. I want to dance around the room! Maybe sing. Hell, I want to do a whole big Old Hollywood-style musical number! In consideration of everyone else, I settle for snagging a cup of coffee from Myrna and impatiently waiting for Miles. It's almost time to start. I thought he'd be here to help set up but he's late. I hope everything is ok. I hope he's as excited about my idea as I am.

My leg is jiggling nervously under the table and I'm absentmindedly tapping my mug with my fingernails when Miles walks in. There's a line etched deep between his eyebrows and his shoulders are hunched. He looks worried and distracted. Leaving my coffee behind, I rush over and wrap him up in a hug. He returns it, but the hug is not quite right. He doesn't hold me close and he pulls away too quickly. It leaves me feeling off-kilter.

"I have news! Well, more of an idea really, but Walter agrees it's a good one. Hopefully, you think it's a good one too. When I tell you, I mean. About my idea." Miles still looks worried, but now also confused. I push on. "Anyway, we don't have time to talk right now, but after? Maybe over dinner?" He shakes his head, suddenly focusing on me like he wasn't listening before.

"I'm," his head shakes again, "I'm on computer duty tonight. I better get over there."

I stay busy but my eyes keep being drawn to Miles. He never looks my way. The cloud of worry hangs over him and he fumbles over things, seeming to struggle with paying attention. His shoulders are even more hunched than usual, swaying him forward and making him appear shorter. I nibble on my bottom lip, worrying about him. For the first time ever I'm rushing through my goodbyes. I don't want Miles to slip out while I'm distracted. I catch up to him while he's shutting down the computer, my empty stomach twisting with my worry.

"So...dinner? What sounds good to you?"

"Ivy," he rubs his hand on the back of his neck, "I can't." He brushes a kiss across my cheek, lips barely touching, and hurries out, his long legs creating distance before I can even process what he said. And everything he didn't say.

I leave Walter to close up and make my way back home, not even paying attention to what I'm doing. It's frankly astonishing that I make it home in one piece.

What is going on with Miles?

Did I do something to upset him?

Is it something with his family?

My stomach is too knotted to want dinner. Instead, I brew some tea and change into my pj's. There is one thing I can do: text Chloe.

ME: *SOS*

I finish my tea, absently flipping channels, but she never responds. I climb into bed, hoping turning in early and to get extra sleep will help me make sense of the weird turn the night took. Grabbing my phone to set an alarm, I spot a missed text alert.

MILES: *can't text driving to Philadelphia*

Miles wouldn't move back to Philadelphia and not even say goodbye, would he? Maybe that's what he meant when he said "*I can't.*" Maybe it hurt too much to tell me. I certainly hurt too much. My heart aches and there's too much pressure behind my eyes. Overwhelmed, I cry myself to sleep.

I'm less than useless all day Friday. I'm confused and sad and angry that I let myself get this wrapped up in Miles. But I don't even know if there's something to be upset about and I'm a mess. The whole day is one big blur. I try reaching out to him with no results. When I get a text alert I grab it and hate how disappointed I am when I see it's Chloe and not him.

CHLOE: *Sorry about last night, Sweets. Liam and I were busy. Not exactly busy, more like BIZ-AY! *wink wink**

It doesn't feel right to pump her for information. I'd rather hear it from Miles. And I don't have it in me to joke right now.

ME: *No worries*

This whole thing is starting to feel too familiar. I don't think I can take being punished with silence again. I end up making a vague excuse to skip yoga and spend my evening crying into a pint of double chocolate ice cream before a restless night of nightmares about Richmond.

CHAPTER 23
MILES

Everything that can go wrong has gone wrong. Murphy's fucking law. I was getting ready to meet Ivy at Fresh Start when I got a call from Peter, a big client I worked with last year. He asked me to come in to meet with him tomorrow at noon. He was not forthcoming, wouldn't even tell me what it was about, but insisted I needed to take the meeting and it had to be then. There were too many unknown quantities to consider. My stomach knotted up and stayed that way. It will take me at least 6 hours to drive up there. I should be leaving to help with set up at Fresh Start but instead, I pack a bag and make myself a sandwich to eat on the road. I call Liam, explaining where I'm going and apologizing for the fact that we'll have to reschedule with the lawyer.

I barely make it to Fresh Start in time and I'm distracted, worrying about what Peter wants and the long drive. I have to disappoint Ivy and that sucks. I can't grab dinner with her or spend time talking afterward, I need to get on the road. I think I kiss her cheek but I'm already thinking about how far I want to get before I allow myself to stop for coffee. I'm driving away before I realize I didn't even say goodbye to her. Way to be a distracted asshole.

I pull off not long after I finally get to the other side of the bridge-tunnel, more anxious to text Ivy than I am to push on. And I might as well get some coffee while I'm stopped. I climb out of my car, fumble my phone and drop it on the pavement. The screen shatters. *Fuck.* It's no longer usable. I use talk-to-text to send a message to Ivy. At the very least I want to let her know where I am. Good thing I've made this drive often; I don't need to rely on my phone to navigate. I turn on DNCE, letting Ivy's guilty pleasure fun music accompany my drive. Traffic sucks and it's after 2 am before I get to my apartment and crash.

I'm exhausted and sleep late on Friday, having to rush to the meeting, inhaling a coffee on the way. We're barely through the pleasantries before Peter offers me a job. I've only ever been freelance, liking the freedom I have on my own and the variety in the jobs I choose. I've designed websites, helped small businesses with branding, and created online advertisements. Peter is talking about a full-time position, on his staff. It's good money, benefits, the whole thing. I'd be locked into one role, but I'd also be doing it in a stocked studio with all the latest equipment alongside a whole team of graphic designers. He gives me a tour of their facilities and introduces me to some of the staff. Yet one more thing I need to consider. I tell Peter I need some time to think about it. Thankfully he doesn't pressure me into making a quick decision. He's a good guy. He'd be a good boss. A good boss in Philly.

By the time I make it back to my neighborhood I'm starving. I pick up some food and take it back to my apartment. I'm not entirely sure where the evening goes. Mom used to call it my brain abyss. Losing track of time and getting lost in my thoughts has cost me more than one relationship. Friends and lovers alike have never appreciated this part of me. I'm bogged down in my head, running myself ragged thinking about the job, dad's estate, wondering what happened in Richmond, thinking about Ivy, and worrying if life in Philadelphia is right for me anymore. At some point, I fall asleep on my couch.

By Saturday I'm missing Ivy like crazy. I don't know if she has texted me. I hope she's not mad at me, but how can she not be? I should have said more. I should have taken the time to tell her goodbye properly. The distance between us is weighing on me, pressing on my chest like a medieval torture device. I need to get a new phone. I can't go any longer without talking to her. I consider my options, think about how much I miss Ivy, and waste too much time thinking before actually taking action. Why is getting out of my head such a struggle sometimes?

Replacing my phone is incredibly frustrating. It takes way too much time to convince the sales guy that I don't want or need any of the shit he's trying to push on me. I need a working phone. That's it! Then getting it set up is a pain in the ass. It may have been smoother if I had waited and let him do it for me but my brain felt like a pressure cooker. I had to get out of there. Finally —I have a few missed texts from Ivy. *Shit.*

Ivy: Why'd you run out of here so fast?
Ivy: Philadelphia? Did you make it safely?
Ivy: Miles, are you ok?
Ivy: Did I do something to upset you?
Ivy: I wish you would talk to me. No matter what happens, I'll always be your friend

I don't want to read too much into it since I was the one causing the radio silence but *what does that mean?* I need to fix this.

Me: I hope you're more than my friend

She doesn't respond right away and I feel like insects are buzzing under my skin. I pace, phone in hand, unable to sit still.

Ivy: I'm making an effort to not be too clingy or emotional here but I need to know what's going on with you. I'm really hurt, Miles

ME: *I'm so sorry*

IVY: *Are you breaking up with me?*

ME: *NO!*

ME: *Shit. I didn't even consider that you would be worried about that*

IVY: *So you're not breaking up with me but you brushed me off after Fresh Start and then froze me out?*

ME: *Not intentionally. I fucked this up. Let me explain*

ME: *I had a meeting yesterday that I didn't find out about until right before Fresh Start. That meant rescheduling things, last-minute packing, a long drive I hadn't anticipated...I was distracted at FS, not meaning to brush you off. Then I shattered my phone at a gas station on the way. I just got a new one*

IVY: *That sounds stressful*

ME: *It was. It is*

ME: *And I've really missed you. Not being able to talk to you made all this worse*

IVY: *NGL, I've been thinking the worst*

ME: *I'm so, so sorry. Sometimes I get a little too lost in my head. I'd never purposefully ignore you. That's cruel*

IVY: *I know you're not cruel. I shouldn't have made assumptions*

ME: *I have a lot of regrets about how I left things*

IVY: *I wish you had just told me*

ME: *Me too. I was an idiot*

IVY: *I worried that you not even telling me goodbye meant something significant*

ME: *Sorry. My mind was already 3 steps ahead, thinking about the drive and my stops and how late I'd get in. Can you forgive me?*

IVY: *I already have*

ME: *You know I haven't really kissed you, good and properly kissed you, since that evil volleyball attacked us?*

IVY: *That is true. I've been referring to that incident as Boob-gate*

ME: *Bahahaha! It wasn't that bad*

ME: *If I could go back I'd drag you out of FS and kiss you senseless that way you'd have no doubts about how I feel about you*

IVY: *You should have done that. Do-over when you get back?*
ME: *Count on it*
ME: *I need to get food and pack some stuff I want to bring to Dad's. Can I call you later? I can't go another day without hearing your voice*
IVY: *I'll be waiting*

I breathe out a sigh of relief. I still have a lot of decisions to make but at least Ivy isn't upset with me. I've come to rely on her friendship and crave her presence. Virginia would be much less bearable without her.

It's much later when I'm finally able to call Ivy. She ended up having dinner with her mom. I didn't want to interrupt their time together. She answers and I feel the knot of tension in my chest loosen at the sound of her greeting.

"It's good to hear your voice." I stifle an audible sigh.

"You too." We're a little tentative at first. I know we're good, but it's still a bit awkward moving past the feelings of yesterday. Before long we're back to our more comfortable rhythm, joking and teasing.

"Didn't you say there was something you wanted to talk to me about on Thursday?" I remind her.

"Right, that. I've liked having you at Fresh Start. Everyone has. I talked to Walter and we both think it would be great—if you want it that is—if you took on a more permanent position with us. It wouldn't be paid at this point, maybe an occasional stipend like you got for the website stuff, but we'd have you to rely on for things like designing our fliers, keeping up with updates on the website, and so on." Her words speed up like she's nervous. "No pressure, of course. And regardless of what you decide about your future, the offer still stands. If you like the work we do and want to be a regular part of it you can do it here. Or, you know, remotely. From anywhere. Like Philly. Or wherever." She blows out a shaky breath.

"You think what I'm doing warrants a permanent role?"

"Definitely! You don't think that?"

"I hadn't thought about it. I mean, that's cool. I wouldn't say I'm used to this sort of thing."

"Job offers?"

"No... acknowledgment. Or like, appreciation."

"Oh," she says softly.

"And you talked to Walter about creating a role for me at Fresh Start that I can do even if I stay in Philly?"

"Um, yes. That's essentially it."

"You're taking care of me," I whisper in surprise.

"I mean...you said you didn't have anything that fulfills you. You're good at what you do and it seems like you enjoy helping the ladies at Fresh Start. I like you and I want you to have things in your life that make you happy." I can perfectly imagine the curve of her shy smile as she speaks.

"Thank you, Ivy. That's probably the nicest thing anyone has ever done for me. I'd love to have a real role with Fresh Start."

"That makes me very happy."

I feel like the Grinch with his suddenly swollen heart. It's overwhelming to think Ivy truly sees me. Usually, the trend is: I'm seen for who I truly am, then all contact ceases. Especially if they've experienced the brain abyss or its antipode: hyper-focus. I've never had someone get to know me this well and want to stick around. "I've really missed you. Getting to talk to you makes my day better. I wish I was there instead of here."

"I wish that too," she sighs. She clears her throat and her voice drops a little. "What would you do...if you were here?" My heart isn't the only thing feeling suddenly swollen. I swallow hard, lowering my voice too, feeling the intimacy of the two of us even with all these miles between us.

"Do you want to hear what I'm thinking about, Ivy? Or would that make you uncomfortable?"

"I want to hear, Miles. I've, um, missed you. A lot."

"You're the boss. You tell me if you want me to stop and we will, no questions." I breathe deeply, suddenly nervous. "Where are you right now? And at the risk of sounding cliche, what are you wearing?"

"Should I show you?"

Fuck yes. "I'd like that." I get a text alert and there's a photo of Ivy waiting. It's a shot down her body, her feet standing next to her bed. She has on a short nightgown. Wow. I need to sit down. "I wish I could touch you, Ivy. You're beautiful."

"Your turn." I take a photo the same way, shooting from above my body as I perch on the edge of my bed. There's no way to hide the obvious erection straining my boxer briefs, even if I wanted to. "Whoa," she sighs.

"That's what you do to me." I pause. Gotta set the scene here. "Imagine us in your bedroom. Right there where you're standing. I want to kiss you. Softly at first. Slowly. Running my fingers through your hair, massaging your scalp, and tilting your head so I can kiss you deeply. I want to taste you, Ivy." I pause, working to keep my words slow and even. "Your lips are sweet and soft, I can't help but nibble on them. I want you to open your mouth to mine. Will you do that for me?" She hums her assent. "I could kiss you forever. It's my favorite thing. But I need to taste more of you. Your skin is as sweet as your lips. I want to kiss a path down your neck and across your collarbone, tracing the path with my fingertips." I breathe deeply again, calming my speeding heart. I feel like a fucking teenager, fumbling around with shaky nerves. "I'm thinking about nibbling on your earlobe and licking the sensitive spot on your neck underneath it before biting down on that tendon on your shoulder." I hear her suck in a shaky breath. "Do you want that, Ivy?"

"Yes," she whispers. "Keep...going."

"I'm sitting on the edge of your bed now, Ivy. Like in the photo. I want you standing in front of me, between my legs. I'm going to run my hands up your thighs, soaking in the silky feel of your skin, bringing my hands up underneath the bottom of your nightgown. The curve of your hips and thighs is so sexy. I'm addicted to your curves."

"I want to touch you. To feel your skin," she tells me shyly. "Can I do that, Miles?"

"You can do anything you want to me, beautiful."

"I'm...I'm thinking about being in that hallway, Liam's shirt forgotten on the floor." She's taking control and it is unbelievably sexy. "Do you ever think about that, Miles?"

"Only every night."

"Me too." I'm so hard, an aching need pulsing in time with my heartbeat.

"What do you do when you think about that, Miles? When you remember me licking my way up to your chest?"

"I think you know what I do, Ivy."

"Are you doing it now?"

"Do you want me to touch myself, beautiful?" We're barely whispering now.

"Yes."

I didn't think I could get harder but apparently, I was wrong. "Will *you*? With me?"

"Yes. Hold on a sec." I hear her shift in the background. There's the whisper of fabric on skin. "I'm naked."

"Fuck. Give me a second, Ivy."

"You're sitting on my bed, Miles. I want to climb in your lap, straddling you." I groan. "I want to kiss you. I want you so badly. I want to feel all of you. More than I've ever wanted anything." I growl out, imagining Ivy in place of my hand. She's growing more confident and it is such a turn-on. "I want you to move underneath me. Against me. Right where I need you." Her breath quickens. "Will you put your hands on me? I want you touching me. Only you."

"I want that too," I groan. "I want to slide my hands under your nightgown, all the way up your sides. I want to cup your breasts in my hands, touching you the way I've been dreaming about. Your body is my ultimate fantasy, Ivy." I'm stroking faster, imagining the feel of her body against mine. The sound of her breathing in my ear spurs me on.

"Miles! I'm so close," she gasps.

I growl, speeding up my speech to match the pace of the fantasy. "I want my hands on your ass, pulling you hard against me. Fuck, the way I want to squeeze you and touch you. I want you rolling your hips, taking everything you need. I want you throwing your head back, completely lost in the moment. I want to give you everything you need, Ivy. Everything." She cries out and I'm right there with her, warmth spurting over my torso. We're both breathing hard. She laughs, sounding a little nervous.

"I've, um, I've never done that before."

"Neither have I."

"That was really hot, Miles." I can almost hear the blush that has to be creeping up her cheeks. *I wonder where else that blush would spread.* "Is it weird that we had phone sex but we didn't talk about...actual sex?"

I collapse back on my bed. "I don't think so. I assumed if you wanted to take it all the way there you would. I told you, you're the boss."

"You were right. I'm not ready to go that far, even over the phone."

"That's fine. I want anything with you. Was that ok? It won't be weird when I see you, will it?"

"No. I feel really good and that's not just the orgasm talking." I laugh, surprised by her candor. "Did you mean everything you said?"

"I'd gladly do any and all of the things I said I wanted to do with you, Ivy."

"I mean, the things you said about how I look," she clarifies.

"Oh. Definitely! You question that? Fuck, everything about you is sexy. Your body in reality is better than any fantasy I've ever had."

"Wow. Um, thank you. That's...wow. You make me feel really good. Did you know that?"

"It's probably good that you don't understand the power you have over me."

"I'm not sure I could handle it. That sort of thing could go straight to my head. The world is not ready for Power-Hungry Ivy." She giggles. "I'm not as good as you are at saying this stuff but...you should know that you are, without a doubt, the sexiest guy I've ever seen. In my life. It kind of blows my mind that I even get to talk to you let alone touch you."

"I'm glad you can't see how hard I'm blushing right now."

"Are you coming back soon?"

"Tomorrow."

"Good. I can't wait to see you. I'm going to go to sleep now. You wore me out. Good night, sexy."

"Night, beautiful."

I fall asleep, dreaming of Ivy over me, under me, in my arms. I'm pulled out of my dreams by my cell phone. It takes me a minute to figure out what the sound means and a minute more before I'm awake enough for the words to register.

LIAM: *Get your ass back home, it's baby time!*

CHAPTER 24
IVY

Liam calls me at 3 am to let me know they're headed to the hospital. Chloe has been in labor for 6 hours already and her contractions are now close enough together and painful enough that she's unable to keep resting in their bed. I turn my coffee maker on, get dressed, and toss the socks I bought for Chloe in my birth bag. I pause long enough to pour coffee into a couple of travel mugs for me and Liam and walk to the hospital.

They're getting settled in their room when I arrive. Liam is a bundle of nervous energy, pacing back and forth and bouncing on the balls of his feet. I need him to get to work so I can. I put a hand on his forearm, rubbing it until he focuses on me.

"Liam. There's a cup of coffee for you on the tray by the bed. Go ahead and help Chloe get into her gown." He looks relieved to have a task.

"Chloe, I brought you some soft grippy socks. The floor stays pretty cold in here and you may find you're more comfortable standing and walking for now." She nods, grimacing through a contraction. "Liam, the socks are right here." I put them on the bed behind him." Once she's changed you can put them on her."

I don't think it's bragging to admit I'm in my element. Early morning labors are like magic. It's dark and quiet. The world is

153

still. It feels like everything is holding its breath, waiting to welcome this new life. I love it. I bustle around the room, unpacking my bag and putting Chloe's things within reach. She has a little Bluetooth speaker and I set it up on the tray, ready for her playlists to stream. She's still a ways from transitioning; relaxing is going to be our focus for a while. I set up my small diffuser and turn it on to send a cool lavender mist towards the bed. I've found that certain fragrances help laboring mothers relax and there's no downside to a nice light, fresh scent, especially in a sterile hospital room. I dim the lights and go out to the nurse's station to get Chloe a cup of ice chips. When I get back Liam is putting the clothes Chloe came in back in her bag. I can see now that I need to keep assigning him jobs at this stage or he'll make Chloe anxious with all his pacing.

"Liam, can you cue up Chloe's relaxing birth playlist?" Soft music fills the room. I recognize one of Chris Thile's instrumental pieces we discussed early on, it's a good choice. Liam looks at me expectantly. "Chloe, what feels good right now?" She opens her eyes slowly, thinking about it.

"I don't want to lie down. Being upright is ok. Moving helps but I don't want to walk."

"Ok, we've got you. Liam, I want you to stand in front of your wife like you're slow dancing at a middle school dance. Chloe, loop your arms over his shoulders. You can lay your head against him if you need to. Liam put your arms underneath hers and around her back. I want you ready at all times to hold all of her weight with those giant arm muscles, ok? Chloe is going to plant her feet as wide as she wants and sway. You are her support. Keep her safe, keep her steady, keep her comfortable." I bring my voice down, talking softly but keeping up the rhythm of my speech. "It's just the two of you together in this moment. Your love for each other brought you here. Your love for each other created this little person and before you know it he or she will be in your arms. Focus on each other. Relax into the contractions. Let gravity bring the baby lower."

I back into the corner and sit in a chair, out of the way, watching them. Liam is whispering in Chloe's ear and kissing her temple gently. She moans, still swaying, and he kisses her again. I melt a little seeing them so wrapped up in each other, laboring beautifully together. They're such a good team. I keep an eye on them, whispering encouragement as needed. A nurse puts a monitor around Chloe's belly but they hook it up to allow her to keep moving. She's progressing nicely and doing it like a pro. They sway for a while, then Chloe wants to walk. Then she bounces on the labor ball for a bit and goes back to swaying. Liam is right there the whole time, supporting her through whatever feels best. When it's time for her cervix to be checked again I pop out to refill the ice chips. She's at 8 cm, nearing 9.

"You are doing so well, Chloe. You're such a badass." She's bent over with her elbows resting on the bed, still swaying. "Liam, raise the bed so her back is flat." She rests her face down on the bed and Liam massages down along her spine. I watch the contractions getting stronger on the monitor. They keep building in length and intensity and it won't be long now before she's ready to push. Sarah, the midwife, arrives. Chloe is no longer able to talk through contractions—time to move her onto the bed.

"Liam, why don't you change the music to her energetic birthing playlist?" Sweat dots Chloe's forehead and her lips look dry. I'm about to mention it but Liam's already taking care of her, wiping her brow and smoothing lip balm on her. "Good job, Daddy. Keep looking after her like that. Sarah will direct her, you don't need to worry about coaching. You keep doing what you're doing."

Liam climbs behind her, letting her rest against his chest. A nurse and I each get one of her legs and give her something to brace against. She's moaning deep and low in her belly with every exhale, eyes closed. Her chin is down, resting on her chest and Liam's face is alongside hers. His arms are around her and she's bracing against them as she bears down. I've never seen Chloe this quiet and still. I run my fingers down her face, along her tightened facial muscles. "Relax up here, Chloe. Release that tension. Direct all that energy down. Baby is right there. You're so close."

Sarah guides her pushing, Liam wipes her forehead with a cool cloth and I keep whispering encouragement. Chloe is completely focused. She doesn't even open her eyes, every bit of her energy is directed inward. The only time she makes any noise other than the continual, low moans is as the baby crowns. The moan climbs up to a ragged scream and Liam's fingers turn white as she squeezes them. They don't call it the ring of fire for nothing.

She opens her eyes then, scared. "I can't do this! It hurts too much, I'm so tired! I need to stop!"

I stare hard into her panicked eyes. "You've got this, Chloe. The head is right there! I've been here with mamas many, many times. That feeling, like it's too much and you can't handle it, is your body's way of telling you your baby is right there, ready to be born. This is it. It's about to be over. A couple of good pushes and we're gonna be celebrating! Let's go, Chloe!"

And then she's done. It's extraordinary, no matter how many times I witness it, and Chloe is awe-inspiring. Sarah places the most perfect baby boy on Chloe's chest. He's not crying, he's making soft, sweet mewling noises. I, however, am sobbing. As is Chloe. Liam's eyes are shining and he keeps kissing Chloe's face and stroking her sweaty hair. Once the little guy is free Chloe unbuttons the shoulder of her gown to slide her son inside, against her skin. Sarah gives them a few minutes before taking him across the room to get his measurements, promising she'll bring him back. This hospital is very supportive of immediate skin-to-skin contact. Once they've checked him over Chloe should get a good hour before they worry about bathing him or anything. Liam and Chloe are kissing and whispering to each other. I give them space and begin to clean up my things. Liam steps out to get some more coffee while Chloe finishes up the less exciting, but no less essential, parts of the delivery.

Sarah brings the baby over, sporting a tiny diaper and a clip over his umbilical stump.

"Would you like to try breastfeeding? The lactation consultant isn't here right now but I'd be happy to help." Chloe smiles at me, nodding happily. She puts him back inside her nightgown, his little body resting on her now soft belly. I help her position her breast, pinching the nipple to help him fit his little rosebud mouth around it. He latches on easily and she starts crying again. "Does it hurt? Do we need to pop him off and try again?"

"No," she sobs. "It feels super weird but ok. I'm not hurting. I just can't believe he's here! Or that I'm DONE! Thank God that's over!" She smiles down at him, tears streaming down her cheeks as she strokes his while he eats.

"Holy shit! You're breastfeeding!" Liam exclaims, striding back in with his coffee. Chloe laughs, still crying a little.

"I know, Babe! He's like a little baby genius! He latched right on."

"You look so beautiful like this, Chlo." Liam snaps a photo and then leans down to kiss them both. "I don't think you've ever been more beautiful."

Oh, my heart! "Do you guys have a name?"

Chloe looks up at Liam. "Now that I see him, I'm thinking Caleb. For your dad." Liam nods too choked up to speak.

"Caleb is perfect. He's such a gorgeous little guy. And look at those broad shoulders! Good job pushing him out Mama, I have a feeling he's going to take after his Daddy! Is there anyone in the waiting room? Do you need me to pass on any messages?"

Liam clears his throat. "Miles should be here soon if he's not out there already. Other than that... Chloe's parents live in Florida now. They'll be up to visit in a few weeks. It's just us." A shadow passes over his eyes. Even I can feel the weight of who is missing.

"Alright then, I'll get out of your hair. Congratulations, you two. The nurse will be back to help you get cleaned up and moved to your room soon."

Miles is sitting in the waiting room when I get there, purple shadows under his eyes and a jittery, shaking leg. He jumps up when he sees me.

"How is she? Is everything ok?"

"She's great. She did a remarkable job. And you have a nephew!" He grins. "If you want to wait they should be moved into their room in a bit and you can go see them."

"Listen, I know you've been here for hours, but would you wait with me?"

"Sure."

He wraps his arms around me, a sense of safety and comfort settling over me. I'm still running on an adrenaline high from the delivery and I'm not looking forward to the crash that's coming. It's my least favorite part. I sit in an empty chair and text Liam to let him know Miles is here and waiting to see them once they're settled. I look up from my phone and realize Miles is gone. I'm in the middle of texting him, wondering where he went, when he walks back in, carrying two cups.

"I figured at this stage more coffee wouldn't be a good idea, but I got you some tea."

"You're the most thoughtful man. This is perfect." I stand to take my coat off and Miles drags me down into his lap. He kisses my cheek and I close my eyes.

"Mmm," he murmurs against me, "this is nice. I missed you so much." We sit that way, sipping tea until he gets the ok from Liam. He links his fingers with mine, leading us down the hall. I'm not complaining about seeing the baby again. Chloe is propped up in bed looking tired and content. She has a big, late breakfast on the tray in front of her. Liam is standing next to her, holding a little swaddled burrito of a baby in his big arms.

"Uncle Miles! Come meet your nephew, Caleb!" Miles tears

up at the name, the same way Liam did. "Here, you gotta hold him, bro. There's nothing better." The baby is passed from brother to brother and Miles sits down, cradling Caleb awkwardly but gently. He looks over at his sister-in-law. She's shoveling pancakes into her mouth like someone is about to take them from her.

"Hey, Chlo. You don't look like this little dude exited your body this morning."

"Well, my lady bits *feel* like he did, but I appreciate the sentiment."

He chuckles. "Guys. You have A BABY!"

"Right?! I can't believe it either and I was there!" More pancakes go in.

"How'd she do, Liam?"

"Shit, man, Chloe was a rockstar!" Liam kisses her temple, awe in his eyes.

"She was," I agree.

"I thought she'd be one of those that screams and insults everyone and makes a scene, being all dramatic." Liam winks cheekily and Chloe gives him the side-eye. "I was prepared to have to talk her down! Instead, it was all fuckin' Zen in here. She labored in almost total silence!"

"Whoa. Chloe? Silent?" Miles cracks.

"You Bennett boys can shut right the fuck up." Chloe glares between bites.

"No," Liam interjects. "I'm serious. She was so focused, totally locked on. Babe, I've never been more proud of you or more in love with you. You were incredible." He presses a kiss on the top of her head and she sighs.

"I guess I'll keep you." I sit next to Miles and he passes Caleb over to me. I bring him close, leaning in to inhale that sweet baby smell. Chloe notices. "It's like crack, right? I'd like to bottle that up and make a fortune on New Baby scented candles!" His skin is ridiculously soft. He has the sweetest full lips and long lashes. Absolutely precious.

"You know who else was a rockstar? Your girl here!" Liam pretends to give me a standing ovation.

Chloe agrees. "You should have seen her, Milesy. This girl is straight-up magic." She tears up looking at me. "Ivy, I don't even want to think about what this morning would have been like without you. And not just because you're my best friend and I love you. You are so good at your job. That shit hurt but it was the most wonderful experience of my life and you made every element perfect for us. Thank you so, *so* much for being here."

I can't help but cry. I've never had someone talk to me this candidly about their birth, while it's still fresh. Usually, I'm gone by this point. I'm locking this away in my own mind vault. I never want to forget how I feel right now, holding this darling baby while surrounded by his family. They chat back and forth a little and I rock Caleb, high on the haze of love in this small hospital room. Chloe has finished eating and looks like she's about to pass out. I gesture to Liam and he dims the overhead lights. Her eyes are getting heavy and the best thing for her right now is sleep. Liam pulls the blanket over his wife and takes his son from me, settling in a chair with him.

I speak quietly so I don't disturb his sleeping family. "Final doula tip: next time the nurses come to take Caleb for a while, get Chloe into that shower *with you*. She's tired and her body is sore and probably feels a bit foreign to her. She can do it herself but she'll benefit from you taking care of her right now and loving her where she is. There's not a ton that you can do for Caleb in these early days, the majority of that workload is going to be on her. She *needs* you to make it your mission to take care of her. Not just when she asks. Anticipate her needs, and make sure she feels loved. Don't let this room be the last place you talk about how incredible she was today." I kiss his cheek and we tiptoe out, closing the door softly behind us.

My exhaustion is starting to catch up with me. I know I should be thinking about food but I'm too tired.

"Did you walk?" Miles asks. I nod sleepily.

"I'm in the parking garage. Let me take you home."

I invite Miles up. I know I should let him get to his dad's house, we're both beyond tired, but I've missed him. He sits on my couch, taking in my small apartment, and I go back to my bedroom. I'm going to be a little brave. Not a big step, a little one. A baby step. I change into my pajamas. Not a nightgown, that would feel too much like I was trying to set a scene. I open my door and Miles turns to look at me.

"Miles? Would you stay with me?" He walks around the couch, never breaking eye contact. He grabs my hands, reading my face.

"Are you as tired as I am?" I shake my head yes, the full weight of my exhaustion hitting me all at once. "Come on, let's sleep."

He leads me to my bed, pulling back the covers. I slide in, watching him while he takes off his socks and shoes, then his shirt. "Would you be more comfortable if I sleep in my jeans?" I shake my head no. He takes off his jeans and tosses them onto his shoes. If I wasn't so bone-tired I'd probably combust at the sight of him in navy blue boxer briefs. A photograph versus in person is no comparison. As it is, though, I can barely think. He lowers the shades on my windows and climbs into bed next to me, lying on his back. He's being Mr. Careful, not touching me, not kissing me, giving me space. But I'm not worried about him being here; I want to be held! I roll against him, tipped over on my side, laying my head on his chest and stretching my arm across him. He brings the arm that is underneath me around my back while he caresses my outstretched arm with his other hand. I throw a bent leg over his hip, getting as close to him as I can. He's cozy and I'm safe and I fall asleep easily.

CHAPTER 25
MILES

Today has been a whole lot of unexpected. I drove for 6 hours on very little sleep, I held my nephew, and I just woke up next to Ivy. In her bed. She's still asleep sprawled across me and she's so lovely it makes my chest ache. There's something about this level of comfort and affection that feels like more than anything I've had in the past. There's an ease that has always been missing. I like being in Ivy's presence, period. I'm not sure if she'd want me to let her sleep or wake her up since it's nearing dinnertime now. She feels right in my arms I'm reluctant to change anything. If I could, I stay in this moment forever. She begins to stir and I run my fingers through her hair.

"Mmmm," she sighs. "That's nice." She yawns, her breath warming my skin. "Thank you for staying. That was the best nap I've ever had. You make a good pillow." She rolls onto her back and sits up, leaning back against the headboard so I sit up next to her. Stretching with a yawn, her breasts press tightly against the fabric of her tank top. She sees me looking and gives me a coy little smile. "You know, Miles, I believe you still owe me a kiss." My eyes widen. I can get on board with this.

"I think you're right." I'm wondering if I should get up. We could go into the living room. We haven't talked about where her lines are drawn and I don't want to overstep. Ivy makes me feel more cautious than I ever have before. I care about her and don't want to hurt her or make her uncomfortable. She climbs onto my lap, straddling me, while I'm still pondering what I should do, catching me off-guard.

"Pay up, Bennett. I want what I'm owed." Kissing me she laps her tongue into my mouth, eager and playful. I hum against her. This is way better than whatever I would have thought of.

"I've missed this. Missed you." She kisses me hungrily and I can feel myself hardening beneath her, cock straining against my boxer briefs. She rocks back slowly and I growl low in my throat. Fuck, that's good. Her nipples are hard, pebbling against her top and I skate my palms across them.

"Miles!" She gasps. "Again."

I brush my fingers across her nipples once more and then run my hands down her sides, holding her waist. She leans back, rocking against me again. I bend forward and gently bite her nipple through her shirt then suck it, with the fabric, into my mouth before doing the same thing on the other side. Ivy is circling her hips and crashes her mouth into mine. I slide my hands up, inside her shirt, feeling the silk and ridges of her ribs before moving up to cup her breasts. She moans into my mouth as I squeeze gently.

"You feel so good. Is this still ok?"

"Yes," she gasps out.

"I need to taste you, Ivy. Can I do that? And can I see you?" She looks me over carefully, biting her lip, and then pulls off her tank top. I can't breathe.

"Fuck. Me." I'm staring hard enough to feel like my eyes are going to pop out of their sockets.

"One day," she quips. I laugh, shakily.

"No. I mean, awesome. That will be...yes, please. But...FUCK. I can't even think. Look at you, Ivy! And you're going to let me touch you?"

"Please," she whispers. My cock twitches at the soft plea. She's not only going to let me touch her, she's *asking* me to. I run my palms over her breasts, squeezing gently. I trace my fingers lightly over her skin, circling her nipples. She closes her eyes. I lean forward and trace the same circles around her pink peak with my tongue then gently suck it into my mouth. I suck harder, then harder still until she moans, and I bite down. Then I repeat the cycle on the other side.

"Better than a dream," I murmur, my mouth still on her breast. She's grinding against me and it all feels good. Too good. She kisses me, pressing her breasts against my chest. Our tongues are tangling and she's nipping at my bottom lip. I'm getting close and I don't want that. It's been a long time and if anyone comes it's going to be her. She rolls her hips again and all I can think is that I need to move out from under her, switch places. I slide my hand up her back and stop on the back of her neck, intending to stop us only long enough to alter positions. Something changes though. It's like a switch is flipped. The second I start to squeeze on her neck she jerks away. Her eyes fly open and she doesn't look confused or turned on.

She looks terrified.

The flat of her hand lashes out, striking me in the throat. I wheeze out a breath, shocked and in pain as she scrambles off of my lap and falls off the bed. I'm frozen, not sure what is happening. I don't seem to have a fight or flight response, I'm like a block of ice. She's on the floor, scooting away from me, her breathing ragged. I still can't breathe. Ivy is shaking uncontrollably, then she's crying.

I clutch my throat, struggling to swallow or talk. Standing shakily, I start to go towards her, but she backs up against the wall, curling up into a ball. I wave a hand out in front of me, trying to signal that she's safe and I won't come any closer.

"Ivy? What'd I do?" My voice sounds strangled and involuntary tears are leaking from my eyes. She's sobbing and it's scaring me. I take a step forward to touch her arm but she flinches away from me. Tears are burning my eyes and now it's not just from the throat strike. She's afraid. Of me.

"Go," I *think* she whispers. It's hard to hear over my pulse hammering in my ears.

"Ivy?"

"Please," she sobs louder. "Please go. Get out." I don't understand what's happening but the way she's looking at me is like a knife stabbing right into my chest. I scoop up my clothes and hurry out the door.

CHAPTER 26
IVY

I'm having a panic attack. Logically I know that's what's happening, but it's hard to be logical when your body is being overwhelmed by anxiety. My thoughts are skittering away from me and I can't get a handle on anything to talk myself down. My pulse is racing and my stomach hurts; my chest feels tight, every breath painful, my own body a vice. I push my fist against my mouth, trying to stifle the loud sobs. Sliding sideways, I collapse on the floor, crying so hard I can't breathe. I don't know how long I'm like that. Eventually, my throat is raw and I feel like there isn't any moisture left in my body. I lie there, trying to box breathe the way my therapist taught me, willing my heart rate to slow down. Miles' shirt is on the floor in front of me. I feel too exposed. I drag it towards me and pull it on, my limbs heavy like they're made of concrete. It smells like him. His scent is comforting. I don't even mind that it's a little snug. My eyes are swollen and I can't breathe out of my nose anymore. The adrenaline is still coursing through my body and I'm shaking.

What did I do? I hit Miles, self-defense-drilled-instincts kicking in. I flipped the crap out and kicked him out of my apartment. Apparently, I'm not completely dried up because the thought of Miles has me crying again. I'm sobbing his name into my floor. I hear the creak of a door and see bare feet padding towards me. Arms are around me, holding me close. Miles picks me up and carries me to the bed. He puts me down carefully and then leaves which makes me cry even more. I need him. I don't want to be alone here. I'm croaking on repeat like a scratched record, "Miles, Miles, Miles..." He comes back a minute later with a warm, damp washcloth and a box of tissues.

"I know you told me to go," he croaks, his voice hoarse, "I couldn't." He cleans my face, wiping carefully with the washcloth, and puts the box of tissues within my reach. "I tried to stay outside. I needed to know you'd be ok. But I heard you saying my name. Outside your door was too far away." He steps out of his jeans and then climbs in behind me, spooning me and wrapping his arms around me, so gently and carefully. I told him to go but he's here, taking care of me. He sat outside my door, shirtless, shoeless, injured, unwilling to leave me alone like this. This is what love feels like. I sob harder. He strokes my hair softly and holds me close.

"Shhhh. You're safe. I've got you. You're safe, Ivy." It's a mantra he repeats as he holds me. I start to warm up and the shaking slows then stops. The adrenaline is gone and I crash in its absence. I doze off and when I wake he's still wrapped around me, telling me I'm safe. He gets up, assuring me he'll be right back. I can hear him moving around the kitchen. He comes back and turns me towards him, so gently, like he's afraid I'll break. "Can I help you to the living room?" He gives me his hand, but after I'm up I need to stand on my own.

"I'm going to go to the bathroom first."

I can hear him back in the kitchen while I'm in the bathroom. I wash my face, both appalled at my appearance and unable to fully care. Miles is waiting for me when I come out. He leads me to the couch with his arm around me for support, wraps me in a blanket, then brings me a bowl of soup and a big glass of water. He turns off everything but the small lamp on the end table then comes back, bringing his meal to the coffee table and sitting next to me. Close but not touching.

"You should eat," he gestures to the bowl, "and drink that. You'll be dehydrated." His face is concerned and serious and it's breaking my heart. He talks even though it seems uncomfortable to do so, pausing often and swallowing carefully. "I'm here for you. If you want to talk to me, I'll listen. But you don't have to. You don't owe me anything. I can just sit here if that's what you need."

We eat in silence. I know I need to talk to him but I'm scared. I'm not sure why, though. I can't imagine his reaction to my story could be any worse than the look on his face when I told him to get out. I finish my soup and turn to face him. He looks solemn. Worried. I think I may have made him cry and that hurts me worse than anything else.

"I want to tell you. I *need* to. But, Miles, I'm scared that you'll look at me differently. I *like* how you see me. Would you," I breathe deeply, trying to calm my nerves, "would you hold my hand?" He slides his fingers through mine and I focus on them, afraid to look at his face.

"Is this about Richmond?" His voice cracks and I hate that I hurt him. I get up, shuffle to the kitchen, and wrap a bag of frozen peas in a kitchen towel, pressing it to his throat before resuming my seat and answering his question.

"Yes," I breathe out, thankful he's helped me start. "Richmond. I told you I went to school there. I had a boyfriend, Vance. He was rich and popular, handsome and charming. And a narcissist. He swept me off my feet, made me feel pretty and special and desired for the first time in my life. It was a whirlwind romance, like something from a book. He knew all the right things to say, the right compliments to give, and for a girl who had never even had a real kiss before, it was like being drunk on affection. Vance asked me to move in with him. Mama wasn't happy about it, said it was way too fast, but I didn't want to hear it. He loved me, so why not? I jumped in with both feet, but I was still nervous to immediately start a physical relationship. I wasn't ready. He was...displeased at our pace but he didn't pressure me. At first."

I gulp water, keeping my eyes on our intertwined fingers. "My doula training took a lot of my time and I was volunteering a couple of afternoons a week. I love helping people. It's important to me. That sounds apologetic but I don't mean it to be. I don't want to apologize for who I am and what I value. I wasn't always so sure of myself, though. Vance acted like he was, I don't know, jealous? Like he didn't want me spending my time and energy on other people. I thought it was flattering that this handsome guy wanted me all to himself."

I take another long drink of water, momentarily putting off saying any of this out loud. "He was very flattering about wanting me with him at all times. Then he'd make cutting remarks about how haggard I was looking, how I was wearing myself out and didn't have anything left to give him. He had been so complimentary and the sudden change was hurtful. He played on my insecurities—my weight, my body type, my awkwardness. He'd complain about any time I spent with my friends the same way and I didn't want to give up volunteering so I stopped seeing my friends. I thought it would appease him. That's what started the cycle of abuse and apologies."

I shut my eyes for a moment, wanting to hold back more tears. "I didn't have any relationships outside of our apartment. He didn't want me to work and would constantly bring up how much money he had and how he could take care of me, but being a doula was too important to me to give up. So I gave up volunteering, again hoping he'd be appeased. He was back to being charming, loving, buying me gifts, and treating me so well I could almost question whether the cutting remarks were that bad before. Like maybe I was overreacting. He didn't outright say there was anything wrong with how I looked, more that I appeared tired, overworked. I convinced myself I had made a big deal out of nothing."

I gulp more water, emptying the glass. "His moods were hot and cold. He'd get angry, *so very angry*, but instead of blowing up at me, as I expected, he would freeze me out, punishing me with his silence. I'd end up apologizing for how *he* hurt *me*, taking responsibility for the way he treated me to get him to talk to me again. And it wasn't even all that hard to do because no matter what happened he made me feel that every problem was my fault. When we started dating I thought he was a social drinker—the occasional beer at a party kind of guy. In actuality, he drank a lot and he got angry when he was drunk. And sloppy. Normally he was all about control but when he was drunk?" I shook my head as if I could knock the memories right out of it.

"One afternoon a meeting with a client went a little long and I dawdled walking home, enjoying the sunshine. When I unlocked the door he was waiting for me. He demanded to know where I'd been but when I told him he didn't believe me. He screamed at me, calling me a liar and a whore. He was convinced I was cheating on him. I swore I wasn't and apologized over and over, but he was super worked up. He wouldn't listen. He threw his bottle of beer at me. It clipped my shoulder, breaking on the edge of the counter behind me. I stepped back, away from him, and cut my feet on the glass." My voice is wobbly and I sneak a glance up at Miles. He looks frozen in place.

"I locked myself in the bathroom, sobbing, and bandaged myself up. He banged on the door for hours. Screaming in rage, pleading, begging me to come out, promising he was sorry and he'd never do it again. When I finally opened the door the next morning, after sleeping in the bathtub, he was passed out on the floor. He woke up and pulled me into his arms, crying and rocking me, pleading for my forgiveness. I let him convince me. I comforted him even while I was injured from his temper. And then I cleaned up the mess so he could get to class."

I trap my shaking hands under my arms and take a steadying breath. Miles is still holding the makeshift icepack against his throat, his expression unreadable when I let myself look at him. "I wish I could say that was the end of it. I wish I could tell you I was strong. I stopped calling my mom because I knew what she would say and I didn't want to admit what a mess I'd gotten myself into. I didn't have friends or my volunteering. Vance started pushing me to have sex every time he would drink and getting angrier and angrier with every no. He picked at my looks, telling me I should go to yoga more to *lean out*, or commenting on how my food choices were going right to my *fat ass*." Miles clenches his jaw, grinding his teeth.

"But then the next day he'd be full of apologies, saying it was just the alcohol that was talking and he loved me. That he only pushed because he wanted me so much. That I made him crazy. Looking back it doesn't make sense that he kept demanding I have sex with him while also insisting that I was unattractive. My therapist says it was simply another way for him to make me feel like I wasn't enough. Like I needed him and no one else would want me. I still didn't see that I'd *never* be enough. He wouldn't let me. I know it sounds crazy. It's humiliating. But when he wasn't hurting me he was this charismatic guy who would take me to nice restaurants to show me off and spin tales about the exotic places we'd travel to and the life we'd have together. I was young. Naive. Embarrassingly inexperienced. I'd never had a boyfriend and I think part of me felt like I was lucky to have someone like Vance want me—if someone like me was going to get the good stuff then I probably deserved the bad stuff too."

Miles is stock still, the veins standing out on his arms and forehead. I feel like the weight of my words, of admitting what happened in Richmond is trying to suffocate me. The need to get it all out is overwhelming.

"One evening a neighbor knocked on the door. He was around my age, good-looking I guess, and had barely finished moving in. He asked if I had a can opener. I invited him in, rifled around the drawer until I found it, then walked him back out, telling him he could bring it back whenever. He walked back to his door and Vance was there, standing outside, his jaw and fists clenched. I backed into our apartment, truly scared, terrified, of what he would do. He growled at me. *That's him? That's the guy you're fucking instead of me? In my bed?* He grabbed my arms, squeezing them. I had bruises." I brush my hands over the spots shakily.

"I told him no. Told him I'd never seen the guy before. Explained he was our neighbor but Vance couldn't even hear me. He shoved me. Hard. I fell, smacking my head on the corner of the wall. I could feel it bleeding, soaking into my hair. He grabbed me around the waist and carried me back to his room, tossing me on his bed with such force my teeth clacked together and my tongue started bleeding. I was crying, incoherent. I remember the veins pulsing in his forehead and the spit spraying my face when he yelled."

I press trembling fingers to my cheek where his spit had struck me, lost in the dark memory. "He yanked my pants down, scratching me with his fingernails in the process. I was bleeding there too. I couldn't get away. He rolled me over on my stomach and held me down on the back of my neck." My hands are shaking hard and I know my voice is barely above a whisper. Miles looks like I punched him and I can't stop the tears. "He was pressing me down so hard...my face was in the mattress...his hands were so big and he was squeezing them into the sides of my throat and I couldn't breathe. I thought I was going to suffocate like that. I thought that was it."

The words are pouring out now. I gesture shakily, "My forehead, my mouth, my side, my leg—I was sticky. Blood was dripping into my eye. My legs were tangled up in my clothes and he was holding me down. Keeping me down. He took off his belt. The sound of the buckle was loud. He hit me with it. I don't know how many times. The leather left welts, the buckle cut. I was screaming...couldn't stop screaming. Later I couldn't talk, my throat was too raw. I lost my voice."

I suck in a rough breath. "He yelled that he might as well take what I was giving to everyone else." Miles is shaking. His fist is clenched and a tear spills over his cheek. "He was bent over me. He was right there. *It* was right there. Pressing into me. The neighbor burst in then. He had already called the cops. He saved me, covered me up so I wasn't exposed." I grab a tissue and wipe my face. I'm puffing like I ran a race. Miles hands me his glass and I gulp down his water and swipe at my eyes.

"And then? What happened to him?" Miles looks like he's carved from stone. Every part of him is rigid and I can feel the waves of anger rolling off of him.

"The neighbor?"

"No. Vance." He growls the name like it's a curse word. "What happened to him?"

"Nothing. He went to jail and his rich parents bailed him out and got him a team of fancy lawyers. It wasn't rape." I shrug. Sort of. My feigned indifference is such a lie I can't even complete the movement.

"But he assaulted you!" He can't yell with his throat injured but the roughness of his voice gives weight to the rage the same way.

"His lawyers tried to argue that he had merely gone a little too far during rough sex."

"Rough sex?" Miles' voice sounds strangled.

"Yes." My respiration is smoother now that I've survived the re-telling. "Super fun hearing it said in court that my physical wounds were caused by over-enthusiastic rough sex. The judge had the comment struck from the record. The police report and rape kit stated I was a virgin and the concussion, staples in my head, numerous lacerations, and of course, the bruises did not match his story. The whole experience—the attempted rape, the hospital visit, the photographs and rape kit, the numerous police interviews, the lawyers—was traumatic. But I had family support, quick evidence retrieval, and a witness. That's more than most victims have. And in the end, it didn't matter. None of that mattered. Someone messed something up in the chain of evidence. A minor detail. Simple human error. But that was all his team of high-priced lawyers needed. Mama packed my stuff for me and I ran home. I wanted to get away. I didn't want to face him again so we let it go."

"And then you started Fresh Start?"

"Yes. And then I started Fresh Start." I blow my nose and wring my hands together. The silence stretches out.

"Ivy?" I look at him, hesitatingly. I don't know if my heart can take it if this was all too much for him. "Can I touch you? I don't know what you need after that but I need to touch you. If it won't be too much for you." Another tear slips over my cheek and I drop the blanket to climb into his lap. I'm straddling him again but this time it's not sexual, I need as much of my body touching him as possible. I need the comfort of a kind, human connection. I wrap my arms and legs around him like a monkey and tuck my face into the crook of his neck, breathing him in and dropping tears on his skin. He's running his hands over my back, my shoulders, my neck, my hair. We stay that way for a long time, giving and receiving comfort. Finally, I move to see his face.

"Do you still want me? Now that you know?" He searches my eyes and then answers by kissing me so gently, so softly, so sweetly I feel it across every inch of my body.

"Yes, I still want you. Now more than ever." He smooths his hands over my damp cheeks. "Thank you for trusting me." I kiss him, pouring my whole heart into it. Miles is unexpected in every way. He's caring and considerate. He's strong and masculine, but thoughtful and nurturing. I've never felt this way with anyone else.

"I'm very sorry about earlier, Ivy. It guts me to think I made you scared, made you cry." I wipe the tears from his cheeks, running my fingers over the sharp angles of his face.

"You have nothing to be sorry for. That wasn't you. You didn't hurt me. You didn't scare me. You didn't make me cry. I'm sorry I reacted that way. You had no way of knowing that would happen. I didn't even know that would happen. I haven't been with anyone, in any way, since Richmond." I pause to kiss him lightly, giving my words a chance to sink in. I hadn't dared to let myself think about how he would react to my history. If I had, I probably would have leaned toward him looking at me like I'm broken or deciding I'm not worth the trouble. I never could have imagined this outcome. He's better than the best dream I could have. I don't know if I deserve someone with so much emotional intelligence, but I don't want to let him go.

"I'm sorry about your throat. It was a reflex. I started taking Krav Maga after my case was dismissed. That throat strike was instinct after years of practicing self-defense. I don't ever want to feel that powerless again."

"I'll be okay, Ivy. Don't give it another thought."

"If I didn't scare you off today, I guess we'll be more aware, going forward, that there could be some things that are triggers for me."

"No grasping the back of your neck." He touches my neck lightly with the tips of his fingers.

"No. And when it comes to sex, I think it's safe to say I won't want to be restrained. I don't want to feel like I have no control."

"Can I ask, is there anything you did with him that would bring back bad memories?"

"As far as physical stuff...him behind me like that, his dick poking me in the ass? Thinking about that sensation makes me feel sick. I can't be like that. I can't do that. He wasn't the giving type, so no issues there. He said guys don't like that and I should be focusing on him anyway."

"Asshole." Miles grits his teeth again and presses his fingertips to his eyelids.

"But, uh when things had just started getting bad, when I was losing everything meaningful to try to appease him and avoid fights, I tried...pleasing him. I thought I could make him happy. Get him to back off on demanding sex. He was too rough. He hurt me and then he got angry when I didn't want to do it again."

"How was he too rough? What did he do to hurt you

specifically?" His voice is soothing and his sweet patience and understanding are a balm to my anxious heart.

"He was pulling my hair, yanking it out of my scalp. It didn't feel like I was *giving* him something, it felt like he was *taking* something from me. Like my mouth was just some hole for him to fill. He treated me like an object." I feel like a wrung-out dishrag. My emotional tank is completely depleted, but there's also some good there. "You know, a couple of months ago I wouldn't have been brave enough to have this conversation. I've never been so frank or vulnerable, with anyone. You're good for me, Miles Bennett." I'm still wrapped around him and I don't know if I even have enough energy to walk to my bedroom.

"How can I take care of you? Right now. What do you need?"

"Can you take me to bed?"

"Of course."

I sleep soundly with Miles' strong arms wrapped around me, keeping the nightmares away.

CHAPTER 27

MILES

That whole intense night with Ivy was a bit of a mind-fuck if I'm being totally honest. I don't know if I've ever experienced such highs and lows in one short period. First, finding her lying on the floor scared me so much. Caring for her was as much for me as it was for her. I *needed* to hold her, to touch her, to tell her she was safe. I needed to be the one to make her feel like that was true. Her story was much worse than I was anticipating. I thought I was hurt when she told me to get out, but that was nothing compared to having to sit back, the distance between us, and hear her recount what that asshole had done to her. I physically hurt, far beyond my throat. I wanted to hurt him; I have never craved violence so much. Thinking about her creamy skin marred with bruises, cut up from his belt and nails...my stomach roils even now. And following those extreme lows was the candid talk about her boundaries. She trusted me with her history, she's trusting me to be considerate with her body and her emotions. It's such a heavy responsibility but I want it. I want it all. Badly. This is more than simply caring about her. Knowing what she's been through and seeing where she is now, I'm in awe of her. Ivy is remarkable, a one in a million kind of woman.

I'm spending every spare moment with her. No matter how

much I see her, I'm never satisfied. We've settled into a rhythm. Sometimes I take her coffee at work or meet her in the park for lunch, sketching while we eat. Once a week we have dinner with her mom after I walk them from yoga. We work at Fresh Start. In between, I squeeze in work, the gym, Caleb time, and painting. I sleep over most nights. It's never more than sleeping but, after sleeping with Ivy, I hate sleeping alone.

I haven't given Peter an answer yet but the idea of going back to Philadelphia is less appealing every day. Thankfully he's not pressuring me since he knows I still have the will and estate stuff hanging over me. Since Ivy has an appointment-free afternoon, I park at her apartment and walk over to meet her. Maybe we'll grab some cookies from Louise and walk in the park. While I'm strolling I notice a mom with two small kids. We've seen them a few times before. The kids are sweet but look like they have a crazy amount of energy, not unlike me and Liam as kids. They're constantly running and climbing all over everything while the mom sits at a picnic table in a tired daze. This gives me an idea. An Ivy kind of an idea. I bet she'll be game and I've got that finishing-a-project buzz thinking about it. She's coming out of the door when I cross the street and her smile is better than freshly baked cookies.

"Where to?"

I link our hands and lead her to The Foundry. "Pick out something sweet for us, I'm going to grab some stuff." I grab one of the smallest fruit trays and a couple of bottles of water. Ivy is pointing out cookies to Louise and I ask her to add one of the huge brownies and a $5 gift card.

"Feeling hungry today, Miles?"

"Nope, I'm feeling like Ivy!" They both stare at me with matching confused looks. "You'll see." They don't look convinced, but I'm already on my way out the door. Ivy catches up, clutching our cookies. "I don't have a card, but they won't know the difference."

I lead us over to the rambunctious kids and their harried

mother. I'm glad Ivy is with me, this gesture might not be received the same way coming from a random dude, alone. The mom glances at us but goes back to watching her kids, probably assuming we're passing by. I'm not sure what to do now that I'm over here. Probably should have made a plan first instead of running on impulse.

"Hi! I'm Miles and this is Ivy. We see you guys here pretty regularly. It's nice watching your kids having so much fun together, it reminds me of me and my brother when we were small." She smiles at me but still looks wary. "Anyway, Ivy and I are going to enjoy a snack, is it cool if we share?"

Her smile looks less hesitant now. "You can take the other side of this table. But you don't have to share your food, we'll head home before too long." Her little boys are circling closer, still chasing each other and laughing.

"We'd like to share. I have some things I'm hoping they'll like that won't get them all hopped up on sugar." I put the fruit and drinks on the table."Is this ok?"

"Sure, thank you! They'd never turn down a snack!"

"Do you mind if I tell them?" She agrees and Ivy is already chatting with her as I turn around. The kids are watching me now, curious. I get down on their level. "Can I tell you guys a secret? My girlfriend and I brought some snacks for you! But before you can have them, I need you to give something to your mom. Can you do that?" They both nod solemnly. "It's a pretty important job. I have something for each of you. All you need to do is give them to your mom *and* tell her one thing you love about her. Got it?" I hand one the brownie and the other the gift card and they take off running for their mom. I stand back, wanting to see the interaction without being in the way.

Brownie boy hands his gift over, hugs his mom, and declares that he loves how she reads to him. Gift card boy then shoves his brother out of the way, presents his gift, and tells her that he loves how she sings to them at night. Not to be outdone, Brownie hugs her again and yells that *he* loves the food she makes, then Gift

Card is shouting that he loves her food more AND he thinks she's the "bestest" mom ever. Ivy is laughing and their mom joins in with tears in her eyes.

"Ok, that's good. You both love me, I love you, let's have a snack you monsters!" She kisses their heads and hands them each a water. Ivy joins me and I catch the mom mouthing thank you as we turn to leave. I walk us over to a bench and sit, pulling Ivy into my lap.

"That was you feeling like me?"

"Yep. I wanted to do something nice for no real reason other than I can. It's a move I like to call *The Ivy*."

"I have a move, do I?" She breaks off a piece of cookie, popping part of it in her mouth and the rest in mine. The crunch of walnuts and gooey, still cooling chocolate chips are delicious.

"Yes, you do," I mumble around my bite, pausing to finish chewing. "The Ivy looks like intentional kindness—keeping care packages in your car for houseless people, sending cards to people who need a kind word, carrying gift cards to The Foundry around in case you see someone who looks like they could use a cup of coffee..."

She interrupts, "Or maybe buying a tired mom a brownie and reminding her how much her sons love her?"

"Now you're getting it. The Ivy."

"You're ridiculous. And that was a nice thing you did." Her kiss tastes like chocolate chip cookies and sunshine. We stay that way for a while, kissing and talking. I love being with her like this but I'm starting to feel antsy. The urge to paint is always there, but I haven't been getting as much time in recently. I *need* to create.

"Would you want to come over to Dad's with me? I need to paint. Or if you think you'd be bored I guess I could go alone."

"Let's do it! I'd like to watch you and I can always work on my cards." She pats her purse.

We drive over to Dad's and it strikes me that it's not too far from her mom's house. Different school districts, but it's strange to think we could have crossed paths when we were younger. I wonder if younger Miles and younger Ivy would have hit it off? I could see younger me being too nervous to talk to her and younger Ivy not being confident enough to see me pining. I set up my easel in the sunroom. I put on Thao & The Get Down Stay Down as painting music. Ivy is wandering the room behind me, examining.

She gasps. "Is this me?" She's holding the watercolor carefully, scrutinizing it up close.

"It does say Ivy on the bottom," I quip. She slaps me on the shoulder.

"It's lovely. When did you do this?"

"I'm not sure how this makes me look but...after that first time at Fresh Start."

"That long ago? You didn't even know me then! I thought you saw me as some weirdo stranger-hugger at that point."

"I never thought that, Ivy," I roll my eyes. "It's yours if you want it." I tip my chin towards the painting in her hands, mine full of supplies.

"Oh no, I couldn't do that. Anyway, why do I need a painting of myself? You keep it." I shrug and go back to setting up my paints. Once I'm painting everything else fades away. I hear Ivy in the background, doing something in another room, then angling the armchair near me, but I'm quickly lost to the art. I use other mediums sometimes, dabbling to stretch myself, but watercolor is my favorite. It feels like emotions, one thing bleeding into the next, the layers creating something new between them. I like that it can be imprecise—no sharp lines, no boundaries. I'm not working on anything specific today, just putting feelings to paper. I create a snippet of the sky at the park, wanting to save the feel of the sun cutting through the leaves of the trees. I spend a lot of time up close, working on that dappling of golden sun, green leaves, and blue sky.

I stretch, taking a brief break, and my eyes go straight to Ivy. I watch her. Study her, in truth. Everything about her draws me in.

Curls loose and wild, her feet are tucked up underneath her and she's as pretty as a picture in the soft light coming in from the windows. She's writing in a card. Her lips are scrunched up in concentration and I'm transfixed by the interesting arch of her mouth, the angles, the shadows, and the determination in her expression. It can be hard to break the hyper-focus when I start painting.

"What are you working on?"

"I'm going to send this card to a guy who lives on my mom's street. He built the cutest free library by his mailbox and keeps it stocked with books for the neighborhood kids."

I look back at my painting, deciding I'm done with it for now. My back is begging for a break and looking at Ivy's expression has me suddenly less interested in continuing working on leaves. The abrupt change in direction wouldn't do the current piece any favors. I stand up, stretching again, and Ivy stands up too. She closes the card and the front is oddly familiar. Is that what she was doing in the other room?

"Did you get that from my stuff?"

"What? What stuff?"

"My box in the front room."

"Why would I take something from your box? What are we talking about? I'm confused."

"I'm not mad. You can use anything I have. Just curious." I point at the card she's holding. "That's my card."

"No," she shakes her head emphatically, her curls bouncing. "It's *my* card. I bought it. I carry a couple in my bag at all times. I keep them stocked for this very purpose."

"Wait, you *bought* that card?"

"That's what I just said, Miles. You're being really weird about it."

"This whole thing is weird. Let me show you so you don't think I'm a crazy person who is strangely possessive about paper goods. The box is out there." She looks like she's concerned for my sanity but follows me anyway. I pull out the box by the entry table and open the lid. Inside are stacks of card stock and envelopes. I take one off the top and hand it to her.

She wrinkles her nose. "You buy the same cards? What are the odds of that? You have good taste!" She hands it back. She didn't take a card from this box.

"You had *that* card in your purse?" She nods. "I don't buy the same cards, Ivy. These are *my* cards."

"I get that *those*," she gestures to the open box, "are your cards. But *mine* came from my purse." She's still not getting it.

"No, I mean I make them. I painted that. Well, what I sell is printed copies of the originals, but these are *my* cards."

"Wait, *you're* Reflection Paper Crafts?"

"Yeah. That's my online shop. It's something I do on the side. For fun."

"You make my favorite cards! Miles, I use them all the time! Wait," she gasps, "YOUR TATTOO!" She hits the palm of her hand into her forehead and rushes forward, bunching my shirtsleeve up to my shoulder. My eyebrows furrow at my inability to follow the turn in the conversation. "You wrote this Latin quote right?" She taps my arm. "I thought the script looked familiar! I brushed it off since that's not the type of thing I would normally know. I don't know fonts, but I do know your calligraphy!"

I look down at my tattoo. *Dum Spiro Spero.* She's right, it is in my script. I wrote it out for the artist. *She sees me.* She notices things no one else does. "I can't believe you caught that. How weird."

"Weird but awesome! Your artwork and your words have been a part of what you call *The Ivy* for quite a while, Miles. I didn't even know you yet and you had already been an important part of what makes it special to me."

"I love that I've sort of been with you all this time. Like we were always supposed to be together." I *need* to be touching her right now. Using my senses. I draw her to me, enclosing her in my arms. She fits, she feels like home. The sight of my girl is bittersweet. A good ache under my ribs. Her skin is soft and warm. Her scent now calls up deep and affectionate feelings. The taste of Ivy is arousing and fulfilling in a way nothing else can compare to. The sound of her voice, sharing with me, is the only soundtrack I want. I can't deny the things I've been feeling for a while now. Liam used to joke that I was way too "*in my feelings.*" Usually, I imagine he wanted me to lighten up or feel less. Be less. But one advantage to feeling so much is that I'm not afraid of feelings. I can put a name to them. I can be confident in what is there. Holding Ivy like this, all of me engrossed in her presence, I feel like more than when I'm on my own. It's not that I can't be happy on my own. I can. But why would I want to be when with Ivy, it's more. Better. Fuller.

"Ivy, tell me if this is too much. You don't have to reciprocate, no pressure, but I need to say this. I always want to be genuine, so I have to be fully honest."

"That's all pretty vague, but I think I can say *ok* fairly confidently."

"I guess I'm asking that you hear me. If it feels like it's too much too soon for you, tell me that. It won't change things for me, but I'll do my best to keep it to myself. Until you're ready."

"Oh-kaaaay. I'm ready to hear you." She tilts her head up and kisses me, her expression saying she's not taking this very seriously. I kiss her back, wanting to pour these feelings into the kiss. Maybe she'll feel what I'm feeling and be more receptive.

"Ivy...I love you."

Her soft brown eyes are wide and her mouth drops open. "Um..."

I push on, wanting to tell her everything in my heart and also, possibly, wanting to keep talking that way she can't tell me it's too much or she doesn't feel the same way. Saying she can tell me won't make that hurt any less. "You may feel like it's too soon, but I'm sure. I love you. Completely. You have the best heart. I love talking to you and serving beside you. You're funny and beautiful and caring and passionate. You're my favorite person." I want to kiss her again but I'm not sure if that would seem like I'm trying to push her to reciprocate. My overthinking rivals my over-abundant emotions. Her eyes have tears pooling along her bottom lashes. She swallows hard.

"Do you know when I knew for sure that I loved you?" I feel like time has stopped. Did I hear her right? "When you cleaned my face with the washcloth before holding me, comforting me down from my panic attack. I was at my lowest, my most broken state, and you took care of me and made me feel safe. That whole night, instead of being about how I broke down, became, for me, about how you took care of me. You sat through all that ugliness and still chose me. The attraction was *always* there and I knew that I liked who you are, but right then I saw your heart. What could I do...but love you." I kiss her. I feel like I'm filled with helium, ready to lift off the ground, or like my whole body is full of sparklers, bright and buzzing.

"I love you, Ivy."

"I love you, Miles."

We move to the living room, stretching out on the couch together. We get lost in each other, each kiss and touch speaking the love we've confessed. It's slow and gentle, not a frenzy of lust but comfort and caring. She rests her head against me and I hold her, tracing soft circles on her back. I've never felt this way before. I've never been this close to someone outside of my family, never wanted someone else's happiness and comfort over my own. I tell Ivy as much and she says the same. *First love.* It's better than I could have imagined. Firsts are momentous and I'm glad this woman in my arms is my first true love. And she loves me back. This line of thinking does lead me to a question I've had niggling at the back of my mind.

"Ivy, I've been wondering about something you said. From when you told me about Richmond." I expect her to stiffen but she stays snuggled against me. Maybe some of the power the memories held was lessened in the sharing. I hope so. "You said there was proof you were a virgin. And you said you haven't been in any kind of relationship since Richmond. So that means..."

Her yes is barely audible. "Vance was my first real boyfriend. My *only* boyfriend until you."

"You didn't date in high school?"

She scoffs. "I was awkward and dorky and pretty much only hung out with my mother. I was invisible. Needless to say, there weren't teenage boys beating down the door at the Hughes house. Vance was the first guy who saw me. Or at least I thought so at the time. I'm sure that's why I let myself get so lost. I didn't know enough to know I couldn't trust him. I thought he cared about me and I was desperate to be loved." I keep caressing her back, sadness for the younger Ivy making my breath catch in my throat. "So, um, that's me. Awkward teenage non-dater, former abusive jackhole's doormat, 24-year-old virgin. Have you, um..."

I sigh, suddenly wishing we were both starting at the same level with all the same firsts. "Not for a while but yes. I'd sort of unintentionally become a celibate hermit in Philadelphia. But before that... High school was hard. I was the tall, too skinny biracial kid obsessed with being unique, authentic, and angsty. I had art—which was not cool like sports—and too many feelings. Dad helped me focus my emotions and Liam took me to the gym with him. By the time I got to college, I was...pretty cocky. Girls were noticing me for the first time and I felt all this pressure to get out there and experience everything. It was like a challenge, learning women's bodies, figuring out what made them feel good."

I clear my throat. "I guess it served me well if experience is all I wanted. But it was all empty. I pursued pleasure but never had any real connections. On the rare occasion I tried to get close to someone, I'd let them in and they'd leave. After a while, I equated being known with being rejected. And I couldn't separate sex from emotions. When I did it left me empty and depressed. I feel too much. I'm not capable of casual physical relationships.

Everything means too much to me." She doesn't comment at all. I continue, ignoring the worry of how she will see me now.

"I had a girlfriend in Philly, after college. I thought the connection we had was special, that it was leading somewhere, but for her, it was just sex. Fun. I found out she seeing someone else at the same time and I stopped dating. Completely. I thought she broke my heart at the time. I know now I never loved her. She hurt me but you're the only one who has ever had my heart."

I don't know if my confession bothered Ivy more than she's letting on. She isn't distant though; I won't let myself worry. She loves me back. We while away the rest of the day, entwined in each other, sharing stories and kissing in a perfect world of two.

CHAPTER 28
IVY

This is what love feels like. I didn't think twice about telling Miles I love him too. It was obvious. He's the first person I want to share things with, the last thing on my mind before I fall asleep, and the first thought when I wake up. I've never known someone so intuitive, loving, and affectionate. I think the version of me he sees is better than who I actually am but he makes me want to be that Ivy and to be worthy of his faith in me.

His confession about his sexual history surprised me. A lot. I'm not sure why exactly. There's no way a guy can be that good with his hands, mouth, and...everything else with zero experience. It still kind of threw me though. I think learning about it right after the "I love you" was what made it difficult. I was on this high, my insides bursting like tiny bubbles in a glass of seltzer, wanting to be as close to him as physically possible. But then, every time he kissed me, they'd be there in the back of my mind: all the women who came before me. I'd get nervous thinking about them, comparing myself to them, worrying about how I could possibly stack up. Strangely enough, thinking about Vance helped me figure things out. At least that jerk was good for something.

Miles tells me he has something special planned for Friday night. It will mean skipping yoga but Mama insists she's happy going solo. She's almost as smitten with Miles as I am. Chloe even leaves Caleb with Liam for a couple of hours that way we can go shopping together. She lends me her magic shopping skills and finds exactly what I'm hoping for and gives enough encouragement to leave me feeling like I can pull it off. Our time is too brief but once she complains that she's aching, desperate to get some relief by breastfeeding, I send her back home.

I'm equal parts nervous and excited. It's not like Miles and I don't go out, we do, but this date feels like a bigger deal somehow. I make it through work (the teensiest baby boy with the biggest blue eyes I've ever seen) and Fresh Start and it's finally Friday evening. I take my time with everything: a long shower with the works, special attention to my hair, date night worthy makeup, and my outfit made entirely of Chloe-approved items from the ground up. She made me buy these high peep-toe heels that have a vintage feel and dang if she wasn't right; they make me feel sexy! I'm finally getting a chance to wear the green wrap dress from our first shopping trip. I think it highlights all of my best parts. I hope Miles thinks the same thing. I feel confident and pretty. The doorbell rings and I force myself to walk, calmly, to answer the door. I shouldn't skip like a schoolgirl in these heels unless I want to risk tripping and breaking something. Miles is waiting on the other side, a single peony in his hand.

Hot. Damn.

I mean, *Granny's famous gravy*, I'd like to eat him with a spoon!

He's wearing a slim-cut suit without a tie and it hugs his body in the best way possible. He looks suave and sexy. The best part, though, is the way he's looking at me like he's never seen anything better.

"Holy fuck, Ivy! You're gorgeous!"

"You're looking pretty gorgeous yourself."

He steps inside, kissing me softly. "You are stunning. Have I told you how much I like you in that green? Good color theory does it for me."

I look him up and down. He has on his lace-up boots and his pants hit above their tops like his jeans always do. It should probably be ridiculous, but it's very him and I love it. I tap his toe with mine. "Thanks! You remind me of my favorite Doctor."

"Doctor? Doctor Who?" He jokes.

"That's the one!" I love that he gets my dorky humor. I take the flower and find a vase. "Peonies are my favorite."

"I may have gone to your mom for help."

"In that case, you both did good. Ready to go?"

Miles kisses me again, slowly and firmly until I'm melting. He groans against me, adding to the heat factor. "We should go before I forget why we should." He pulls back reluctantly and leads me out the door. When we get to his car he takes off his jacket, laying it carefully on the back seat. He has on suspenders and I die a little bit. Apparently, forearms and dressing like an old man drive me wild. My entire body is on high alert next to him. He's completely gorgeous and he's all mine. I still don't know where we're going but I'm happy to let Miles surprise me. I am one lucky girl.

I was not mentally prepared for this level of surprise.

Oh my stars and garters, I might actually die.

Can you have a coronary from extreme romantic thoughtfulness?

I don't want to cry off my makeup, but it's taking a lot of effort to keep it together. We're seeing the Virginia Symphony Orchestra. And they're performing Gustav Holst's "The Planets." We take our seats and Miles threads his fingers through mine, looking at me expectantly.

"Do you like it?"

I kiss him hard then sniff as a tear tries to break free. "I love it! This is incredible. How did you even know?"

"You mentioned it at Chloe's, the first time we hung out there. Remember? You told us about your dad and the records."

"I can't believe you remembered. This means so much to me."

"I'd do anything to see you this happy."

The whole experience is pure magic. Hearing it performed live is a bucket list experience and sitting next to the man I love, remembering my dad with the perfect soundtrack, is overwhelming. My heart is thrumming and my whole body is buzzing like a live electrical wire. I'm filled to the point of overflowing with love and joy. It ends and I drift like seafoam, anchored to Miles' hand in mine.

Miles starts the car and I put my hand on his thigh. "Will you take me home?" There's a brief flash of disappointment but he agrees. I don't want to go to a restaurant or a coffee shop, but I don't have the words. All the feelings are taking up too much space. The ride is quiet. I'm fit to burst, feeling a million things at once, and Miles seems contemplative. He walks me inside my apartment and I close the door before he can try to say his goodbyes. His face tells me we're not on the same page, but I can fix that. He must think I didn't want the date to continue. That couldn't be further from the truth. I'm afraid I'll stumble over my words, though, and make a mess of things. I may not be able to say it well, but I can show him. I slide his suit jacket off and hang it over the back of the couch. He doesn't stop me but looks at me questioningly. I take him by the hand and lead him through the door to my bedroom. The lights are all off but there's bright moonlight shining in the windows. It's enough to help me feel more comfortable.

"Love?"

I put a finger over his lips. I can't talk or I'll get too nervous. I press my lips to his, tasting him, but step back when my heart starts pounding. He opens his eyes slowly, watching me. Breathing deeply I reach over and untie my dress. His eyes widen and I open my dress, letting it drop off of my shoulders to the floor. I can tell by his expression that Chloe was right on the money. I wore the negligee she picked out as a slip under my dress. It's lacy and sheer, skimming the tops of my thighs. Chloe said it was ladylike and sensual. I feel that way.

"Did you wear this for me?" His low whisper feeds the fire burning through me.

I nod, biting my bottom lip. Miles is looking at me like he wants to rip the lace off, but he stays standing a couple of feet away. He's so good to me. He's restrained, letting me lead, still protecting my heart and making sure I feel safe. I soak up the sight of him, letting him watch me, enjoying the building tension, and giving myself time to be brave. He licks his lips and I can't wait any longer. I go to him, sliding his suspenders off of his shoulders and stepping closer to unbutton his shirt. My hands are trembling with as much excitement as nerves as I finish and pull his shirt out of his pants, leaving it hanging open. I smooth my hands over his chest, making myself linger, unhurried. He smells freaking delicious. He finally moves but only to finish taking his shirt off. I love that my comfort is so important to him, but I *need* his hands on me. I press myself into him, kissing him deeply. He finally relaxes into the kiss, his tongue swirling with mine. His hands tangle in my hair and my hands are on the move, touching every inch of skin I can reach.

I kick off my heels and he stops long enough to take his boots off before claiming my mouth again. His hands drop down, teasing my nipples through the lace and I moan. His hard length is pressing into me and I make quick work of undoing his pants, pushing them down and off of his hips. I run my hand over his erection, heady with the thought that I do this to him, and he growls low in his throat. He slides my straps off of my shoulders and then he's pushing the cups down and worshipping me with his mouth. I let the negligee slide down my body and I'm left in my black panties ("cheeky" at Chloe's insistence), more exposed than I've ever been in my life but completely at ease. Or at least as *at ease* a person can be while also being this turned on. Miles is sucking and biting and I'm on fire. He kisses his way up to my face and looks at me, his eyes heavy with desire.

"You're in control, Ivy."

I don't want it. The realization is freeing.

"Miles? I want *you* to be. I trust you. With everything. Can you," I suck in a steadying breath, "take the lead?"

He tips his chin slowly and then kisses me like I'm all he's ever wanted. He's still restrained but that restraint is such a turn-on. He's strong and completely in control. He runs his hands down my sides, pushing against me then walks us backward, towards the bed. He steps back from me, taking his time, letting his eyes roam over me. Feeling bold I turn slowly in a circle, letting him see all of me.

"You are so fucking perfect. Lie down on the bed, Ivy." It's a command but it's gentle, not domineering. "I'm going to take my time tonight." I lie down, stretching my arms up over my head, reveling in his slow perusal of my body. "I'm going to make you feel so good, beautiful."

He holds his body over mine, up on his forearms, placing himself between my legs. He's right where I need him to be and the pressure is delicious. He explores my mouth with his tongue and I lift my hips, rubbing myself against him. This is what it's supposed to be like! He kisses his way slowly down my body. As he moves I lose that perfect friction right at my center, but he keeps things building all the same. He sucks on my nipple until I can't hold in my moan, biting at me to tease. His mouth licks down my torso, his tongue dipping into my belly button before trailing down lower. He licks lightly, over my panties, hitting that small nub of sensitive nerves and my hips rock up on their own. He chuckles against me, that seductive sound driving me higher still, and presses down on my hips with his hands. His mouth is on the move again, loving me and teasing me in equal measure. He works his way down my thigh, sucking gently on the back of my knee before working his way back up. I'm aching for him and he knows it, brushing lightly over my panties before traveling down my other leg. He teases me a few more times, caressing and kissing and nipping up and down my legs but purposefully avoiding where I want him most, leaving me wanting more. Craving him. He lifts his head, tucks his fingers gently under the waistband of my panties, and looks at me, wanting confirmation.

"Please, Miles." He peels my panties down, tossing them aside and bringing himself back up between my legs.

"So. Fucking. Perfect." He locks eyes with me for a moment. "For the record, guys like this. *I* like this."

He licks up my center with the flat of his tongue, leaving me breathless and shaking. His head between my legs is almost too much to take in. Is any sight sexier? I drop my head back, overwhelmed by sensation. Miles licks lightly up and down. He moves slowly, then faster, lapping then circling, testing what I like and adjusting to my reactions.

"You taste so good." It's building and my legs are shaking. He concentrates his mouth on my clitoris and strokes a finger down, sliding it inside me.

"Miles! Oh my gosh," I gasp. He slides the finger in and out, then adds a second finger pressing deeper. I clutch at the sheets, needing something to hold on to. I'm balanced on a razor's edge of pleasure. My hips are pushing up into him on their own and I'm moaning. He circles his tongue once more, then sucks on my clit and I explode in a shower of light and breathy cries. He keeps his tongue on me, licking gently as I come back down. I'm panting, overcome. He kisses my hip bone and slides up my body. He's rock hard against me and even though I'm barely over the most intense orgasm of my life, I still want him. A lot. He kisses me and I can taste myself on him.

"I love you, Ivy." He nibbles on my earlobe. "You cumming is the sexiest thing I've ever seen." We keep kissing but he's keeping things where they are. I want him to lead, I told him to lead, but he's being too cautious now and *I need more of him.* I bring my legs up enough to use my feet to push down his underwear until he's naked against me.

"Love, I don't have a condom. It's fine, this is enough for me, I promise." I reach my hand between us, gripping his cock. I don't have much to compare it to but he feels impressive. He groans, dropping his head against me. "That feels good." I encircle him, squeezing and gliding my hand up from base to tip. It feels good to me too.

"I bought some condoms when I got my lingerie." He looks up at me in surprise. I keep stroking him, loving how I'm making him feel. "But, Miles? I'm on birth control. I'm good with having nothing between us if you are." He pulls my hand away and draws my arms up, linking our fingers above my head and lying on top of me, his full weight pressing me down. Gosh, I love how it feels, being held down by him, trapped under his weight.

"We'll go slow. Tell me if it hurts, Ivy. I don't want to hurt you." He slides his hands down my body, pulling my legs wider and lifting himself over me. He rubs himself up and down my folds, spreading my arousal. "You're so wet for me." He positions his tip right at my entrance, pushing in slowly, letting me get used to him. He's big and I feel tight but it's not a bad feeling. It's really, really good. He pulls out and then pushes back in, going a little deeper. "You still good?"

"So good. More, Miles."

He pulls back and slides himself in, as far in as he can go. There's pain, a slight prickling of tears at the corner of my eyes, but there's more pleasure than anything. He holds himself there and takes in my eyes.

"Are you ok? Did I hurt you?"

I pull his face down and kiss him hard. "More than ok. It's good. I love you, Miles. Make us feel good?" He finally moves inside of me and I groan at the sensation, lifting my hips to bring him deeper. He keeps the pace slow but I can feel another orgasm building and I need MORE. My fingernails scratch down his back. I feel like I can't get close enough to him. I want to be a part of him, somehow even more connected than we are now.

"Fuck, Ivy. You feel amazing!"

I dig my fingers into his perfect ass cheeks, driving him into me. "More, Miles, please? I need more." He growls and rolls us over until he's underneath me.

"I want to see you. Need to."

I lower myself down his length and watch his head drop back, his eyes rolling up. I rest my hands on his chest, bringing myself up and lowering myself down.

"Is this right?"

"Fuck yes, just like that." His hands dig into my hips, setting the rhythm, picking up our pace. I try rolling my hips, getting the friction I need every time our bodies come together. Miles brings himself up taking my breasts in his hands and the sensation pushes me even closer to the brink. My head drops back, my curls tickling my back and his legs. "Shit! I'm so close!" He's pumping up into me, the movements harder and more erratic. My whole being is alight, right at the tipping point. He pushes into me, hitting a spot deep inside at the same time that he bites down on my nipple and I crash over the edge, shattering. I cry out, every muscle tensing, inside and out. He keeps pumping and I feel Miles come undone. He growls into my breast, straining under me, and collapses back, pulling me with him.

Our skin is slick, my hair is sticking to me, and Miles is flushed and dazed. He's never looked sexier. I'm limp against him, every part of me relaxed and sated. He kisses the side of my face, caressing my back. "Stay here, I'll be right back." He rolls me off of him and hops up. This is the first time I've really gotten a good look at all of him and even in my present two-orgasms-limp-noodle state I'm still so turned on at the sight of Miles Bennett naked. He looks like a freaking statue of a Greek god. I want to take a bite out of that ass. It sounds like he's in the bathroom. He comes back in and I get a delicious view of his frontside.

Shitake mushrooms, that was just inside of me?

He's not even fully hard anymore and daaaaaang. He smirks at me and then comes over, using the warm washcloth to gently clean me.

"I hope this isn't weird. I didn't want you to be uncomfortable."

Swoon. "Drop dead gorgeous *and* super thoughtful? How'd I get this lucky?" He puts the washcloth on my nightstand and climbs back into bed, pulling me against him. This has seriously been the best night of my life.

"You cursed, Ivy! I'm scandalized," he jokes.

"I swear! Occasionally." He laughs. "Ok, very rarely but it slipped out! I guess I'm just an old lady at heart!"

"I like it. You keep us classy." I run my fingers along his chest, soaking in our closeness.

"Is it always like that?"

"Sex? No. It's never been like that. That was..."

"Earth-shattering," I conclude.

"Yeah. Life-changing. Mind-melting."

I press a soft kiss into his chest. "For me too. Thank you for taking such good care of me."

"Always, love. Always."

We fall asleep like that, wrapped up in each other, happier than we've ever been.

CHAPTER 29
MILES

I'm walking on clouds.

Bathing in sunshine.

Every sound is like baby angels singing.

Ivy Hughes loves me and the sex last night was unbelievable. In my humble opinion, it was likely the best sex that's ever been had by anyone. Or maybe I only feel that way because it was between me and Ivy. Who can be sure? Every single second was perfect and will be burned into my brain for the rest of my life. The way she took control and then handed it to me, her little moans and cries, the way she touched me and asked me for more... it was fucking perfect. I think Ivy has ruined me. I could never be with anyone else. She's still asleep next to me, dark curls fanning around her head on the pillow. If I stay here next to her naked body I won't be able to help waking her for round two. I don't want to rush things. I pull on my boxer briefs and pad out to make coffee.

I text Liam, wanting to know how they're doing, wondering if they need anything. Liam doesn't respond but for all I know, he's still asleep. The new baby schedule seems to be a crapshoot and he's on paternity leave. Maybe I should have held off until later. Hopefully, my text didn't interrupt their sleep. I'm digging through the cabinet for mugs when Ivy shuffles out, disappointingly no longer naked. She's still sexy as all get out though in a loose t-shirt that's falling off one shoulder. Her hair is mussed and it doesn't look like she has anything on under the shirt. My heart aches pleasantly knowing it belongs to her.

"Kiss," I command, "then coffee?"

"I haven't brushed my teeth," she grumbles.

"Don't care." I point to my mouth and she obliges. I pour and she leans against the countertop next to me.

She smiles wryly. "I might need a little ego boost, so...where are we at? We both still agree last night was the best night ever?"

"100%."

"Phew," she breathes out. "Just wanted to make sure I hadn't oversold it in my dreams or something."

"I don't think it's possible to oversell last night." She blushes and we drink our coffee in companionable silence. "That was... surprising. After we talked at my dad's I thought it might take you a while to be comfortable with me again. I wasn't expecting you to initiate."

"I'll admit I was a little thrown at first. It was hard not to imagine all those other girls, wondering what they were like, worrying that I can't compare..."

"No! Ivy, they weren't..."

She interrupts me, holding her hand up to stop me from continuing. "I know. Really. I *was* worried. I felt self-conscious like I probably couldn't compete. Then I thought about Vance."

"That asshole? How..."

She holds her hand up again. "Vance is my past. Everything that I went through, good and bad, has brought me to where I am now, to who I am now. You didn't judge me or look at me differently or let my history dictate how you thought I'd see you. It wasn't fair for me to treat you any differently than how you treated me. I don't want to give the women in your past a moment's thought. They're part of what made you who you are today, what brought you to me. Plus, I'm the one that gets to reap the benefits of all of that," she pauses a coy little smile blooming, "experience."

"That's very mature of you. You're happy with the results of my experience?"

"You are very good. At all the things." The little smile becomes a full-blown grin.

"I'm happy to use any and all of my skills for you. I'm sure there are still ways for me to improve. Maybe we can work out some kind of evaluation system."

She winks at me, leaning her hip against the counter. The caffeine works its magic and she sighs as she finishes her cup, putting it down behind me.

"Thank you for that." She steps between my legs and leans against me, chest to chest, holding me while I finish my cup. Could every morning be like this? I drink the last drop and she reaches up, taking my mug and putting it next to hers and then she's kissing me.

My lips tingle underneath hers and the electricity spreads throughout my body. She licks between my lips and opens for my tongue. She tastes like dark roast. I slide my hands down and then back up, inside her loose shirt, cupping her bare ass. I'm already hard as she rubs against me. She breaks the kiss and looks up at me shyly.

"I want to do something."

I shrug a shoulder. We can do something else, I guess. Not every hour has to be filled with kissing. I'll admit that thought is disappointing. I drop my arms, trying to shift my thoughts to breakfast or something else but she leans forward, licking then biting my nipple. Before I can get my hands back on her she's sliding down my body, licking and kissing as she goes. She pulls down my boxer briefs, drops to her knees, and looks back up at me.

"Is this ok?"

I think I say yes. I'm not sure. Maybe words came out?

"I may need your help. You can tell me what feels good, give me directions. I want this to be good for you." She bites her lip nervously.

"There's no possible way for this to not be good for me, Ivy. But I can help if you want me to." She licks her lips and puts her hand around me. "You can hold me harder than that. Pressure is..." Was I talking? It's hard to concentrate with her in this position. She grips me more firmly and then licks my tip, swirling her tongue around it. I have to grip the countertop behind me. She does it again and then takes me into her mouth. I let out a shaky breath and when I look down she's looking up at me, needing affirmation.

"It's good, love. That feels good."

She puts her tongue flat against the underneath of my cock and glides it down, squeezing her hand in front of her mouth as she moves lower. I groan. She glances up at me and then does it again, swirling her tongue around the tip when she gets back up to the top. She starts over, the pressure from her hand harder, but this time when she's moving her head back she sucks in. My knees get wobbly and I growl a bit. She pops me out of her mouth and smirks up at me, an eyebrow raised.

"More. Like that." My voice sounds hoarse.

"You taste good." She licks her lips. Suddenly more confident she takes me back in her mouth, working my length with her hand and her mouth together. She hums against me, her apparent enjoyment turning me on even more. Her tongue is teasing, tapping, and lapping against me, and every time she moves back up she sucks in harder. My breathing is ragged and I can feel sparks shooting down my spine, gathering low for my release. She moves faster, licking and sucking me to greater heights. Ivy slides her hands around, squeezes my ass, and takes me deeper into her mouth.

"Shit. I'm almost there, Ivy."

I should tell her she can pull back or we can stop but I can't think straight. I look down at her as she takes me back to her throat again, sucking in, her cheeks hollowing. She looks straight into my eyes as she takes me in her mouth and cups my balls with one of her hands and that combination is my undoing. I come apart, spilling everything I have into her mouth and crying out her name. Ivy swallows, wipes at her mouth primly, and stands up. I know she's going to ask me if it was okay and I don't have any functioning brain cells left to talk right now, so I kiss her senseless. Once I no longer need the counter to support my weight, I open my eyes and breathe deeply.

"Holy shit."

"Not a bad effort, I take it?"

"Let's just say there was a lot wrong with your ex. What a fucking idiot."

As Saturday mornings go, this is one for the memory vault. We shower together and I get Ivy caught up in the orgasm count before we fall into her bed wet and make love. With Ivy, it's more than sex. By the time we're finally dressed (thankfully I'd started leaving clothes for sleepovers so I didn't have to put the suit back on) it's past lunchtime. I want nothing more than to stay wrapped up in Ivy all day and night but we finally had the meeting with the lawyer yesterday and I need to talk everything over with my family. Of course, Ivy understands. She's wonderful like that. I leave her after a solid half-hour of goodbye kisses, promising to be back with dinner. *I really fucking love her.*

I must glide over the air into Chloe and Liam's house because they both look at me like I've grown an extra head and start grilling me before I can even sit down.

"What's up with you, bro? Why does your face look like that?"

Chloe screeches, "YOU HAD SEX WITH IVY!" Caleb starts crying down the hall. "Shit, Milesy, you made me wake the baby!"

"I'll get him, you sit, Banshee." Liam hops up. We can hear

him through the baby monitor, talking to Caleb and changing his diaper.

"How's he doing? Rocking at the dad thing like he does everything else?"

"You can't distract me, Miles. I'll get the truth out of you. But yes, he's killing it. Best baby daddy ever," she clutches her hands over her heart. "We're the luckiest."

Liam comes out, cradling his son, and hands him to Chloe. She starts arranging him on this weird pillow thing around her waist and Liam leaves then comes back with a big glass of ice water for her and beers for us.

"Fair warning, the boobs are coming out 'cause this guy needs to eat. It's too hot to cover him up; you're just going to have to get over yourself, got it?"

"Ok. It's cool, Chlo. I won't be staring at your boobs, but I'm not going to be the jerk who begrudges my little dude sustenance."

"Excellent, now spill. Did you or did you not bone our little Ivy?"

"Nice, Chloe. Real classy. We did not *bone*. How old are you? We're two adults who are madly in love and we had sex while expressing that."

"Whoa! Shit, back up. Did you say in love?" Liam chokes on his beer and Chloe's head jerks up.

"Yes. I love her. Totally and completely. I'm in love with Ivy. And she loves me. And last night was the best night of my life."

Chloe starts crying and Liam immediately jumps up, bringing her back a box of tissues, even wiping her cheeks so she doesn't have to adjust the baby. She was not kidding, he is rocking this.

"Milesy," Chloe sobs, "that's the best thing I've ever heard! My plan worked. I got a front seat to your romance!" She sniffles. "Stupid fucking hormones."

"Dude. Ivy is great. Way to lock that shit down." Liam grins widely at me.

"Now that we got that out of the way, can we talk about what we learned at the lawyer's?"

Some of the details of the will were quite a surprise. We weren't expecting much other than clarification on what he had wanted us to do about his house, maybe a clearer picture of his finances. Dad was a pretty private guy. Instead, we were told that not only was Dad's house paid for but he also owned his parents' old house. He didn't have debt and there aren't too many hoops to jump through. He left our grandparents' house to Liam and Chloe. It has rental tenants in it right now and the income will be going to them. He left me his house.

Liam takes another swig from his bottle. "Chloe and I talked about Grandma and Grandpa's house some last night. Since there are already tenants and we don't know where my next set of orders will send us, we're going to leave things as is. We'll have a little more money in the bank with the rental income which will balance out the extra we'll need to spend on a property manager and taxes. Once we know what the next couple of years looks like, we'll talk about it again. Ultimately we'd like to live there but for now, the rental income will be helpful. What are you thinking?"

I've spent the last few months with all of my options stirring around in my brain, feeling untethered and unsure about what direction I should go. Today, the ground is finally steady beneath my feet.

"A lot of things were clarified for me yesterday, things I was leaning towards but was too unsure or afraid to admit to myself. Hearing the will gave me the final push I needed."

"Are you sure it wasn't Ivy's magic body?" Chloe snorts.

I roll my eyes. "Ivy plays into it. A lot. She's the most important thing in my life, honestly. But having sex with her wasn't the deciding factor. I don't have anything in Philadelphia. We all know that. I'm done. I want to move into Dad's, work from here, volunteer at Fresh Start, be with Ivy, do family dinners with you guys, the whole thing."

Chloe does a tiny happy dance, careful not to jostle Caleb too much. "You're really staying, Milesy?"

"Yeah. I want to see you guys more. I want to be a part of Caleb's life for as long as you're here."

"We'd love that, bro. We want you around more. We've missed you."

"Holy shit, Miles, please say you'll make Ivy my sister! That's the only thing that could trump best friend!"

"Babe, bring it down a notch! Don't put too much pressure on the guy, we don't want to lose her!"

Man, I love these two. How did I stay away so long? "I don't want to freak Ivy out but, yeah, that's the plan. I want forever with her."

Chloe screams, startling Caleb. "Sorry baby boy, it was necessary! Milesy, when I'm done over here I am going to hug the crap out of you!" I don't think I'll mind. It's nice that they're excited for me.

"When you get a chance I'd like to have you guys over to look through Dad's stuff. We can pull out anything sentimental that we want for ourselves. Any excess I'd like to see what Fresh Start can use and then maybe sell whatever is left and give them the proceeds. If that's ok with you guys." They both chime in their agreement. "I'll have to go back to Philadelphia briefly. I need to talk to Peter about this new job offer and pack up my apartment, but then I'll be here permanently. I'm putting the finishing touches on the website stuff for Fresh Start this week and I'll probably drive up there next weekend. Maybe I'll take Ivy with me, show her around. All that shit will be better if she's there."

"You've got it bad!" Chloe teases.

"I get it," my brother adds, "out of the two of them I'd pick Ivy too."

"Asshole," I throw back with a grin. "But hard agree."

We chat a bit more and I get a turn holding Caleb after Chloe hugs the crap out of me, as promised. I thought briefly about texting Ivy to come over here for dinner but I don't want to share her yet. Instead, I pick up takeout on the way back to her apartment. As I'm parking I'm struck by the best idea for the website. I know exactly how I can humanize their mission, how I can connect donors with a more personal story, and how I can show Ivy how much I believe in her. I've got that familiar buzz. It's going to be perfect.

CHAPTER 30
IVY

I didn't know my life could be like this. I was made to do my job, I have hobbies that fulfill me, I have a second family in Chloe and Liam, and now I have my own epic love story kind of relationship with the best guy on earth. Miles is so considerate, so kind, so sweet, so freakin' HOT and the sex is beyond description. Seriously. How is this my life? It's too soon to be thinking about it but, honestly, I can't imagine my life without Miles in it. I don't even want to. I'll keep that to myself until a time when it's less crazy to mention, but I know, deep down, that I've found my forever love.

Tuesday I have a light afternoon and Miles takes me to Back Bay National Wildlife Refuge. There are the cutest wooden walkways, gorgeous stretches of beach, and I love all of the greenery and lily pads. We walk and talk and Miles takes pictures of scenes he might like to paint. He also keeps making me stop to take pictures of me. I feel a little silly playing model but he's so earnest and genuine, I can't say no. I sneak in photos of him too and we take a couple of ridiculous selfies before another couple takes pity on us and gets a real photo.

I immediately change my phone background that way I can see it all the time. Miles is leaning against a wooden railing. It's perfect, quintessential Miles: tousled dark curls, swoon-worthy amber eyes, angular face, that long lean body with his sexy tattoos, fitted jeans rolled up over his boots—my freaking walking fantasy. He's looking right at the camera, one corner of his mouth pulling up in that smile that makes me melt, his arm around me. And I'm tucked up against him, curls blowing, smiling up at him. I want to print it out and frame it. I wish we could stay longer but we already have dinner plans. We take food out to Chloe and Liam's house and they have zero chill about how happy they are about our relationship. I love it. I love how much they care about and support Miles. They joke and tease, they're loud and crass, but they all have each other's backs. I'm looking forward to introducing them to Mama.

Wednesday starts with a birth, the most perfect squishy baby girl that took her sweet time and made her mom work for her. It was a long delivery and all the pushing without much progress made us concerned we were going to need to call a doctor in for a c-section. Thankfully baby was not in distress and the combination of relaxation techniques and a different position made all the difference. Exhausted but happy is a good way to leave a birthing room.

Miles is hunkered down finishing up the website. He tells me he and Walter have planned a big reveal at Fresh Start! They're both super excited about it. They are trying to keep the details from me, but I heard Myrna has been baking, old graduates are coming, and Mama is bringing flowers. It'll be like a party! Miles comes over to my apartment for lunch and we get a little time to talk over sandwiches. Everything is better with him. I'm embarrassed to say I'm a little bummed he won't be sleeping over tonight, but he expects to be burning the midnight oil to finish whatever special project he's working on. Knowing how much he pours his heart into everything he does, it's going to be great. I'm so proud of him.

I don't have a single thing to contribute to all the frenzy around prepping for the party. It's a regular Thursday night for me. I am looking forward to Myrna's treats, though. And finally seeing the result of all of Miles' hard work. My last appointment runs long and I don't end up having enough time to go home to change before I need to be heading to the church. I guess I'll be partying in my work clothes. At least my jeans and blouse are cute. I park and there's a flurry of activity coming in and out of the building. I spy Mama with her arms full of flowers and Walter and Miles are walking, heads together, looking at some remote thing very intently. I slip inside and start helping with set up. I keep hoping I'll get a moment to say hello to my boyfriend, sneak a kiss or a hug, something to get my Miles-fix, but we stay too busy. I have to settle for smiling across the room and mouthing "I love you." Mama catches him mouthing it back and beams at me. I know I'll hear about it later. I'm looking forward to it. Mama has always been my closest confidant and I've loved finally having good things to share with her.

Everything comes together beautifully. There are bunches of gerbera daisies in an array of bright colors, pans of Myrna's famous cookie dough brownies, and ladies are pouring in, grabbing cups of coffee and tea while chatting with each other. It's making me emotional to see so many of them together in one place. Why haven't we done this before? We should make it a yearly thing—invite them back, check in, and celebrate their successes. I make myself a quick note to talk to Walter about it later. Everyone is mingling and I take a little time to join in, wanting to hear how jobs are going and see pictures of growing kids and hug every single person I see. I spy Phoebe, standing tall and proud in a pretty outfit from the boutique she works in, talking to Amanda. Amanda is one of our more recent graduates and it has been a joy to witness her blossoming. She came to us battered but determined. She worked harder than anyone, nailed her interview, and is now working as a receptionist at a small accounting office while taking college classes. Her employers are helping her and have told her there's a job waiting for her, as an accountant, when she graduates. My posture straightens and I walk taller, filled with pride for what all these women have accomplished. They make it all worthwhile.

Eventually, Walter whistles to get everyone's attention and calls Miles up to the desk where he's standing. They make an odd pairing, Miles tall and dark while Walter is short, round, and grey.

"Hi everybody! Thank you all for coming tonight! It's been so great to see all of your lovely faces and hear about how your lives are growing now that you've left us. I want to introduce you all to Miles. Say hey, Miles." Miles waves awkwardly and flashes a smile. Gah, I've got it bad. Mama wolf whistles and everyone laughs. "Miles here has accepted a position as our graphic designer, without pay, lucky duck." There are a few chuckles but no one laughs as hard as Walter does. Typical. He loves his own jokes. "Before that though, Miles was hired to design a brand new website for us! It's going to help us do even bigger things here, but instead of telling you all about it, he thought we could show you. If you would, Miles?"

Walter steps to the side and Miles leans down and does something on the computer. I'm definitely not staring at his butt. That would be inappropriate. Who am I kidding? I totally am, it's a masterpiece. He turns back, remote in hand and what was on the computer screen shows up on the larger screen they have set up. Fancy.

"Hey, guys. A lot of what I did was more corporate branding: making a logo, creating business cards and flyers, setting up Fresh Start social media accounts, that sort of thing. This is the new logo that is featured in all of those places." He brings up the logo and tears prick my eyes. It's beautiful. Perfect.

The circle emblem features a watercolor sunrise inside two clasped hands, "Fresh Start" penned below in Miles' graceful script. Everyone oohs and ahs, applauding. Miles lets the clapping die down and continues.

"We've also got a sign, with this image, on its way for the outside of this building. But, as Walter said, my main focus was the website. First of all, one of the big things you want in any good website is maneuverability. It needs to be user-friendly. I won't bore you, but I do want to point out the menu over here. You can navigate anywhere from it and it stays with you when you go to a new page. It should be easy for anyone to find their way around. Even Walter can use it!" We all laugh and Walter gives a big thumbs up. "The biggest issue we wanted to address was making it easier for people to donate money and goods. Not only did we need to streamline things, but we also wanted to free up some of Walter's time. He needs to spend more of it being an administrator and less of it picking up donations and waiting on drop-offs."

Miles navigates through the other pages and my sense of pride keeps growing. "We have a portal set up here where you can give online, pull up the address to send a check, or get time and location information to drop off donations of clothes and things. There are also connections to businesses who are stepping up to build working relationships with us, offering internships with a funnel into employment and other jobs that will be available solely through Fresh Start." A loud cheer goes up at this. There are so many incredible things here it's hard to absorb them all. This is much more than a new website.

"We've provided a form here so anyone can apply to volunteer with us without needing to come in. There are also bios for the permanent staff of volunteers. There's a lot of helpful information on here and I hope everyone will check it out on their own." He's personable and confident up there. Everyone is eating up what he's saying.

"One challenge I came up against was the struggle to get donors and businesses to see the very human side of what we do here at Fresh Start, the *necessity* of our mission here, when there is a real security issue in sharing your stories." Miles is serious and earnest and my heart is so full. I love him so much. "It's hard to make us human when showing the faces of women who are fresh out of an abusive home could put them in harm's way again. I truly think, to grow and to get more funding, that personal connection is *essential,* but I couldn't see how to humanize the organization *and* keep you safe. But then I fell in love with Ivy Hughes." He smiles at me and the room fills with a chorus of "aaaaawwwwww." Public declarations of love? So swoony.

"If anyone here doesn't know, this whole place is Ivy's labor of love. Everything we do here was grown from her dream and her tireless work. But it didn't start here. Ivy *is* the face of Fresh Start."

He's smiling with such love and pride, but he clicks the remote and my stomach drops. There's my face, one of the pictures he took at Back Bay. And there, on the screen for everyone to see, no, on the *live website for the world to see*, is my story. My private hell. My ultimate shame.

His mouth is still moving but I can't hear what he's saying over the roar in my ears. I scan over the words, barely able to comprehend what he's written.

Words jump out at me:

assault,

attempted rape,

hospitalized.

Why would he do this to me? How could he share this with everyone? With the world?

There's clapping and people are turning toward me. All their eyes are on me. EVERYONE KNOWS. They're smiling and cheering but it feels creepy and distorted, like images in a funhouse mirror.

I can't breathe.

I can't be here.

I think I'm going to be sick.

A sob breaks free and I run out the door, barely able to see the way to my car through my tears.

CHAPTER 31
MILES

I don't understand. One minute Ivy was smiling at me and the next she was running out, crying. Walter tried to smooth things over but everyone saw her. It took me a minute to push through the crowd and by the time I got to the parking lot her car was gone. My stomach hurts. What's going through her head right now? I pull out my phone and text her.

ME: *Where'd you go? Are you ok, love?*

She doesn't respond. I call her, but she doesn't answer. I go back in, worrying but doing my best to finish what I was supposed to do tonight. I finally give up, though, because I'm too distracted to answer questions. I spot Kath and work my way over to her.

"She's not answering my calls. What happened? What should I do?"

Kath pats my arm. "I don't know for sure but if I had to hazard a guess...Ivy is a pretty private person. She puts all of her energy into everyone around her but she doesn't let very many people in. I don't personally know anyone that she has told that full story to, outside of you."

The weight of what I've done knocks the air right out of my lungs, as completely as if I was punched. "Shit." That doesn't feel like enough. "FUCK!" People turn to look in my direction but I couldn't care less. I'm dragging my fingers through my hair, pacing. "I didn't know. You have to believe me, Kath, I didn't know! I heard four separate people reference Ivy's problems in Richmond before she ever told me about it herself. I thought people knew. I thought everyone knew that's where her passion for Fresh Start came from. I thought it would be a good thing if everyone coming to Fresh Start could see how far she's come. She's so inspiring!"

Kath smiles softly, sharing some of her calm with me by placing her soft hands on my cheeks and holding me still. "You guys will figure it out." I hug her, feeling desperate, and run to my car. I'm on the verge of full-blown panic.

I have to make this right.

I love her.

I have to find her.

I love her.

I drive to her apartment but she's not there. I go to Kath's house but it's dark and empty. I walk through the park and half run to all her favorite places nearby but I can't find her. I feel almost numb with worry.

I keep calling her but it goes straight to voicemail. I try texting again.

ME: *Please talk to me.*
ME: *I love you, Ivy*
ME: *Please, beautiful, let me know you're ok*
ME: *I'm very worried*

I drive out to Chloe and Liam's house. I pull up and when I see her car isn't here either I snap. I stumble out of my car and vomit into the grass, my clenched stomach finally rebelling. My headlights must have alerted Liam to my arrival because he comes out his front door and runs toward me when he sees me bent over his yard.

"Miles? Are you ok?"

I can't even answer him. I just sob, dropping to my knees on the ground. I can't hold myself together anymore. It's not that she left me. That's happened before, numerous times. But I've never been so vulnerable, so invested, and it hurts so much more. He does the last thing I expect and drops down in front of me, wrapping me in a hug. I'm shaking, sucking in sharp jagged breaths, being held by my giant older brother. What a fucking mess. There are footsteps and then Chloe's next to us.

"Babe, let's get him inside."

Liam half carries me into his house I'm so useless and Chloe fusses around me, mothering me in ways I don't deserve. They sit on either side of me on the couch, sandwiching me between them, holding my hands while I completely shut down.

My throat is scratchy,

my eyes are glassy,

my head hurts,

my mouth tastes like puke,

I feel too much. Everything is too much.

I sit and stare in front of me, retreating into my head. Chloe is the first to lose patience although I'm sure she's a little nicer than Liam would have been. I keep waiting for him to try to punch some sense into me.

"Milesy? Tell us what's happening. Please? We're here for you but you have to tell us what's wrong."

"She's gone," I croak.

"Who's gone, Boo? What is this about?"

"Ivy. I hurt her. I didn't mean to, but I did. I hurt her and she's gone." I curl up on myself and Chloe pulls my head into her lap, stroking my hair.

"Where did she go?"

"I don't know." My voice cracks and I tear up again. "I looked for her. I called her. I texted, but she won't answer. I can't find her. She hates me and I love her so much."

Liam pats my shoulder and gets up to go take care of their son who is making noise in the nursery.

"Do you want to tell me what you did?"

I tell her everything, the whole story pouring out like my vomit on their grass. It's unpleasant and bitter in my mouth. She keeps stroking my hair until I've talked myself out.

"Miles, you had no way of knowing it was a secret. You didn't do it to hurt her. She'll see that when she's less upset."

"I wanted everyone to be as proud of her as I am, Chlo. I wanted them to see how far she's come and all the good that was born from her hurt. How did everything go this wrong? I should have known I'd make her leave. I always do."

At some point I pass out, my phone still clutched in my hand. In my dreams I'm sprinting, chasing Ivy but she keeps disappearing, turning into mist when I reach her.

The next day Ivy doesn't go to work (I check). Her apartment is still empty and Chloe hasn't heard from her. I drive around looking for her for a while, then go back to Dad's house. My house, I guess. Ivy doesn't even know about it. I didn't even get to tell her my plans. I change and go to the gym, lifting weights, then running on the treadmill until my legs threaten to give out. Exercise quiets my often over-stimulated brain and gives me energy, but today I finish feeling more tired than ever. I shower, make myself eat something, and lose time. *Hello, brain abyss.* I can't paint, I can't eat, I can't focus on tv or books. I end up lying on the couch, scrolling through my phone, looking at pictures of Ivy. By dinnertime, I'm going stir crazy. I drive over to Kath's house and Ivy's car is in the driveway. I sprint up the front stairs, banging on the door. Kath opens the door and I pretty much yell at her.

"I need to see her!"

Kath motions me inside. "She's not here, Miles. She *was* here. Your sister-in-law came and made her go get something to eat with her."

I drop into a chair, my legs giving out. "She's ok?"

"She's safe," Kath amends.

"She still won't talk to me. How can I tell her how sorry I am if she won't talk to me? I don't want her to leave me. Everyone leaves me." I drop my forehead onto the table, struggling not to cry again. "What is going on with me? I'm a fucking mess."

"I mean this with all sincerity, Miles, so I hope you take it that way: I can give you the number of a good therapist. After I lost Ivy's dad, then Richmond...it's done us a lot of good. But honey? Your parents didn't want to leave you. That wasn't their choice. And Ivy? I'll bet she needs space to work through things, not permanent distance."

"I love her. So much, Kath! "

"I know, Miles. And she loves you too. She does. When Ivy gets scared or upset she pushes people away and runs. It's what she's always done. You're a good man, Miles. You're a good man *for her*. We have a very open relationship, my daughter and I. She talks to me. So I know that up to now, every time Ivy has run, you've chased her. You found her at Fresh Start, you gave her some space and then went after her and convinced her to give you a chance. Hell, she kicked you out of her apartment and you waited outside the door and then barged back in and took care of her. Deep down, Ivy knows that she can trust you. I want you to know that while she is upset and her feelings are valid, you didn't do anything wrong."

I shake my head. It doesn't feel like I didn't do anything wrong. It *feels* like I ruined the best thing I've ever had.

"I know enough of you, Miles, to know that you wouldn't intentionally hurt my daughter. And if I know that, then she knows that too. I think that the two of you are going to struggle with retreating from problems as long as you're together. You're going to have to work hard to run towards each other, to lean on each other when you're hurt. This time, I think you need to let Ivy run toward *you*. Give her some space, Miles. Let her work this out and make this decision on her own. I think my girl needs to learn to trust herself. She'll come back to you. Meanwhile, you try to trust her. Trust that she loves you."

She hugs me and walks me out. I guess it wouldn't qualify as giving her space if I'm still here waiting when Ivy gets back. I'm not normally the one to jump into action, but everything in me is screaming to make Ivy hear me out, make her understand, make her come back to me. Kath is right, I need to trust her and let her do this on her own. I get it but I hate it. I hate that I hurt her. I rattle around my empty house but all I can feel is the dark pressing in from all sides. I know where this road leads if I keep internalizing and retreating into my head and it's only going to make things worse. I need to get out of here. I throw some stuff in a bag and lock up. I let Liam know that I'm leaving and text Ivy one last time.

ME: *I love you. I'm here whenever you want to talk*

CHAPTER 32
IVY

I feel as if my heart was ripped out and now I'm walking around with a gaping, empty hole in my chest. I call in sick to work and spend the whole day hiding in my mom's house. I spend a good hour in her tub, sobbing until the water is cold and I can't stop shivering before I get out and continue the party, except this time in a robe on my old bed. I'm lost and hurt. I haven't eaten since lunch yesterday but the thought of food makes me feel sick. I ache with missing Miles and that hurts as much as my broken heart does. Mama hasn't lectured or tried to talk me down, she's given me space. I can't even think I'm so sad. I've been listening to all my angstiest music. Dashboard Confessional's album "The Places We Have Come to Fear the Most" has been on a loop. All I can do is cry and stare off into space. The doorbell rings but I ignore it. It's not my house and I don't want to see anyone anyway. A minute later, Chloe marches in.

"Ok, Sweets, get up. You have 5 minutes to wash your face and put on some clothes. I don't care if it's sweats, put something on your body and meet me in the kitchen. Otherwise, I will come in here, strip you naked, and dress you like a giant fucking doll. You know I will. 5 minutes."

I can't handle any more humiliation and Chloe's right, I know she'll do it. I do as I'm told. She drags me into her car and then out for pho. We go to a little hole-in-the-wall shop where we're the only diners. She gives me long enough to have a big bowl of flavorful broth and Vietnamese goodness in front of me before she says anything.

"Ivy, are you ok?" I merely shake my head. "I've gotten the gist of the situation, but I'd like to hear from you what's going on."

"Miles shared my story with everyone, without asking. He used what I told him in private, during a very vulnerable moment, for his job. It's like we paid him that stipend to humiliate me. And I loved him." My tears drip down my face and plop on the tabletop.

"Let's address those points. Did Miles know it was a private story that you hadn't shared?" I pause. I don't have an answer for that. "I'm going to assume by your silence that you didn't tell him it was a secret or ask him to keep your confidence. If you think about it, you'll also recall he knew that you had told me about it and I've known you the same amount of time he has. You didn't tell *me* it was a secret and the only reason I didn't speak candidly with him about it was your mutual attraction. I was hoping you'd end up together and that you'd tell him yourself."

I feel like I'm shrinking under the weight of her candid assessment. I'm not sure anyone has ever spoken to me so frankly, but with kindness.

"It also seems like a reasonable assumption for him to think this was something people who know you know of."

I nod, reluctantly. "Now that you say that I, um, don't think I said it was a secret. Or ask him to keep it one."

She ticks the second point off on her fingers. "Do you honestly think he wrote about you on the website because it's a job and he wanted the money?"

I shake my head no, embarrassed. She's not angry or judgmental. She's looking at me with love in her eyes and somehow that's harder to take.

"You *loved* him? Past tense?"

I shake my head again. "I love him," I whisper.

"Did you read what he wrote, Sweets? On the website?"

Another shake no. I'm starting to feel ashamed of myself—like I got this wrong. Chloe pulls out her phone and brings up the Fresh Start website. She reads aloud.

"Fresh Start is Ivy Hughes' labor of love. It is her passion, drive, and incomparable work ethic that keep it on track. What's even more impressive is that Ivy's dream for Fresh Start was born from her own pain. The mission of Fresh Start is dear to Ivy because she has personally risen from the ashes of hurt at the hand of someone who claimed to love her. Just like the women she empowers at Fresh Start, Ivy is more than her story. She isn't defined by the abuse she suffered. Ivy survived an assault that left her bloodied and bruised, covered in lacerations, with a concussion and staples in her head. An attempted rape that left her hospitalized and fleeing the place that had been her home was not the end for Ivy, but a new beginning. She left her abuser, she built herself a full and rich life on her terms, and she used her experience to create a place that would nurture and empower women with her same brave spirit—women who have walked through hell and come out the other side stronger and more compassionate. Ivy understands where our ladies are coming from, she knows how hard they're working to survive, and she has a true love for them and a gentleness of spirit from walking that same, hard path. Ivy pours her heart and soul into Fresh Start and no one who comes in contact with her can come away unchanged."

My pho is sitting forgotten on the table. Tears are now streaming down my face.

"Do you hear him, Ivy? Do you *truly* hear him? He's proud of you. Miles *loves* you. He wasn't sharing your shame with the world, he was sharing his love. He was telling everyone how impressive you are. *You* made Fresh Start special and he believes in the work because he believes in you." Thank God we're the only customers because I am loudly sobbing now. "I don't want to rub salt in your wounds, but you should know that what you did is the absolute worst thing you could do to Miles. I feel like if you've talked as much and as deeply as you've said, you should know this. He lost his mom as a small child. His brother left him to go to college, then ended up getting married, commissioning, and immediately deploying. He didn't mean to, but Liam graduated high school and never came back. Miles held his dad while he passed and had to handle all of it alone. When he's been particularly low he's shared countless stories about letting people close only to have them cut off contact. When it comes to Miles, he keeps everyone at a distance because he can't trust them to stick around. I love you, Sweets, but you fucked this up. Bad. You reacted without all the information and abandoned him like he's convinced everyone eventually will."

"What have I done, Chloe? I need to see him! I need to apologize! I love him and I keep hurting him!" My voice is getting louder and louder and she shushes me.

"Hush. Step one: eat. You need food." I dig into my pho, the warmth of the delicious soup filling me. "Step two: go back to your mom's and sleep. Don't argue, I'm a mother now, I know things. You're a fucking mess, Ivy. You're making yourself sick. Get food in your belly and get a good night's sleep. Tomorrow, after a long, hot shower and some coffee, things won't seem quite as bleak. You can go to Miles when you are a human and not a walking snot rag."

I cry/laugh. She's not wrong. Chloe pays for dinner and drops me off with a big hug.

"*You* need to fix this, not Miles. I love you, Sweets. We all do. Everything will be ok."

I don't deserve the Bennetts but I am very thankful they're in my life.

The next morning I do feel more human. A shower, good coffee, and clean clothes all help. I drive straight to Miles' dad's house. His car isn't there. I text Chloe.

ME: *Miles isn't at his dad's house*
CHLOE: *I should have texted you. Liam told me last night that Miles left.*
ME: *Where is he??*
CHLOE: *He went back to Philly, Sweets*
ME: *No! Why is he there?*
CHLOE: *Liam said it was something about that job*
ME: *What job?*
CHLOE: *the full-time graphic design job with the firm up there, from that meeting before*

I don't know what to say back. I screwed everything up. Once again I reacted and ran. And I was dead wrong. I want to tell Miles how wrong I was. I want to tell him I love him. But I'm too late. He's gone and is seeing about a full-time job 6 hours away. Dejected, I go back to my apartment.

The weekend is a haze.

I can't cry anymore.

I'm completely numb.

I love Miles so much, but I missed my chance. This is my fault and I don't deserve him.

I want to tell him how I feel but I can't face the end being spelled out in no uncertain terms. As long as we don't talk I can keep pretending it's all a misunderstanding, right? I never claimed to be mature. I think the evidence shows I am the opposite of mature. I consider texting him but the immediacy is too much. I'll know if he reads it and doesn't respond and it will kill me. And it will be worse if he does respond and confirms my fears. Even if he's settling back in Philadelphia, he'll have to come back to sort through his dad's house. I need to write one last card. I'll leave it there and he'll find it eventually. I'll pour my heart out and then make myself leave him alone. I don't think I'll ever get over loving Miles Bennett. I know how strong I am, though. Given time, I can find my footing and resume the life I've built, on my own. However long that takes.

CHAPTER 33
MILES

Being back in my old apartment drives home the point that I do not belong here anymore. It feels empty, foreign. Even with the void left in Ivy's absence, I'm finished with Pennsylvania. I want to be in Virginia. I want a life down there. I wrap up Philly as quickly as possible. Peter is very understanding and even promises to keep me on for any freelance jobs that come up. I don't have any regrets about turning down the job. Philadelphia is not my home anymore. Ivy is. I hope she knows that. I hope I get the chance to tell her that. It's depressingly easy to pack up my life here. Most of my furniture is old bits and pieces I found at thrift stores. It's not even worth hauling them home. I spend the afternoon selling the bigger items locally and then take everything else to be donated. What is left fits in the back of my car: the rest of my clothes, a couple of boxes of books, my record player and albums, and my art supplies. Those take up most of the available space. I have various sizes of canvases, my easel, sketchbooks, pads of watercolor paper, and my one piece of furniture: a chest with a lot of small drawers filled with brushes, watercolor tins, acrylic paints, and different solvents. It will be nice to have all of my supplies in one place. It's a tight fit but I get everything loaded up.

I spend Sunday cleaning then turn in my keys. I thought it would be more nostalgic to leave. It's not — I'm ready to start the next chapter. I had planned to stay at a hotel and start early on Monday, but I'm too anxious to get back. I drive through the night and crash as soon as I get in.

The next morning I still haven't heard from Ivy. The only thing I can do is unload all of my things. I can't push her, no matter how much I want to. Once that's taken care of I can ask Chloe and Liam to come over to sort Dad's stuff. I'm carrying my first load in when I see a card taped to the outside of the front door. I drop everything and pull it open, excited and scared to see what's inside.

Miles,

This is the hardest card I've ever had to write. I'm so very sorry. All of this is my fault. Thank you for the wonderful things you said about me on the website. I wish I was half the woman you think I am. I'm sorry I made such a mess of everything. If I wanted my past to be a secret, I should have told you that. You didn't do anything wrong. I overreacted and ran away. Again. I'm most sorry that I didn't come to my senses in time to stop you from leaving. It makes me sick thinking that I hurt you so much you had to go. All I wanted was to run into your arms and tell you how I feel, but I was too late. I missed out on the best thing that has ever happened to me. I love you, Miles. I'll always love you. I'll be forever grateful that our paths crossed in that park. Knowing you has made my life much richer. I hope your life in Philadelphia is wonderful. You deserve everything good that life has to offer.

Love, Ivy

Somehow our wires have gotten crossed. My time with Ivy has helped me become more proactive, spurring me into action instead of living in the wishes and dreams. I have some planning to do and this time I'm going to rely on the people we care about to make sure every detail is right. After all, this is the most important thing I'll ever do. I send out a flurry of texts and hurriedly unpack my car. I don't need to be hauling my life around in the backseat while I'm driving all over Hampton Roads, taking the necessary steps to seize control of my future.

CHAPTER 34
IVY

It's not easy to go on with my regular life as if I'm not missing a piece of myself. I wish I could crawl into bed and hide until the part of my heart that beats for Miles dies and puts me out of my misery. Unfortunately, I-drove-my-boyfriend-away isn't an excuse recognized by my employer, leaving me to slog through my week like a zombie. Every day I fight myself over the overwhelming urge to drive up to Philadelphia and beg Miles to take me back. I imagine myself driving all night, showing up in this grand gesture...but I don't dare take it further and picture how he'd receive me. I'm too scared. I can't bear that I hurt him so much he didn't stay. If he needed to leave then I owe it to him to let him find what he needs in Philly. I love him too much to keep hurting him. If only it didn't hurt me. I know Chloe said I need to fix this but I don't know how.

Chloe keeps checking up on me. I'm thankful I haven't lost her too. I try not to cling too tightly though. They're family and she's only my friend. I can't see us staying this close in the future when Miles is with someone else. One day she'll have a sister-in-law and my presence will make things awkward. The thought of Miles with someone else, marrying someone else, is like a pile of hot stones in my gut. I hate whoever gets to make him happy.

Thursday night Walter calls me and insists I take the night off. He says a lot of people are too sick to come in and there's not much to do. I don't buy it. Sweet old man. I start my evening off looking at pictures on my phone until it gets to be too much and the crying overtakes me again. I force myself to put my phone away and spend the rest of the night bingeing on ice cream and the 11th Doctor. Matt Smith is like comfort food. Except for the part where his boots and pants remind me of Miles. I take the bittersweet pain though until I pass out on my couch.

By Friday afternoon I'm desperate for yoga with Mama. I'm feeling emotionally drained and sluggish from all the lying around and stuffing my face with junk. I love and miss Miles, but it's ridiculous to wrap so much of who I am up in him. I'm not going to cease to exist because I'm single again, no matter how much it hurts. I worked too hard to stand on my own two feet to throw it all away, again, for a guy. I need to start actively working at not moping. All I want today is to distract myself with gossip and move my body. My hopes to slip in the back unnoticed are immediately thwarted by Sophie and Lauren. They yell as soon as I make it in the door and I find myself buried in a big group hug. I'm a sniffling mess, but this time the tears feel good.

"Ivy girl, we've missed you! Where have you been?" Lauren asks way too loudly in my ear.

"Give her some motherflippin' breathing room, Lauren!"

Sasha steps up and hugs me quietly, her sweet nature bringing the crazy down a notch. "Is it Miles, honey? We haven't seen you guys in a while."

All I get out is a nod before the tears are back with a vengeance.

"Good going, Sasha, now we've got waterworks!" Lauren elbows her, but good-naturedly. It seems Sasha is part of the mom crew now. I'm happy for her and am not above using it to distract myself from my broken heart. "*Is* it that smokin' hot tall drink of water? Do we need to form a posse? I fight dirty. Sophie packs a mean punch. We could at least rough him up a bit." Sophie ruffles her pixie cut and flexes, trying to look tough.

I giggle and some of the ache in my heart eases. I'm not as alone as I thought. "It wasn't him, it was me. It's my fault. I hurt him and drove him away and now he's gone. The end."

Sasha rubs my arm, her kind eyes finding mine. "Something tells me this isn't the end."

I shake my head. "I wish. More than anything, I wish that. But he moved back to Philadelphia and I need to let him go."

Sasha quirks one side of her mouth up and looks like she thinks I'm being stupid. "He looked at you like my Shawn looks at me. It was real. You're meant to be together. Someone reminded me," she looks at me pointedly, "when I needed it most, that I should give myself grace. You should do that too. I don't know when, but you'll both get there. I'm sure of it." I want to ask her how she knew the card was from me but the teacher is looking impatient upfront and we are here for yoga, not group therapy. She pushes us harder than usual and it's exactly what I need.

When we leave Mama turns us away from our route home. "You and I need some pampering, Sweet Pea. What do you say to some salon time, my treat?"

I squeeze her into a hug. "You're the best, Mama. That sounds wonderful."

I get a much-needed trim from my stylist who is the bee's knees at working with curly hair. We get facials and Mama even pushes me into getting a manicure. I never get my nails painted and it makes me feel girly and pretty. By the time we walk back for dinner I'm feeling more human than I have since that awful night last Thursday. I might even manage to leave my house not looking like a hot mess in the near future. Fingers crossed.

When I wake up Saturday morning, my heart still hurts but things don't feel as dire. It's a pleasant change. I savor my cup of coffee and decide a little makeup will make me feel good. Instead of spending the day in my pj's, I put on my green top and favorite jeans. It makes me feel pretty and I focus on how Miles made me feel when I was wearing it instead of thinking about how much I miss him. I can focus on the good times, right? It's going to take a lot of mental gymnastics to keep from falling over the edge into sadness and tears, but one step at a time. Today, enjoying a nice outfit is enough. I don't feel like I'm becoming one with my couch cushions so I'm calling today a victory and it's still breakfast time. Maybe I can do this. I hear a text alert.

CHLOE: Sweets, are you up? Can you do me a huge favor pretty pretty please?
ME: Whatcha need?
CHLOE: Can you run out to that park in front of your place? I think my phone fell out under the bench by the path this morning.
ME: Your phone? Aren't you texting me with it?
CHLOE: Right. Mom brain. I meant my wallet.
ME: Wallet. Ok. I can do that
CHLOE: Now? Not to be a jerk, but I don't want it to get stolen.
ME: I've got you. I'll text you when I find it
CHLOE: THANK YOU

A walk sounds good anyway. I can grab Chloe's wallet, then spend some time in the park. Maybe I'll drive it out to her and get in some baby snuggles. It's a beautiful morning and the sunshine is doing me good. I need to remember how much better I feel when I exercise and spend time outside. Holing up in my apartment was not doing me any favors. I'm zoned out, thinking as I approach the bench. When I focus on it though, I become rooted in place, shock making my brain and feet freeze in tandem.

"Miles?"

Am I hallucinating?

He looks good enough to be a figment of my imagination.

He has a gorgeous peony and his smile is brighter than the

sun. My heart speeds up and I'm blinking too much, trying to make sense of this. I'm sure I look like a lunatic.

"Um, are you looking for Chloe's wallet too?"

He laughs at me because, clearly, I'm an idiot. "No, she just said that to get you here."

Cheese and rice, he's here for me! I'm not having a total mental breakdown, he's actually standing in front of me. I close the difference, needing to touch him more than I need air. Oh, cripes, please don't let me mess this up. I step straight into his arms, inhaling his delicious Miles scent and running my hands along his back. I've missed him so much. I can't even talk, I let my touch do it for me. I soak him in. He pulls away to look at me and I feel his absence like I've lost a limb.

"Hi. I missed you."

"Hi." I suddenly feel shy and unsure of myself. *Why* is he here, like this? "I, uh, need to say some things to you, Miles. But I'm going to turn this way," I slip my hand into his and swivel to stand next to him, looking straight ahead instead of into his eyes, "because it's easier without eye contact."

He turns too so we're side by side, holding hands, and I feel like I might be able to speak now that I can't see his gorgeous face.

"I have this bad habit of shutting down when I'm upset. It never helps things. I need to work harder to stop doing that. I need to handle myself better. I shouldn't have run. But even if I needed to get some space initially, I shouldn't have stayed gone and cut you out. I'm sorry. I wanted to go to you, to tell you I was wrong, but it was too late. You'd already moved."

He squeezes my hand. "Ivy, I didn't move. Well, I did, but not the way you think."

"So you did move? Or you didn't?"

"I went back to Philadelphia to move out of my apartment."

"But Chloe said you went back because of a new job."

"That was misleading. I *was* offered a full-time position, but I turned it down. Philadelphia isn't home. I want to be here."

He drops my hand and puts his arm around my shoulder, holding me close but still allowing me the space I need to talk. *Holy Moses,* I really, really love this man.

"I moved into my dad's house, Ivy. He left it to me. I'm staying here permanently." I'm about to turn to him, needing more connection than his arm around my shoulders, when his words hold me in place, too afraid of where the conversation might be headed for eye contact. "There's something else too."

Oh no, did I read too much into things again? I can't handle the rollercoaster of my stupid emotions! *Calm down, Ivy!* My stomach is knotting up and I'm fighting down feeling like I'm going to hyperventilate.

"I didn't only come back because of the house. I came back for you. I want you, Ivy. Forever." My heart is back to racing. "You're it for me, beautiful. You're everything I could ever want in a friend, a lover, a partner. You make me more open, more caring, just...more. I want to be more because of you. I love you, Ivy, more than anything."

I feel a tear trace down my cheek but I'm too frozen to even wipe it away. I'm afraid if I move I'll break the spell and none of this will be real.

"I don't want to get down on one knee in front of you like I'm presenting some prize for you to consider because *you*—a life with you—is the prize. I want nothing more than to be like this forever, standing right next to you, facing the good things and the hard things together."

I gasp, unable to hold it in. Is this happening?

"Ivy, my love, will you be my wife?"

I finally have enough control over my body to turn to look at him. Those golden eyes are shining and his smile scorches a path straight to my heart. I throw myself forward, kissing him, pouring into it all my love, all of my longing, everything that has been building up inside of me while he was gone. My skin is tingling and my heart is bursting, growing bigger and fuller like the blooming petals of a peony. His lips are soft and familiar and he feels like home. My home.

"You didn't exactly answer my question," he whispers against my mouth.

"Yes, Miles! A thousand times yes."

He pulls a ring out of his pocket and slips it on my finger. It's the most gorgeous thing I've ever seen. A thin rose gold band with a setting that looks like vines, crisscrossing and accented with delicate little diamonds. There's some kind of pink stone sparkling in the center.

"The oval stone is morganite. It reminded me of you, bright and feminine."

I can't stop staring at it. "Miles, this is exquisite! I love it."

He looks pretty pleased with himself. "Did you know Myrna's husband is a jeweler? When I told him about you and showed him a picture he knew exactly what I needed."

I kiss him again, happy and in love. He flags down a man walking by. "Excuse me, would you mind taking our picture? This gorgeous lady said she'd be my wife!" The kind stranger gives us our own mini photoshoot, congratulating us before resuming his walk. I'm thankful he thought of that, now we'll have pictures to look back on. "There's something else too."

"I'm not sure I can handle anything else! My heart's already about to explode out of my body," I tease.

He shows me his right forearm. Where there used to be bare skin there's now a vintage-style heart, intertwined with vines of ivy. I run my fingers over the still healing skin.

"This is me." He nods. "You did this for me *before* you asked me to marry you? What if I had said no?" Like that was even an option! But still.

"I hoped you'd say yes! But even if you had turned me down, it wouldn't have changed how I feel. I love you. You're part of me. I wanted you here," he points at his arm, "like you're here." He places my hand over his heart. SWOON.

"I love you, Miles Bennett."

"And I love you! Ivy Bennett has a nice ring to it, doesn't it? Let's make that happen soon, ok?"

"Miles? What would it take to get you naked and in my bed?"

He grabs my hand and starts jogging us towards my apartment, making me laugh. "You're the boss!"

The day passes us by in passionate hours I will never forget. Miles gives me everything I need and more. There's slow savoring, hurried fervor, the repeated melding of hearts and bodies. I'll never get enough of him. I can't believe I get this for the rest of my life. We're lying together, legs entwined, leisurely kissing in a post-orgasmic haze. Miles presses a featherlight kiss on each of my eyelids and sighs softly. "I never want to leave this bed."

"As much as I agree, I don't think that's an option. Needs will persist." I giggle as his stomach growls as if on cue.

"We should get up and put on some clothes. I hope you're feeling up to being with other people, your mom is expecting us for dinner."

I pout in mock frustration. "I guess I can put on some clothes for food."

I'm surprised when we get to Mama's and Chloe and Liam are there too. Mama is holding Caleb, cooing and looking every bit like a doting grandma. On the wall behind her, in a frame, is the watercolor of me, now signed and matted.

"Where did this come from?" I tilt my head towards the wall.

"Isn't it breathtaking? Miles gave it to me. My future son-in-law is quite talented."

I hug everyone, giving Caleb a little kiss. Or twenty. His fat little cheeks are irresistible. I whisper to him, almost unable to believe it myself. "I'm going to be your auntie!" Turning away from Caleb's addictively kissable face, I address his parents. "I'm not complaining about your being here, but *how* are you here? I hadn't even introduced you yet."

"Oh, Sweets, we had a whole pow-wow to bring you back from zombie status and get you to that proposal!" Chloe explains. "Now show me that ring!"

She squeals over it and pulls Miles into a hug. "You did fucking awesome, Milesy! That thing is gorgeous and so Ivy."

Liam pulls me into a side hug, squeezing me breathless. "Welcome to the family, sis."

John Brown it (as my Grandaddy used to say), he got me with that one! The big lug.

"You were in on this too, Mama?"

"Of course! They're family, right? I needed to do what I could to make sure I get to keep this tiny little heartbreaker in my life!" She smooches Caleb. "They won't technically be mine, but you'll be a Bennett and that's close enough."

Chloe smacks Mama's shoulder and then wraps her arm around her. "Please, Grandma Kath, you're never getting rid of us. Miles and Liam don't have their parents anymore. We *need* you." Mama wipes her now damp cheeks and smiles. Looks like Chloe has laid claim to another Hughes. I love her for it.

Dinner is loud and joyful, full of delicious food and laughter. We need to do this every week!

Family dinner.

I have a whole family now.

Long ago, I discovered a part of myself when I reached out to encourage a stranger. Through awkward adolescence, moves, and trauma; while recovering, rebuilding my life, and rediscovering who I am, looking for the good in others and finding ways to show them they're seen and appreciated has given me a life with intention. It's given me something to focus on outside of myself. It allowed me to keep hope alive. I never could have imagined, when I picked out that first blank card, that these notes, these little things to pass on kindness, would lead me to my calling, my forever love, and my family. Whatever they may have started as, I can never see them as random acts of kindness again. There's nothing random about any of it. They gave me a purpose. They have a purpose. And that's how the notes—how *I*—will be moving forward into this full and fantastic life I've built. With purpose. With intention. Intentional kindness with overwhelming love.

EPILOGUE: MILES

The weather is crisp and cold, with a hint of snow in the air. Maybe it's weird but winter is my favorite season. I love the pause when even nature lays low and takes a break before blooming again. Too many people forget to give themselves time to rest, to be quiet and still. I revel in the stillness. I'm also a big fan of snuggling with Ivy under piles of blankets until we're too hot to stay covered. I wanted to marry Ivy right away, but all the work we had put into Fresh Start resulted in a big influx of new donors, new business relationships, and more shelters wanting to join us. Planning a wedding while expanding to accommodate more ladies and more volunteers would have been too much on her plate. And we all know she would have driven herself to exhaustion trying to take care of everyone else. It's a fiancé's job to want what's best for his lady and make it happen. So I convinced her to push the wedding back. I think the waiting did us good. We had time to get better at communicating through our hurts, we grew even closer, had regular family dinners, and built a life. We also worked on the house. It has good bones and Ivy isn't very materialistic, but I wanted it to be *our* home. We've painted, refinished cabinets, and made small changes that have made it feel more like ours., a place to begin our own fresh start.

Liam pats my shoulder. "They're ready for us."

We join the minister at the front of the church, standing where dad's casket was. Oddly it makes me feel close to him. Liam leaves me there and makes his way back to the foyer. Our part of the ceremony is small and unfussy, just the way we wanted it, but we couldn't keep the numbers as intimate as we had hoped. There were too many people who love Ivy and wanted to be here to celebrate. It's not a bad problem to have. I feel antsy. I'm not nervous, I'm excited and anxious for Ivy to get here, to get started. I wouldn't care about what I'm wearing except for the fact that I know Ivy likes me in this suit with my boots. What my love wants, my love gets. Easy.

The inside of the church is a riot of blooms and the smell is intoxicating. Kath outdid herself and I know a lot more about plants now that I spend time at the shop regularly. The arrangements are surrounded by dusty miller and eucalyptus with their distinct silvery and mossy green colors. There are pops of deep red in the winter berries and delicate cream blooms of small iceberg roses and full petaled ranunculus. They're going to photograph beautifully and I'm already itching to paint them.

The music begins and it's finally time to start. Kath takes her place in the front row. She thought Ivy needed to walk in on her own. My mother-in-law is an intuitive and thoughtful woman. Next comes Liam and Chloe. She's pregnant again and glowing. They stand on either side of me, the best man and matron of honor. Then Caleb toddles up the aisle, making everyone ooh and aww over his little dress pants and suspenders. That kid is the cutest. He climbs up in Kath's lap—Grandma Kath to the rescue. Then everyone turns towards the back.

It's time.

It's *finally* time.

Ivy steps in and takes my breath away. I bring my hand to my chest, tears stinging my eyes, and will myself to breathe slowly and savor every step she takes toward me. She's stunning. She stops inside the door, taking me in the same way I am her. When she resumes walking, her eyes never leave mine, a shy smile on her lips. She looks like some kind of winter princess. Her dark curls are pulled away from her face and tumble down her back. The top of her dress is cream lace that hugs her body and the sleeves are sheer with vines of lace trailing down her arms. It cuts in at her narrow waist with a belt and the skirt floats out around her. She's ethereal. By the time she reaches me, I can't help but kiss her.

"It's not time for that yet, bro!" Liam quips, drawing a laugh from the pews.

I ignore him. "You are gorgeous, Ivy."

"Thanks, you too." She taps on the toe of my boot with hers, our little inside joke making her smile broader. I take her hand and the minister starts. The whole ceremony is a blur. All I can see is Ivy. The minister talks about love as an action, we say our vows, and we exchange rings. I can't remember the specifics of any of it. I'll never forget how she looked at me, how I felt, but the rest of it is simply hazy background noise. He pronounces us husband and wife and I'm finally able to take her into my arms. My wife. Our kiss fills me with warmth and light. She's soft and sweet and Liam clears his throat like we've been kissing too long. Dick.

The reception is just right. We're not party people but this celebration is tailor-made for us. We're surrounded by people who care about us. There's a brunch with coffee and tea, pastries, and a buffet-style continental breakfast. I didn't want to start our first night as a married couple by crashing into bed, too tired for anything but sleep. When we leave we'll be able to nap and still have the rest of the day, and night, ahead of us. I know, I'm a genius. I put my fingers under Ivy's chin, tipping her face up to kiss her. I savor the taste of her, her tongue velvet against mine.

"Hey, wife."

She nips at my lip. "Hey, husband."

"How much longer do we need to stay before I can take you home and strip you out of this dress?"

Her eyes glow with desire. "Give me 5 minutes to say my goodbyes and then I'm all yours. Forever."

It's 5 minutes too long. I watch her giving hugs and shaking hands but I'm impatient to have her all to myself. We cannot get home fast enough. Ivy has had her fill of being the center of attention and our family helps us skip out, avoiding the crowd-pouring-out-and-watching-us-leave tradition. It takes the two of us to get her full skirt safely inside the passenger side. Once I'm in I slide it up and slip my hand in, on her thigh. Maybe it isn't the safest thing but I tease and caress her while I drive. I can't keep my hands to myself. I don't want to. I want her ready when we get home. I carry her over our threshold and take her straight to our bedroom.

She takes my jacket off and runs her hands along my suspenders playfully. "You know how much I like you in these. Very sexy."

I kiss her firmly, backing her against the wall and boxing her in with my arms. "So, wife, you decide. Should I slowly strip you down until we're both naked? Or should I take you right here, like this?"

In answer, she slowly slides her skirt up and removes her panties.

Holy fuck, my wife is hot.

She undoes my pants and reaches in, pulling out my cock and stroking me with her small hand. My eyes close on their own. I kiss her hard and she shoves her tongue into my mouth, hungry and messy.

I groan into her mouth. "I need to be inside of you right now, Ivy. Hard and fast. That ok?"

"Please, Miles. Hurry."

She pulls her skirt up to her waist, as desperate as I am. I grip her ass, lifting her and bracing her against the wall. Her eyes lock onto mine and I push up into her. The feeling, that sliding in, our bodies joining together, is perfect. I was made for her.

"You feel too fucking good." I pull back and slam back in,

speeding up. I grind my pelvis against her clit, driving her closer. We're utterly in synch, matching pace, everything building. With every thrust, my heart is beating out: *mine, mine, mine.*

"More, Miles. Harder."

Our tongues are tangling and I'm driving into her harder, feeling my release gathering in my balls. Her fingers dig into me as she moans.

"I'm right there!"

She squeezes around me, gripping my cock with her inner muscles as I hit up into her center, then we're both crying out. She collapses against me and I kiss her neck, carrying her gently to the bed. "I don't think I can move, Miles. You broke me with sex."

"You're ridiculous, Ivy. I love you. And I've got you." I gently undress her, covering every inch of skin I expose with soft kisses before taking off my clothes. We slide under the covers, snuggled up and content.

"Today was perfect. I loved every minute."

"Me too, love. Thank you for marrying me."

We nap in each other's arms, wake and make love again, slowly and tenderly this time. Hours later we answer the door to a dinner delivery courtesy of our family. We let them take care of us and take care of each other. Just the way we will for the rest of our lives.

PLAYLIST

- Hold Out Your Hand by Brandi Carlile
- Smooth Sailin' by Leon Bridges
- Is It Any Wonder? by Durand Jones & the Indications
- We Get Along by Sharon Jones & the Dap-Kings
- Brown Eyed Lover by Allen Stone
- Lay Down by Son Little
- I Loved You by Alice Russell
- Somewhere Between by Eli Paperboy Reed
- I Need You by Jon Batiste

ALSO BY DREA BRADDOCK

O'AHU NAVAL OFFICERS SERIES

(prequel) One Night in Waikiki

(Book 1) Like a Good Neighbor

(Book 2) Like a Good Wife

(holiday novella) Small Packages

(Book 3) Like a Good Roommate

About the Author

Drea lives on the beautiful island of Oahu, Hawai'i with her husband, a Navy SWO, and their 5 children. She drinks a lot of coffee, reads a lot of books, has a lot of tattoos, and likes to put the people she dreams up through the emotional wringer before giving them their happily ever after. When not writing, she can be found weightlifting with her sailor, avoiding social engagements, and singing and playing guitar with their church worship band.

Follow her on:
Website: www.dreabraddock.com
Facebook Group: www.facebook.com/groups/hanamaucollective
Instagram: www.instagram.com/author.drea.braddock
Twitter: www.twitter.com/authordrea